KV-389-424

TO LOVE AGAIN

Denise Robins

'After long loneliness and bitter pain
How sweet, how sweet it is, to love again!'

D.R.

Chivers Press • **Thorndike Press**
Bath, England **Waterville, Maine USA**

This Large Print edition is published by Chivers Press, England, and by Thorndike Press, USA.

Published in 2003 in the U.K. by arrangement with the author's estate.

Published in 2003 in the U.S. by arrangement with Claire Lorrimer.

U.K.	Hardcover	ISBN 0–7540–8905–3	(Chivers Large Print)
U.K.	Softcover	ISBN 0–7540–8906–1	(Camden Large Print)
U.S.	Softcover	ISBN 0–7862–5126–3	(General Series Edition)

Copyright © Denise Robins 1959

All rights reserved.

The characters in this book are entirely imaginary and bear no relation to any living person.

The text of this Large Print edition is unabridged.
Other aspects of the book may vary from the original edition.

Set in 16 pt. New Times Roman.

Printed in Great Britain on acid-free paper.

British Library Cataloguing in Publication Data available

Library of Congress Control Number: 2002115682

CHAPTER ONE

It did not seem to be any good trying to avoid the thought of Christopher. Always she remembered him; it seemed as though the world conspired against her to make her remember. Wherever she went, she had at some time been there with *him.* The music she heard, they had listened to together. When she read a new book some stray word or paragraph called to mind a remark of his; or she wanted him to read and discuss it. In the cinema, there was bound to be a film which contained an incident with her—or an actor who reminded her of Chris.

Always together, Helen and Christopher, always planning for their future. Poor, both struggling artists—but so rich in their love and their enthusiasms. The shared jokes, the mutual understanding, the friends they had made and who were for the most part as impecunious and hardworking as themselves—all these had vanished with the death of Christopher.

She was thinking about him now as she walked with her uncle into the 'Ritz' for lunch.

Actually, it was Helen's birthday lunch. She was twenty-two today. It meant nothing to her. But Uncle George insisted upon what he called 'a little beano' and she had come so as not to disappoint him.

When she sat down to table with her uncle, loosened her coat and took off her gloves, she tried to smile and be cheerful. Dear old Uncle George was such a pet. Like a father to her. She had made her home with him and Aunt Mary for the last five years.

They wanted her to go on living with them but she could not do it. They were not well off. Mr. Shaw was a retired Civil Servant with small private means which were deteriorating steadily through increased taxation. She, Helen, was over twenty-one now and must earn her own living. With her uncle's help she had taken up the training she had always longed for in the School of Art. But since Christopher's death she seemed to have lost all interest in it. Indeed, she shrank from all things artistic. Beautiful paintings, lovely music—those were the joys she had shared with *him*. She could no longer enjoy them without him.

Everybody had been very kind—all her friends tried to induce her to carry on with her art, but now that Christopher was not here to advise or share in it, she seemed to have no desire to continue her career.

It was six months since Christopher had died. Three months of the six she had spent in Sussex with Lady Pilgrim, Chris's mother, who was as broken-hearted as herself. The other three she had spent in trying to take up the threads of her old life, but had dismally failed. Now she was looking for a job. Everybody said that she needed hard work; that Time and Work were the best antidotes for a sorrow such as hers.

She heard her uncle saying:

'I must confess the birthday girl is looking very nice today. A pity she has only got her old uncle with her, eh?'

He had meant to be flattering and kind but it only gave Helen a pang. Of course! Christopher should have been there. And she would have been his wife by now.

She had tried so hard not to feel bitter against the fate which had robbed her of the one man who had seemed right for her. But bitterness was in her very soul today as she glanced at her reflection in the mirror behind their table.

'The birthday girl' was looking very nice, was she? Perhaps! She was wearing a new grey-blue tweed with a crisp white pleated blouse and a blue-grey felt with a feather in it on the ash-blonde head which Christopher had adored. She had never cut her hair but wore it in a shining loop in the nape of her neck. She had grown thin since he died. And she was very pale. The large dark grey eyes with their long dark lashes were a little sunken. She knew that she had been beautiful and gay when Christopher was with her. Today she felt plain and dull. Her aunt had accused her, recently,

3

of letting herself go—of becoming apathetic. Helen supposed that was true there was only one thing to do, work; not dabble about with art but take a job quite unconnected with it. What *could* she do.

Her gaze wandered around the room and was suddenly caught and held by a party at the adjoining table. A strange trio. An elegant woman—still a girl in her late twenties perhaps, or early thirties—exquisitely dressed—a smart man-about-town, rather large, inclined to stoutness. He had a small dark moustache, and wore horn-rimmed spectacles. Between them, looking most incongruous with the smart pair and in a place like the 'Ritz', sat a small thin girl, aged, perhaps, ten or eleven. It was the little girl who captured Helen's full attention.

She wore school-uniform, dark green, the felt hat bearing a green and yellow band. The cream-coloured shirt and striped tie looked fairly new and so did the blazer.

She was not a pretty child. She had carroty hair, done in two short plaits, and a gold band across her teeth. She had bony wrists and hands. Her shoulders were hunched in a dejected attitude. What struck Helen most forcibly was the fact that the child was crying.

Quite quietly but desolately, she was crying, and every now and then lifted a crumpled handkerchief to wipe away the tears. She ate nothing. Once or twice Helen saw the woman

4

lean forward and put her hand on the child's arm as though to comfort her. She heard her saying:

'Patty, darling, do try to cheer up and eat something. You had no breakfast. You will only be sick in the train if you don't put something in your little inside.'

Bright words spoken in a bright voice. But the child shook her head and whispered, 'No, thank you.' And the plate before her remained untouched.

The woman, obviously the mother, then abandoned her efforts to console, and entered into a conversation with the man who looked to Helen bad-tempered and made little response other than a few nods and grunts. He did not address the child. She did not look at him. Just now and again she cast a brief heart-rending look at her mother.

Helen found herself becoming immensely interested, and deeply sorry for the child. It was September. Schools were reopening. Yes, of course, the poor little thing was going back to school this afternoon and this was the last lunch. How well Helen remembered her own school days and what torture they had been. She needed no imagination to realize what this child was enduring. Helen had always suffered in the same way but it seemed that so few parents realized what their children went through in this way. *'It is good for a kid to go to school'* they said—*'children need discipline*

5

away from home'—and so on. But Helen and Christopher had agreed that their children should never be made to go to boarding-school—never forced to break their hearts like this child, Patty, at the next table.

She leaned across to her uncle and began to talk to him about it. Mr. Shaw looked over his glasses and nodded.

'Yes, it is hard,' he agreed, 'what a poor little thing the girlie is. The mother is a handsome creature. Is that the father, do you suppose?'

Helen had not quite made up her mind about the man—but the more she watched the more she became convinced that he could not be Patty's father. She in no way resembled him and he would surely, if she were his own daughter, have joked with her or endeavoured in some way to dry her tears. But he ignored her and kept looking at his wrist-watch.

Helen had a very vivid imagination and let it run riot. She decided that he was Patty's stepfather, and that the woman was trying to conciliate him and that the child was not wanted really by either of them.

She heard her speak more firmly to Patty.

'You really must make an effort to stop crying, darling. After all, the term will soon pass. It is only three months to Christmas.'

The child nodded and said nothing, but pressed her handkerchief against her lips. Helen was filled with compassion. She knew

6

how long three months could be in the life of a child. She could almost *hear* Patty ticking off the days and weeks. Three months more. Twelve weeks. Ninety-two days—and so into hours and minutes until the stretch of time became longer and more unbearable.

Helen longed to move to the side of the desolate figure in the ugly uniform and put her arms around it, and give Patty all the warmth of her deep understanding. She herself had been hurt so badly lately—she could not bear to see another hurt—watch a small girl being assailed by the pangs of homesickness even before she left her mother's side. Suddenly the child got up. Helen heard her mother say:

'Yes, dear, that's right—you run along and wash your face and I'll join you in a moment. Nigel and I will finish our coffee first.'

'So I am right,' thought Helen, 'she speaks of the man as Nigel. He is not Patty's father.'

She saw the figure of the little girl walking forlornly through the big restaurant and was suddenly seized by an impulse to follow—to speak to her—

She murmured an excuse to her uncle, took her coat over her arm and stood up.

A moment later she was in the warm softly lit ladies' room where Patty, hat off, was dabbing cold water against her swollen eyes.

Helen made pretence at washing her own hands, then glanced at the child and said:

'I do hate big crowded places to eat in—

7

don't you?'

Patty looked up. For a moment a pair of red-rimmed mournful blue eyes with sandy lashes regarded the fair, slender girl doubtfully. Then she muttered:

'Yes, I do.'

'On a sunny day like this, it would have been nice to have a picnic, wouldn't it?'

Patty went on regarding this stranger with a child's natural suspicion and reserve.

'Yes, it would,' she said, and sighed a little.

'Going back to school?'

As Helen asked the question she saw Patty's thin hands clench.

'Yes.'

Helen made no attempt to glorify school life. As one child to another, she said:

'It's rotten, isn't it! It makes one feel quite *sick*, going back. Nobody ever understood why I cried so much before term started.'

Then a new look—one of relief—crossed Patty's face.

'Nobody understands why I cry, either,' she said, 'and it makes *me* feel sick. That's why *I* couldn't eat my lunch.'

'Is it a nice school?' asked Helen, 'I mean as nice as school can be.'

'No, it is horrid,' Patty muttered.

'So was mine,' said Helen with a grimace, 'but they kept telling me how nice it was and how good for me, and how lucky I was to be there.'

8

'Oh!' exclaimed Patty and dropped the towel and drew nearer to Helen, drawn now as though by a magnet; elated by so much understanding. 'That's what they keep saying to me. At least Mummy does and Uncle Nigel agrees. I think Uncle Nigel made Mummy send me there.'

Helen put an arm lightly around the child's thin shoulders (the blazer was too big for her).

'Where is your horrid old school?' she smiled.

'Bexhill,' she answered. 'And it's called "St. Cyprian's".'

And suddenly Patty's reserve broke down. A torrent of words rushed out. It was as though she felt, intuitively, that she could trust Helen. She told her that her name was Patricia Wade. Daddy used to call her Patty. Daddy was marvellous. He was a doctor, and they lived in the country which Patty adored, and she had adored her father. But, young as he was, something went wrong with his heart a year ago and he had died. Since then, Patty's home life had changed. The old home was sold up. Mummy took a flat in London; then Uncle Nigel came into the picture. His name was Mr. Cressland. He was not really her uncle but a friend of Mummy's. Now Mummy said that she was going to marry him. Daddy had promised that she, Patty, should never go to boarding-school. But Uncle Nigel had persuaded Mummy to send her to one. It was going to be awful because he was going to try and take Daddy's place. He did not like her, either. She *knew* he didn't. Once she had even heard Mummy telling him to be nicer to her.

Helen listened. It was a tragic little story and more than ever she yearned to comfort the child. She let Patty talk until she had got it all off her chest. Then Helen said gravely:

'Never mind, Patty. It may not be as bad as you think and Christmas is coming.'

'But Daddy won't be here,' said Patty.

Helen could hardly look at the child's woebegone face. How well she understood the feeling of sick despair, when you had to face a Christmas without the person you loved most in the world.

Patty was adding:

'Next hols, Mummy wants me to have a sort of holiday governess; someone to look after me, because Mummy will want to be more with Uncle Nigel'—the lower lip quivered—'I suppose he will be living with us, then.'

Helen deliberately avoided discussion of this. She pressed Patty's hand.

'Perhaps the governess will be very nice.'

Patty regarded Helen with a new look of friendship and confidence.

'Oh, I wish it could be someone like *you*— oh, can't *you* come and be my holiday governess . . .?' Then she gave a little laugh and stared at the ground, adding: 'I suppose that's awfully silly. I don't even know your

10

name.'

'My name is Helen Shaw and I am like you—I have lost someone I love very much and I don't look forward very much to Christmas, either.'

The little girl's hot thin hand squeezed hers convulsively.

'Oh, don't you? How simply rotten! I say, *do* come and look after me. It would be simply terrific. Oh, *do!*'

The words gave Helen a slight jolt. She had never for a moment thought of doing a job like that. Yet she wondered suddenly, why not? She loved children. It wouldn't be at all disagreeable for her to have to look after someone like Patty.

At that moment Patty's mother came hurrying into the room.

'Are you ready, darling . . .?' she began. Then paused as she saw the fair girl in the grey tweeds holding Patty's hand. Helen rather shyly smiled at the older woman.

'I hope you don't mind—Patty and I have been having a talk.'

Mrs. Wade smiled. And that smile bred in Helen an immediate and instinctive dislike of Patty's mother. It was so artificial. Like the high-pitched voice, it had a glittering quality: like the woman herself for she was glittering too, exquisitely dressed in a black and white ensemble, with a little Persian lamb cape to which was pinned a large exotic orchid. In time

11

to come, Helen was to associate Rita Wade with orchids, or some other expensive flower.

As she drew nearer Helen, Mrs. Wade brought with her a subtle perfume—the aroma of the Turkish cigarette held between nervous-looking fingers, very long with pointed, red-laquered nails. Helen decided that she must have a touch of Italian or Spanish blood because of the dark, heavily fringed eyes which were the only soft and beautiful thing in an oval face that was as flawless, but hard as chiselled marble. She put no colour on her cheeks. Only the thin lips were a scarlet line and betrayed a quick, nervous temper. She gave one the appearance of a woman who lived on her nerves. She wore a hat that spelled 'Paris', with a curled ostrich plume sweeping down to the slender neck. One could glimpse the Titian-red hair, which, Helen reflected, accounted for the reddish tinge in Patty's. When she spoke to Helen she was charming, but Helen felt that there was no warmth beneath that charm and that it was merely a façade.

'How perfectly sweet of you to bother about my little girl. The poor angel is always so upset before going to school but once she gets there, she really adores it, don't you, Patty?'

Patty remained silent but her hot moist fingers held more tightly on to Helen's.

'We must hurry, Patty,' added Mrs. Wade. 'Nigel went to order a taxi; you mustn't miss your train.'

Helen glanced at the child and noted the expression of despair which crossed her small face. Then Patty broke away from Helen and flung her arms around her mother.

'Oh, Mummy, I do wish this lady could look after me during the hols. It would be super! Mummy, please, *couldn't* she?'

Helen began to murmur a protest:

'Patty, really . . .!'

'But Mummy, why couldn't she? She's simply marvellous and—'

'Just a moment, darling, hold on!' broke in her mother with a short laugh and put her powder compact back in her bag. Hastily she rouged her lips, and glanced in the mirror at Helen's reflection. The girl was standing just beside her. Quite good-looking, she decided; lovely fair hair, otherwise ordinary. Too thin a bit round-shouldered and badly dressed. What an awful felt hat! And cheap tweeds. But she had a nice voice and was obviously well educated. She wondered how Patty managed to pick her up, and to get so intimate in so short a time.

Really, children were very tactless and trying. She was awfully fond of poor little Patty but since Tommy died it had not been easy— without much money, and with a position to keep up, and having to pay the school bills and Patty's clothes *and* her own. Of course, she knew in her heart that the child hated boarding-school and she felt an occasional pang of compunction, but what could she do? Everybody said it was good for Patty to go to school. It would be wrong for her to live in a London flat with no companion of her own age.

It never entered Rita Wade's head to sacrifice her own inclinations towards a town life, and a good time, in order to keep her child in the country, which she could have done. Rita's love of life and excitement was far too strong for that. To be a widow of thirty-four with a child of eleven was death to her, and she hated admitting that Patty was so old or that she, Rita, was more than twenty-nine.

Besides, there was Nigel—Nigel with whom she was so much in love and who had money and could give her everything that she wanted. She had had one or two battles with him over Patty. It was a bit trying that he so disliked children. She meant to do her utmost for her small daughter—but only up to a point. Beyond that point lay herself and her own selfish whims.

Certainly she had intended getting a holiday governess for Patty at the end of this term. She closed the big lizard bag which Nigel had sent her last time he was abroad, and turned to Helen.

'I'm afraid my daughter is a bit impulsive and embarrassing,' she said with a little laugh. 'You really don't know her!'

14

It was Patty who replied for Helen and with an excitement which made her small face look quite pretty. Helen could see that here was an ugly duckling who might eventually achieve some of her mother's beauty.

'Oh, but I do know Miss Shaw quite well already, Mummy. We've had a terrific talk and I would *adore* her to live with us.'

Mrs. Wade laughed again, put an arm around Patty and glanced nervously at her wrist-watch.

'My sweet, how you do exaggerate! But really, we have no time to go into this now and I am quite sure Miss—er—Shaw is it?—has not the slightest wish to look after you, my poor poppet!'

Patty had turned such beseeching eyes to Helen that the girl found it impossible to wipe away that new touching look of pleasure and eagerness.

Without a second thought, she turned to Mrs. Wade and said:

'I might like it . . . Actually, I am looking for a job of some kind. I am devoted to children. Of course I know I am a complete stranger to you and this is most unorthodox but I could give you plenty of references, and if you like to see me when you are less busy . . .'

She broke off, a little flushed, and astonished by her own temerity.

Then Patty confirmed it by a torrent of beseeching words, hugging her mother who

15

eventually extricated herself from the child's arms, laughed quite good-naturedly, opened her bag, found a card and handed it to Helen.

'Well, well, we'll see, darling. That is my address if you'd like to drop in tomorrow morning before eleven—Miss—er—Shaw. Patty seems to have taken such a violent fancy to you. We might as well meet.'

Helen smiled and put the card into her own bag.

'I would like to come and talk things over with you, Mrs. Wade.'

Then Patty flung herself into Helen's arms. She whispered: 'Oh, Miss Shaw, *promise* you'll go and see Mummy. I shan't mind the term nearly so much if I feel you will be at home for Christmas.'

Helen kissed the flushed little face and felt her eyelids stinging with a strange emotion of mingled tenderness and compassion. It struck her forcibly that Patty must lack all real understanding and human contact in her young life if she could feel so strongly about a stranger who had only given her a few encouraging words.

CHAPTER TWO

It was Mrs. Wade herself who opened the door of her flat to Helen, just before half past ten

16

that next morning. Helen had entered the handsome block of flats in Knightsbridge feeling slightly foolish; the whole thing was ridiculous after such a brief meeting with a weeping schoolgirl to apply for a job as her holiday governess! And yet—all night she had been haunted by the memory of Patty . . . geated between those two at the 'Ritz'; the glittering mother and the sulky man-about-town . . . silently weeping. And she could not forget her promise to Patty.

Patty's mother, dressed in a dark green tailored ensemble this morning, was looking tired and cross, but greeted Helen quite affably.

'Oh, it's you—Miss—er—Shaw—do come in. So you didn't forget my funny little daughter's suggestion!'

'No,' said Helen. 'I didn't forget!'

Mrs. Wade guided her into a sitting-room in which there was none of the pale light of the dull autumn morning. All the electric lamps were switched on. It was one of Rita's habits—to live with all the lights and fires full on. The place struck Helen as being unbearably hot.

'I'm never warm . . .' Rita stated, as she motioned Helen to a chair and rubbed her thin long fingers together and offered Helen a cigarette which she refused. Rita lit one for herself and began to talk rapidly—about Patty, her husband's death, her subsequent difficulties and her impending marriage.

17

'You'll quite understand, Miss Shaw—Nigel—Mr. Cressland—is very sweet with Patty but naturally he won't want her always with us and I anticipate being married again next month.'

Helen nodded. So far she had not put a word in but listened attentively. But she thought:

'Nigel is *not* sweet with Patty! He resents her. And she, this woman, is fighting between her natural affection for her own child and her passion for the man. How awful!'

Rita talked on; she was flying to Paris—should be leaving the day after tomorrow, to buy her trousseau. She used to have a first-rate maid, a half-Swiss girl named Louisa, who looked after her, and mended for her and Patty, too, in the holidays, and did the breakfast (they ate most of their other meals out—there was a restaurant in the building) but now that beastly Louisa had walked out on her last night at a moment's notice—obviously been offered more money by someone else. She was left in the lurch—just when she was most busy, and she hated leaving the flat empty while she was away—she liked someone to stay here, to look after things.

A torrent of words poured from Rita's lips, her hands clenching and unclenching nervously, the long fingers flicking the cigarette ash on to the carpet. Helen continued to listen and learn. Several things

18

struck her; mainly what a dreadful life it would be for Patty alone here, in this overheated and artificially lighted apartment. It was full of soft thick carpets, painted furniture, everything modern and expensive. The cocktail cabinet, the radio-gramophone, the off-white walls and chair covers, the satin cushions and curtains, the frilly net, excluding all possible views of the outside world.

A prison for a small girl—no room for a game—for a little healthy untidiness, for a puppy or a kitten. It was the woman's flat— imbued with her taste and personality.

'Poor Patty . . .' thought Helen anew.

'Now what I want,' she heard Rita's high voice, 'is someone to take Pat out—or even away occasionally to the seaside—someone young—to amuse her. You're young, aren't you?'

'I was twenty-two yesterday.'

'And no ties—I mean—not engaged or— about to marry, yourself?'

Helen's fingers interlocked. A wave of red dyed her pale, thin young face. She said in a low tone:

'No—I was to be married but my fiancé— died—of infantile paralysis—six months ago.'

Rita Wade dragged her thoughts from herself to expend an instant's sympathy on the younger girl.

'Oh, I'm so sorry . . .' she murmured.

Helen bit her lip and changed the

19

conversation.

'Actually I have nobody in the world now but my aunt and uncle. They are not well off and I want to earn my own living.'

She explained her position and her abandoned art.

Rita Wade said:

'Oh, how nice—you might teach Patty to draw. She loves drawing—'

Helen, suddenly grown cynical, thought:

'It's only because she thinks the drawing will keep the child occupied—not because she wants Patty to find something she really wishes to do . . .'

Rita then went, tactfully, into the question of references.

'Of course,' smiled Helen, 'I'm just someone Patty talked to in an hotel.'

She gave Rita three names: her uncle's banker, her vicar who had known her since she was confirmed, and Christopher's mother, Lady Pilgrim.

The title impressed Rita Wade, as Helen knew it would do. It made her slightly scornful of Patty's mother. What a shallow worldly creature—behind that wonderful beauty. And it *was* wonderful. Helen could imagine that men 'fell' like ninepins before the slim, graceful figure which showed no signs of thickening despite the fact that Rita was in her thirties; that alabaster skin, those brown slumbrous eyes with the dark red hair could be

20

accounted for now. Rita's mother had been an Italian.

'But my father was thoroughly English like my late husband. Patty inherits their looks. A pity she's got those pale blue eyes and sandy hair. Why couldn't it have been a real red like mine?'

'She's a very sweet, sensitive little girl,' said Helen.

Rita yawned, looked at her watch and rose.

'Oh, yes, she's sweet, but I don't pretend to understand children. I'm sure *you* will be marvellous with her. She adores you. You made a great hit yesterday.'

Helen also stood up.

'Then you want me to take the post at the end of the school term, Mrs Wade.'

'Definitely. But how about the three months before—you say you must find a job—'

That started a new line of thought. And it was then that Helen, herself, suggested that she might take the place of the Swiss girl, Louisa, and start work immediately in the flat.

'I know I used to be an artist—or meant to be one—but I'm very domesticated. I went to a French convent and learned to sew well. And I can cook, too . . .' (oh, those marvellous picnic-meals in the studio, with Chris—aeons and aeons ago—how he had loved her omelettes, she thought desolately).

Mrs. Wade, a little startled, stared at Helen. Her dark eyes gleamed hopefully.

21

'You really would do *that*—mind my flat while I was abroad—and look after my clothes, as well as Patty? Of course, we'd find a daily in the holidays, when you had Patty—but now—you wouldn't mind a little housework?'

'Everyone has to do it these days,' smiled Helen.

And after that, swiftly and thankfully Mrs. Wade engaged Helen. At five pounds a week. She could start to live in the flat at once—and take complete charge.

'If you're lonely you can ask a friend to stay!' said Patty's mother. 'I don't mind at all. There are two beds in Patty's room. I use it in the term time for guests.'

That was typical of her, as Helen was to discover. The sudden generous impulses and kindnesses which made Rita Wade so attractive—as well as the latent meanness, crass selfishness, even cruelty, the unreliable streak—along with the sudden violent temper and jealousy inherited from her Sicilian grandmother.

But today she was all charm—because Helen Shaw had come just at the psychological moment, and seemed just the right person for Patty, and for *her*, in the flat.

Helen was quiet and tactful, Rita considered. She wouldn't get on Nigel's nerves. Neither would she interest him—she was much too 'Jane Eyreish', too quiet and retiring to amuse most men, although

22

admittedly she had lovely fair hair and those deep grey eyes.

'But I need never bother about her with Nigel,' thought Rita. 'Beside me—she's insipid.'

And she consoled herself with that thought when—two hours later—she met Nigel Cressland in the 'Berkeley', as arranged. After lunch he was driving her down to Sussex where they were both to be guests for the week-end in a big country house.

She was in her best mood—delighted to have discovered Helen Shaw and got Patty 'settled' for Christmas, to say nothing of replacing Louisa at a moment's notice.

But before the week-end was far advanced, Rita was feeling far from good-humoured and a little anxious. Nigel was a difficult man. She had long discovered that. He could be most amusing and charming. When they had first met in this very country house, he had fallen violently in love with her. But he was one degree more selfish and self-centred than she. They alternated between feverish love-making and hot disputes. They were always rushing around in pursuit of amusement, in town or in the country or by the river—racing, motoring, playing bridge or poker, spending much more money than Rita could afford.

Dr. Wade had had a big practice, made money and had small private means also at the back of him, and he had left everything to

Rita. But she was rapidly devouring it up and beginning to spend capital. She was taking a chance about that—hoping by her present mode of life to meet and marry a man of means. Arguing with herself that if her second husband had money, Patty would also benefit.

Nigel seemed to have plenty of money. He was forty, a director of several companies and an inveterate gambler on the Stock Exchange. Whenever he made a 'coup' he gave Rita something expensive. He seemed crazy about her. And she was in love with him in her way, not a very deep way, if at moments she resented the fact that he was not more of a slave—like Patty's father who had so humbly adored her. She thirsted for adoration. Sometimes Nigel was offhand and even unkind to her. When he was thwarted, he sulked for days. He had been sulking a lot lately—over Patty. He wanted her to keep Patty right out of the way. He resented the time Rita spent with the child when she was at home.

'She isn't mine, why should you expect me to like her?' once he had asked Rita in the middle of a row.

Shallow though she was, the mother in her had rebelled at that; hotly she had upheld her child's rights. But in the end, weakly she had consented to keep Patty more in the background. But it did not endear Nigel to her. And she was marrying him, she knew full well, because of the money. Sometimes she felt afraid—horribly under his thumb—because of all those bills he paid for her, bills she had no right to run up, when she ought to have saved for Patty's future, and he had backed her overdraft at the bank.

The one thing Rita tried to do was to avoid discussions of her small daughter with Nigel, but it was bound to come up during the week-end in Sussex.

It was one night after a poker party. After everybody else had gone, Nigel stayed down in the drawing-room finishing a whisky. Rita stayed with him.

'Hellish tired. And I lost a couple of quid. You're all square, aren't you, Nigel?'

'No. I made ten bob on the evening. Chicken feed,' he drawled. 'Hardly worth the effort.'

'Still it was an amusing evening,' said Rita.

A sudden memory of Patty smote her. She said:

'By the way, darling, you remember that day we lunched at the "Ritz" just before Patty went back to school, at the table next to us there was an elderly man and a fair girl in tweeds . . .'

Nigel yawned again.

'Why the devil should I remember them? There were dozens of people lunching all round us, my sweet.'

'Oh, well,' said Rita, 'the thing is that Patty made friends with the girl, Helen Shaw. She had excellent references and is just the type I want, and she's going to look after the flat in Louisa's place and then mind Patty in the holidays. Don't you think it's a good idea?'

Without hesitation he answered:

'I think it's one of your worst, my dear Rita.'

'But why . . .?'

'Because it means another person in the flat, a third, when we want to be alone. Which applies to your place or to any other one we may move to.'

'Never mind. Miss Shaw will keep out of the way, I assure you. She's not the type to thrust herself forward. And, after all, if you want to see more of me, I must have someone to mind Patty.'

'Well, considering this Christmas you're supposed to be on honeymoon with me, I think it's damned bad luck that I've got to have the kid, plus a governess hanging around. I scarcely call it tactful of you.'

Her heart sank. There he was, truculent, bearish, always beastly when Patty's name came up. Hotly she exclaimed:

'Neither is it tactful of you always being so nasty about my child.'

Now a cold sardonic smile appeared on the man's thin lips. Through half-closed eyes he regarded her much as he would regard any *objet d'art* in the room. Damned beautiful woman, Rita, he reflected. He prided himself on his good taste. That black dinner dress with the long tight sleeves sheathed her small

26

breasts and small graceful waist as though she had been moulded into it and billowed into a cascade of tulle from the hips downwards. And what with her flawless camelia-skin, the beautiful red hair and the dark magnificent eyes (not a girl he knew could touch her), all that was sensual and acquisitive in Nigel Cressland had wanted Rita from the moment he first saw her, debts, child and all. The debts he could cope with (so long as his luck lasted, he told himself dryly) but the child was a constant thorn in the flesh and he couldn't think how any woman as attractive as Rita could have produced that plain little object, Patty. If she had been pretty, amusing—like her mother—he might have tolerated her about the place. But Patty, so stand-offish and surly, with the gold band over her crooked teeth and that carroty hair which had just missed being the glorious Titian of Rita's—she was a most unattractive child. No doubt she resembled her worthy papa who, from all accounts, had not been over-blessed with good looks.

'Why the hell can't you find a holiday camp and send Patty there for Christmas,' Nigel suggested after a pause.

Rita's eyes flashed. There were times when the mother instinct asserted itself, times when she wasn't as weak, as ready to sacrifice all her whims to Nigel as he would wish. She snapped:

'Holiday camps, my dear Nigel, are for

27

summer, not winter, and why should I *never* have my child in her own home?'

He put his tongue in his cheek.

'Isn't it shortly going to be *my* home?'

Rita flushed.

'Ye—es—but it will be mine too and Patty is my child.'

'Your greatest mistake my sweet.'

'Oh, don't be so hateful. Other men have married widows with children and been decent to them. Why should *you* be so unreasonable?'

'I can't stand children, and I told you that when we got engaged. We're merely going over old ground.'

She felt ready to cry with frustration—she did not like children herself but the wretched little Patty was her own flesh and blood and besides it annoyed her that Nigel should always get his own way. Of course the person who held the purse-strings always got it. 'Damn and blast,' thought Rita bitterly.

She made a gesture of exasperation then picked up a cigarette out of the gilded Louis Quatorze china box which stood on the mantelpiece behind her. She tapped it on one polished thumbnail.

'Sometimes I think you're not human.'

He stretched his legs and lolled back in the deep-cushioned chair, showing his teeth in a smile which had a touch of malicious humour.

'You make me laugh like a drain, my sweet! Are *you* any more human? Did you not spend the first week we met telling me how dreadful it was for poor Rita to have been left widowed with a child on her hands? And of course the said child was first of all described as being four years old, then six, then when I met her, I found it was eleven. Don't kid yourself that you're any more fond of children than I am.'

'I know I'm not,' she said, furious and scarlet, 'but as *I've* got Patty, I can't totally neglect her.'

'My dear girl, she's at a very expensive boarding-school, for which incidentally I am paying, and could in no way be called neglected...'

Rita chewed her lower lip speechlessly. Of course, Nigel *would* throw it up at her about paying Patty's schooling. And it was all too true, because she had gambled away the money Tom had trusted her with; and she had had to raise the cash somehow when the time came for educating the child properly. Until her meeting with Nigel, Patty had been to day schools. But now, with all this extra expense— the uniform and the huge bills one had to pay for the best schools—she had *had* to appeal to Nigel.

Weakly she said:

'Well, doesn't it please you to think that you're doing something for her, considering you're going to be her stepfather?'

The man got up and threw his cigarette-end into the fire.

'I've no wish to be reminded of that. Neither do I intend to have a repetition of that frightful lunch at the "Ritz", with the kid snivelling in public. In fact, the less I see of my *soi-disant* stepdaughter, the better.'

Tears of rage threatened to play havoc with the black on Rita's lashes. She put down the unlighted cigarette she had been holding, snatched mirror and chiffon handkerchief out of her sequin evening bag and carefully dabbed her eyes.

'Sometimes I think you're a *fiend*, Nigel.'

'And sometimes I think you enjoy deceiving yourself into thinking that you're a good mother, my angel.'

'Well, I try to be . . .' she gulped.

Then he laughed.

'But you will never succeed. You haven't even the making of a fond mamma. You are far too interested in your little self and I'm not surprised. You're extremely attractive. But not when you lug that child around with you. You take my advice and keep her as far away from me as possible, then we won't ever quarrel.'

She made a gesture of anger and impotence. Her large dark eyes flung him a resentful look.

'Well, I'm going to have this Miss Shaw to start off with, letting her mind Patty; and I promise I'll keep them both out of your way,' she said.

'You said you wanted me to try and take you to the Bahamas later on. Would you like to bring Patty *and* the governess too?' he sneered.

'Don't be a fool, Nigel.'

Then he laughed, put his glasses in his coat-pocket, came close to her and with one of his quick gusts of passion, caught the slim alluring body in his arms and buried his face against the red perfumed waves of hair, letting his lips stray down one of the small white ears in which gleamed a gold curved earring which he had given her.

'Don't let's waste time talking about Patty. How about kissing me?'

She gave him a rather wintry smile and offered him her lips. The kiss was a prolonged one, his large hands straying down her back to the slim waist.

'Nobody would ever think you'd had a baby, Rita, my darling; you've got a miraculous figure! When are you going to Paris to buy lovely things for me to see?'

'Next week, perhaps.'

'Let me know how much money you want . . .'

That was better. It was the old generous Nigel who had at first attracted her. She kissed him back with a responsive warmth and after a moment, by mutual consent, they moved out of the drawing-room and up the wide staircase, his arm still around her.

He had forgotten Patty and their difference of opinion. But she had not. And she realized,

31

that night, that she was rapidly falling out of love with Nigel. She wished she could meet somebody else who could satisfy the romantic as well as the mercenary strain in her.

CHAPTER THREE

Meanwhile in the Knightsbridge flat, Helen began a new life in which Christopher and the sweet, sorrowful memories of their love had no part.

She was not unhappy. She liked being alone. And she had plenty to do. Louisa had neglected her job. Helen took down all the frilly net curtains and washed and ironed them. She sorted and tidied Rita's clothes. She had left disgracefully untidy wardrobe and drawers. She mended some of Patty's cotton frocks and let down hems of the winter ones which, her mother said, she had outgrown but which she would need if they could be made to fit.

In Rita's absence, Helen switched off some of the fires, opened wide the windows and let in fresh air and daylight. In the evenings she visited her uncle and aunt or her friends. And she wrote to Patty—long newsy letters, telling her amusing things to make her laugh, and illustrating the letters with comic little drawings, as only an artist could do.

The response was terrific. Long, badly scrawled but worshipping letters came from the love-starved child. St. Cyprian's was as hateful to her as ever, she said, but she was all right because her *darling* Helen was waiting for her. (Helen had told her to call her by that name.) She longed for the 'hols'. She spoke far more of what she would do with Helen than with her own mother. Nigel Cressland she never mentioned.

Sunday came and Helen went down to Bexhill to take Patty out to lunch. It was a huge success. The child looked better, quite rosy and happy after that outing, and with promise of another one soon. It left no doubt in Helen's mind that she had done the right thing in taking this job. She was going to make all the difference to Patty's life, and in helping the child, she, herself, was being helped. Her own deep wounds were healing. She had not felt so peaceful, so eager to build up her life again, since Christopher died.

On the day of Rita's return from Paris, Helen put flowers in the drawing-room and Rita's bedroom, and prepared a small but well thought out meal.

Patty's mother, followed by a porter with her two airways suitcases, swept in just before supper, bringing with her the usual aroma of perfume; elegant, strikingly beautiful with a new chic hat, a delicate shade of olive green, on her Titian head. She seemed in excellent

33

spirits—glowing—quite changed from the moody, ill-tempered young woman who had left London. She greeted Helen affably— complimented her on the lovely flowers and later during the evening meal sang Helen's praises.

'Really, it's divine, coming back and finding all this. You've considered details a domestic would never think of. I'm delighted, Helen. I shall call you "Helen", eh, and not Miss Shaw? And you wrote such comprehensive letters. I felt I need worry about nothing in the flat.'

A faint flush crept up under Helen's pallor. She was experiencing the best side of Rita Wade tonight.

'I'm glad you're pleased, Mrs. Wade,' she said.

After the meal, Rita invited the girl to sit with her by the fire (once again all the heat possible was turned on and the place had become Rita's warm, scented nest as before). Smoking a cigarette, relaxed on the sofa, in her brocade housecoat, Rita chatted to Helen like an old friend. She seemed eager *to* pour out confidences. Having heard the latest news of her small daughter, she said:

'Now, Helen, I am going to trust you with my personal news. I want you to know that I've broken my engagement with Nigel Cressland...'

Helen looked at her with faint astonishment.

'Has he phoned or been here at all?' Rita added, lowering her voice as though expecting the man to overhear her.

'Yes,' Helen answered, 'twice yesterday Mr. Cressland phoned.' Rita then said, authoritatively, that he was not to be told anything she was doing, and that she would always be 'out' when he called. He had behaved badly in Paris and she was 'through with him'.

She wouldn't go into details—sufficient to say that she did not wish to continue their association.

Helen maintained a discreet silence, thinking that the loss of Nigel Cressland was the best thing that could happen for little Patty. Rita then told Helen more news that she was aching to impart. She had met 'someone else' in Paris. She hoped to be able to announce a fresh engagement to him. But for the moment they were just tremendous friends.

'He is a marvellous person—the most fascinating creature I've met for years!' said Rita, her large dark eyes dreamy, yet full of latent fire. And in a few more words she intimated to the younger girl that she had fallen desperately in love with this new friend in Paris. She could not stop talking about him—she described his background, his marvellous good looks, his brilliant mind. He was in Paris on business, recently come to Europe from Kenya, where he had big

35

property. He was expected in London this week-end.

'We have everything in common!' added Rita Wade. 'He is very artistic outside his work—particularly musical. He has given me a list of records to buy. You might get them for me at H.M.V.'s, Oxford Street, tomorrow, my dear.'

She tossed Helen the list. Helen regarded it with astonishment. Classical music-the kind she understood and had so often heard at 'Prom Concerts' with Christopher. Beethoven, Mozart, Bach. Yet Rita had never before suggested that she was a lover of classical music. All the records in this flat were dance music—revue—or musical comedy. 'Obviously,' thought Helen, 'she is trying to impress the new boy friend,' whose name, Rita was now telling her, was Peter Farrington. Everybody called him 'Pierrot'—it had always been his nickname; Rita adored it.

'He is deliciously vital and full of enthusiasms—he made me feel seventeen again!' exclaimed Rita, leaning back on the cushions, sighing.

Helen maintained a discreet silence. But Rita's next confidence made her look at this spoiled beautiful woman with a contempt she found hard to conceal. Rita had not told Peter about Patty. She just *could* not, she said. They had had such a heavenly time 'doing Paris' and been so young together—he could not spoil it by admitting that she had a daughter of eleven. He had guessed her age to be twenty-five so she had let him think it.

'I don't look more, do I, Helen?' Rita asked eagerly. 'Don't you agree—let Peter keep his illusions just now? Later when we're married—I'll confess about poor little Pat. But I *must* marry Peter. He's eight years younger than I am, but as I am so young-looking what matter? I adore him, Helen, I mean to go back to Kenya with him.'

Helen found it difficult to reply. She felt tongue-tied. It seemed to her to be utterly contemptible for a woman to deny existence of her own child just because she was 'crazy about' a man younger than herself.

'Poor little Patty—thank goodness *I* shall be here when she comes home,' the girl thought grimly.

Rita finished the talk by suggesting glibly that Helen should help keep Patty out of the way when she returned from school.

Peter—Pierrot—Peter—the name was never off Rita's lips during the next few days. She let Helen buy the records; played one half-way through then abandoned it. She couldn't be bothered with such heavy stuff, she said laughing, but it would be here for Pierrot. Helen grew sick of hearing the man's name. Already she despised him. A foolish boy allowing an older woman to deceive him—and Rita was even more foolish if she thought to

37

get away with her deception.

Then commenced the most difficult time of all for Helen. The quiet flat became a kind of vortex—whirling with Rita Wade's intense and often unbridled emotions.

Nigel Cressland persistently telephoned or called, and each time Helen was left to cope with him. He refused to believe that his former fiancée was out or away. He sent bitter, even threatening, messages to Rita, and it seemed to Helen that the woman sometimes was afraid—she was certainly nervous—ill-at-ease—whenever they spoke of Nigel, and still determined not to see him.

There were moments when Rita herself doubted whether she would 'get away with it'. She was much more nervous about the affair that she had allowed Helen to think. But under that façade of delicate beauty there lay a remorseless determination. And nothing is more determined than a woman in love with a man younger than herself.

In Paris, Rita's encounter with Peter Farrington had had an extraordinary effect on her. A dangerous one, because with his youth, his charm and his own enormous enthusiasm for life he made Nigel appear dull and horribly blasé in comparison. He appealed to her romantic imagination as well as her passions; her lust for money, for possessions, for all that she had lacked during her mundane life with Dr. Wade.

Peter had so many assets. There would be no shortage of money from his direction. The wife of a well-known banker in Nairobi would never lack means. There had been nothing lately but talk amongst Rita's friends about future prospects in Kenya—no use staying in England—better to get out to the Colonies. When she thought about it it seemed possible that Nigel would eventually find himself hard up with all the taxation and obstruction in the path of individual enterprise.

But Peter lived in Nairobi and his assets were there. It would be the most wonderful thing in the world to get out of England and start life with him in a gay, beautiful sunny place like Nairobi.

She was thinking about him one morning as she lay in bed finishing the coffee which Helen had brought her. Rita, in her charming way, had said to the girl:

'I can't let you bring me trays—you're not a domestic—but I do so love my coffee and toast in bed—' and of course Helen had at once offered to bring it.

On the breakfast tray were several letters including one with a French stamp and Paris postmark. It was from Peter.

'I hope to be finished here and get over to London by the end of next week. I can't wait to see you again. Rita, you don't know what you've done to me. I just

39

didn't think there could be a girl as beautiful or as marvellous. We had a heavenly time together, didn't we? I can well understand now why so much literature has been written about Paris for lovers—to watch you walking through the Bois de Boulogne was poetry itself. I miss you, Rita.

I've never missed any other woman in the same way but then you are not "any other woman", you are a unique person. Thank you for coming to Paris and into my life . . .'

Again and again she had read that letter and her vanity was soothed and flattered, her sense of triumph tingling. It really *was* a triumph to make a handsome and attractive young man like Peter feel this way about her. Again and again she read those particular words *'a girl as beautiful'*. A *girl!* He thought of her as a girl of his own age. That was the most satisfying thing of all. She shut her eyes and ran her hands down her perfect body. Not an ounce of superfluous fat. None of those extra pieces on the hips nor a 'tyre' round the waist, nor the sagging breasts of her contemporaries who had to rush to find strong girdles or take to diet and massage. No one would think she had ever had Patty. She owed that in a way to poor Tom's devotion; after Patty's birth he had taken such good care of her.

Life with Tom—when Patty was a baby—when they had lived in the country—what a long time ago that seemed! Almost as far back as her girlhood. She had had old parents. They lived in a London suburb. She never told anybody about that or what a relief it had been to her when the poor old dears went heavenwards, one shortly after the other, during the first years of her marriage. Rita had always been ambitious, never wished it to be known that she had sprung from very ordinary people and a commonplace home. And it was a mercy that she had her Italian blood; one of those astonishing products of elderly ordinary people, she was a child of singular beauty.

Why had she been such a fool as to rush into marriage with Tom? Possibly because she had wanted to get away from home and her parents and Tommy had adored her so and after all he had had a little money and everybody said that he was a coming man in the profession. One of the bones of contention between them had been that he would never practise in Harley Street as she had wanted.

But all that was over now and after Tommy there had been several lovers—Nigel—and now Peter. Ah! But Peter was going to be her Waterloo. She was crazy about the boy.

She thought of their first evening out together alone. They had danced in one of those small intimate restaurants just off the Champs Elysées.

He had told her many times during the evening how ravishing she was and how perfectly she danced. He was much taller than she, and had a way of drooping his lids suddenly, looking down at her, drawing her a little nearer him, which she found very exciting. They danced all night and then went home together when dawn was breaking rosily over the Arc de Triomphe. He had kissed her for the first time—gently as though afraid to hurt her and then, invited by the warmth of her lips, with a fire and passion which was not altogether inexperienced. And she liked it that way. Peter roused all the warm Southern blood in her and made her realize how hungry she had been for a romantic love all these years. Only that ice-cold brain of hers, that shrewd common sense warning her to play her part with discretion, saved her from losing her head altogether.

But she knew that it was essential that she should keep Peter's respect if she wanted to marry him, and she was gratified when next morning he sent a huge box of lilies to her hotel bearing a little note which said:

'Forgive me if I was a little crazy last night but I couldn't help it. My dear, you're much too attractive but I want you to know that I'm at your feet; let me stay there.'

'PIERROT.'

42

She was only too willing to keep him there and she was equally determined to keep her own head and not spoil his illusions. It was such a relief from the association with Nigel who at times delighted to humiliate her by his references to her financial embarrassment; in fact, the way he treated her generally—as though he had bought her! To say nothing of his attitude towards Patty. Nigel knew altogether too much about her.

Peter thought of her as a young and bereft widow (for him quite virginal and unscathed) and although she had meant to tell him that she had a child, she kept putting it off and putting it off until it was too late.

She knew that she was a traitor—that she had betrayed her child by denying her existence—but she, Rita, wanted Peter Farrington as she had never wanted any other man in her life. No doubt he was not as averse to children as Nigel—quite possibly he would want one of his own—but it would certainly be a shock to him if she produced a child of eleven.

Then Nigel arrived in Paris.

He came to her hotel to see her in one of his worst moods and was very rude. Flushed with her recent triumph—with this new gorgeous young lover behind her—she astonished Nigel (and herself) by giving him back his ring and coolly announcing that she was not going to marry him.

She could revise the scene plainly now as she lay in her bed on this cold, rather foggy autumn morning, her electric fire and lamps blazing.

Nigel, standing in front of her fire in the private sitting-room of her Paris hotel—herself in a silky peignoir, lying on the sofa. She had been resting prior to meeting Peter for dinner and the opera. She had not expected Nigel till next morning. She remembered how unpleasant he looked with his heavy, pasty face and bad-tempered mouth. Of course now poor Nigel stood no chance as compared with Peter—her Pierrot—sun-browned, laughing, quick-witted, with a lot of brain behind that boyish exterior.

Nigel's jaw had dropped when she held out her hand with the big solitaire diamond for which he had paid a great deal of money at the time.

Then he snapped:

'Don't be a little idiot, Rita.'

She shrugged her shoulders, got up and slipped the ring into his coat pocket, then returned to her sofa, running slim fingers through her red waves of hair, yawning.

Of course, after that he had blazed at her. What the hell did she think she was doing? What idiotic game was this? Did she think she was going to walk out on him just a few weeks before their wedding? And so on, until she

44

looked at him through her long glistening lashes and said:

'It's no use, Nigel, I've made up my mind.'

Then he changed his tactics. Came to her side, grabbed her hand and began to make clumsy love to her. She was just fooling—she must know that he was mad about her—it was just that he was disgruntled because some business deal hadn't come off—he apologized for his rudeness—(the first apology Nigel had ever made to her).

She remembered how nauseated she had been by the touch of his hands and by his efforts to kiss her. She was still under the spell of Peter's charming poetic love-making and the tenderness of his brown fine hands. She found Nigel's square-tipped coarse fingers repulsive despite their careful manicuring.

Once again she told him, coldly, that their engagement was at an end.

'As you, yourself, once said, we don't really see eye to eye,' she reminded him.

He had asked her if it was 'because of the kid' and mumbled something to the effect that he would try and put up with 'more Patty' if she wanted it. Rita played on that for a moment and let him think that she was turning him down because it wasn't fair to give Patty such an unwilling stepfather.

But Nigel knew her too well and he was only hoodwinked for a few minutes. Then, with an ugly look in his eyes he demanded the truth.

45

'Come on, own up, there's some other chap . . .'

Rita looked at her wrist-watch.

'If there is, that's my affair,' she said. 'It's quite normal for people to break engagements, my dear Nigel. You needn't look at me as though I'm raving.'

Then he, too, grew ice-cold; and very ugly indeed. He sat on the arm of a chair opposite her, carefully lit a cigar and while he smoked he reminded her of the bills he had paid during the last twelve months and of her overdraft.

That frightened her a little. She had said:

'Well, we've had some good times together, and you've enjoyed them as much as I have—surely you don't begrudge some slight payment, do you?'

He had told her then that it was more than 'slight' and that he begrudged it bitterly and that he was damned if he was going to make her a present of all the furs and jewels and cash just in order to watch her marry some other man.

'Who is this fellow? Is *he* prepared to take on your debts as well as your beautiful white body?' he had asked rudely.

Flushed and hot-eyed, she had bitten her lips and made no answer. But in the silence that had ensued, a variety of feverish and unpleasant thoughts assailed her. Under these circumstances could she let Peter see her as

46

she really was—or know about those debts? As for Patty—she had got herself into the devil of a mess all right. Even if Peter forgave her for being eight years older than he thought her and for having a child aged eleven, he wouldn't forgive the fact that she had flung away Patty's inheritance and allowed Nigel to pay the very school at which the child was being educated.

She had tried argument and pleading in turn with Nigel—to no avail.

Unless she changed her mind and went through with this marriage he would ruin her, he said. He would give her breathing space in which to pull herself together and put an end to this folly but if she still persisted in it, he would withdraw his backing at her bank and her new boy friend could compete.

With this savage threat he marched out of her room and out of the hotel.

Her mind darted this way and that seeking for a way out—and she could see only one loophole. She must marry Peter before he found out either about Patty, her debts or her association with Nigel.

But Nigel had some queer hold over her. Of that Helen was certain. The situation became daily more strained, and it was making Helen, herself, quite nervous. She dreaded the phone or front door bell ringing in case another occasion should arise when she must deal with a furious Nigel. The break was obviously not of his making and he seemed more in love with

Rita now than he had been before. And at any moment Peter Farrington was expected from Paris.

Then, suddenly, a catastrophe for Rita. On a cold October day when she had arranged to go down to Bexhill with Helen to see her child, she was seized with violent pains and a high temperature. Within a couple of hours she was in the London Clinic. It was an emergency appendix—she was to be operated on that same afternoon.

Just before the operation, she saw Helen and clung to her, sobbing convulsively.

'It's a tragedy for me. I had a wire this morning. Peter is coming to London tomorrow. Oh, heavens, Helen, he and Nigel *mustn't meet.* Nigel is malicious. If Pierrot met him and told him about *us*—Nigel would smash it all up—he'd tell Pierrot about Patty, my age—everything. It would finish me. I'll tell Pierrot everything in my own good time. Helen, swear you'll keep those two men apart. And when Peter comes—be tactful—bring him to see me—fix it all for me. I'll *die* if you don't help me.'

She was frenzied. Helen was sorry for her—just as she would be sorry for any human being in physical pain—and Rita was suffering and scared of the operation. Helen tried to comfort her. As far as possible she would do what Rita asked. But inwardly Helen was scornful. She could not bear the thought of

48

that child, down in the boarding-school, being denied. Patty who, when Helen last saw her, had been busy painting a special, touching little Christmas card for 'darling Mummy'.

Rita clung to Helen with feverish fingers, her great dark eyes glittering.

'I rely on you, Helen—and I'll repay you—give you a lot if you promise not to let me down—'

'I want nothing, but I'll do all I can,' said Helen flushing.

She returned to the flat—once more quiet, now that its hectic, restless mistress had departed—half wishing she had not taken this job. It was no easy matter working for Rita Wade. She exhausted one, mentally, as well as physically.

'I shall stay only for Patty's sake—I must try to make some kind of Christmas for *her*,' Helen reflected.

She sat down that evening to write to the child and explain why Mummy had not been to see her, and to tell her to write to the clinic.

She was just about to put the chain on the front door and retire for the night, when the bell rang. Helen quickly regarded herself in the mirror in her bedroom. Heavens, if this was a visitor—how untidy she was! She had on an old grey flannel suit. Her hair was not done. Speedily Helen tied it back with a bow, dabbed her nose with powder and ran to the door.

Just before she opened it, she was struck by

the unpleasant suspicion that this might be Nigel Cressland, himself, coming to make another 'scene'. The last time she had seen him he had grinned at her with a touch of malevolence and said:

'My, my, the beautiful Rita has gotten herself a staunch ally. But do not think I believe that she is always out or away, my dear girl. I'm not a fool. I know she's avoiding me deliberately. But one of these days—we shall meet. Au revoir!'

Helen hoped this was *not* Nigel—especially as she was alone tonight. He might force his way in—try to find Rita—and it wouldn't be pleasant.

Then she opened the door. For a moment she stood staring. It was not the heavy figure of Nigel Cressland that she saw but a tall, slightly built young man in grey, carrying a hat in one hand and a suitcase in the other. He looked down at her and said a trifle anxiously:

'Good evening. I'm sorry to trouble you, but isn't this Mrs. Wade's flat?'

Helen stood transfixed—staring—as though at a ghost. It *was* a ghost, she thought for one crazy moment. *Christopher's ghost.* It was Christopher himself standing there—with that graceful, familiar figure—the chestnut-brown hair—the thin, alert face with slightly hollowed cheeks—the wide boyish mouth. It was Christopher, *come back from the dead.*

All the pent-up emotions, the bitter grief,

the aching loneliness within Helen, so long bottled up and well controlled, broke loose in this unguarded instant. A low cry came from her.

'Chris—Chris—*Oh, Chris!*'

The young man stared, utterly taken aback and astonished. Never in his life had he heard such anguish in a woman's voice. And this woman was so young, a mere child with her long, light hair. As for her eyes-how tragic and beautiful, full of desolation.

It only took Helen a moment in which to recover herself then she felt so hot and embarrassed that she could only draw the back of her hand across her forehead (a forehead that was actually wet from shock and nerves) and gasp:

'I'm most terribly sorry—you must think me quite crazy—really I don't know what to say—please come in.'

He gave a sigh of relief. The nice-looking girl with the long, fair hair tied with that bow at the back of her head, making her look like a schoolgirl, was not mad after all. Obviously it was a case of mistaken identity.

Helen recovered even more and as she led the young man into the sitting-room and switched on the light, she added further explanations.

'I feel an awful fool but you see—you're just the living image of—somebody I knew—we were going to be married—he died.'

The word stuck in her throat—it seemed so long since she had mentioned Christopher's death to anybody—rigidly she had schooled herself not to speak of him, knowing the pain, the grief that it conjured up and she did not want to go on suffering over Christopher, she wanted to start life again and it must necessarily be a life in which he had no part otherwise the very memory of their complete and absorbing love would destroy her.

Peter Farrington dropped his suitcase and loosened the muffler around his neck and looked around him at the subdued lights in Rita's pretty luxurious sitting-room—still as she had left it—chrysanthemums in a tall china vase on the little piecrust walnut table by the window—a new *Vogue* lying opened on the sofa—cigarettes visible through the lid of a plastic box, a big silver lighter, a huge glass ashtray (Rita smoked madly and could not bear small ashtrays).

He found it hot and apparently so did the girl who had admitted him. Speedily she opened a window and let in a breath of the keen frosty air.

Then she turned and looked at him and now that she saw him in the lamplight her heartbeats slowed down a little as did the mad racing of her pulses. He *was* like Christopher but much taller. Chris used to be rather slight and small-boned but this man had wide strong shoulders and a wider more humorous mouth

52

and of course he was as brown from the sun as poor Chris had been pale. This was no artist who spent long hours in a studio slaving over his work with little time for fresh air or exercise. This young bronzed man from Kenya exuded a health and vitality which life had denied to Christopher. But the likeness was still there—painfully and incredibly. The eyes, the high cheek-bones, the straight nose, that thick chestnut hair. And even the way Peter Farrington lifted a hand and ran it through that untidy head. Chris used to do that.

'I'm afraid Mrs. Wade is not here,' she said, trying to speak in a matter of fact voice. 'I—I know she expected you and she asked me to tell you that she got you a room at the Hyde Park Hotel which is only just round the corner.'

Peter Farrington took a cigarette from the plastic box which Helen was now hurriedly offering him. He noticed that her hand trembled and she still looked distressed. Poor little thing! Hell of a shame, he thought, losing the chap she liked so much, and it must have been a whole lot, to have produced this nervous crisis.

He was still a bit upset himself by that anguished cry with which she had welcomed him. He felt that it would haunt him till the end of his days—like that look in those dark grey eyes.

'Thanks awfully,' he said as he lit the

cigarette, 'I know the Hyde Park. And of course I know who you are now. Rita said that she had someone running a flat for her.'

'Yes. I'm Helen—Helen Shaw.'

'I'm afraid it's a bit late to turn up. The plane was delayed. We ran into a bit of fog. But where is Rita—Mrs. Wade?'

'Please sit down,' she said.

He took the armchair she indicated. Helen seated herself rather stiffly on the edge of the Chesterfield, looking more than ever like a schoolgirl, he thought, with her hands locked nervously together in her lap. 'I must apologize to you,' she said, 'for appearing like this . . .' she touched her hair, 'but I—I washed it this evening and I didn't expect visitors.'.

'Please don't worry, it looks charming,' he said, with that quick charm and friendliness of manner which made Peter Farrington popular with men and women alike.

A slight colour stole back into Helen's cheeks. Then:

'I'm afraid I've got bad news for you,' she blurted out. 'Mrs. Wade was taken ill this morning. She had to go to a nursing-home.'

Peter looked startled.

'Ill? In a home? Good Lord, what's wrong? I'm most frightfully sorry . . .'

Helen sat silent for an instant. He was rather naïve and young and the complete antithesis of Nigel Cressland. And he was very nice. Much too young and nice for Rita. In a

54

flash she recognized that fact despite the slight scorn with which she regarded this man who had been so taken in by a woman of Rita's type.

Then remembering her job she set to work to explain what happened to Rita; told him that although he could not see the patient, she, Helen, would keep him informed and that there was nothing to worry about—her surgeon was one of the best in London and it seemed a straightforward affair. They had taken it in time.

Peter received this news with interest and relief, at once jotted down the address of the clinic in a notebook and made it obvious that he was a young man of method; then asked a lot more questions that left no room for doubt that he was very much in love with Rita.

The more he talked about Rita—frankly praising her—saying how beautiful and wonderful she was and how unique, etc.—the colder and more quiet Helen became. Certainly he was nice and honest and rather touchingly gullible. And she had already heard from Rita how generous he was. And what a gay companion. And on top of that to look like Chris . . . That was too much. Bitter to know that Rita had him in her clutches. Bitter to remember Patty, the neglected little girl in her boarding-school living and longing for the first day of what she called the 'hols' and she, Helen, had promised not to mention Patty. It made her feel rather sick.

Peter looked at the girl. The fair head was bowed, he could not see her face but he thought there was a tired droop to the slender shoulders.

He stood up.

'I've kept you up quite long enough,' he said. 'I must get along to my hotel.'

Then Helen also rose and raised her eyes to him. Once more he was a little startled by their beauty and their sadness and he thought:

'She must have loved that chap a hell of a lot—' and this was followed by another, hopeful and exciting: 'Will Rita ever love me that way? It would be wonderful to know that the woman one married was devoted to one— even after death.'

Helen was saying in a polite little voice that she would be going round to the clinic tomorrow to see Mrs. Wade and would give a message to her from Mr. Farrington.

That eager alert look crossed Peter's face (Chris used to look like that when he saw a picture he liked, or heard an extract from one of his favourite composers when he switched on the radio). This was a young man from Nairobi who had fallen in love with a beautiful scheming woman older than himself. The alertness, the eagerness, were all for *her.*

'Tell Rita I'm desperately sorry to arrive in London and find this disaster,' he said, 'and that I'll send a note around for her to read as soon as she's able. And ask her, please, to let me see her as *soon* as possible.'

'Yes,' said Helen.

As she opened the front door and he replaced his muffler, he gave a smile which was so friendly and delightful that she had to respond to it and smile back very faintly. She began to understand a little why Rita had developed such a passion for Peter Farrington. He was a refreshing change from that blasé sardonic individual Nigel. And there was something so boyish and enthusiastic about him-like a breath of fresh air—the keen exquisite air from the mountain peaks of East Africa whence he came. With a deep resentment in her against fate, she thought: *If Chris had lived and we'd gone abroad into the sunshine as we'd planned, he might have looked like this . . .'*

'Well, good night, Helen,' said Peter, 'if I may call you that. My name's Peter, as you know.'

Helen nodded. She thought: 'But *she* calls him *Pierrot.* It's much too whimsical. It doesn't suit him. Peter means a *rock*—there is something rather rock-like about this young man—rocklike and steadfast perhaps. It will take a lot to disillusion him in the woman he has idealized or perhaps he will never be disillusioned. Rita is clever. She might manage to keep his admiration and respect.'

But there was always Patty. Sooner or later

he would have to know about Patty *and* Rita's real age.

Helen went back to her bedroom after he had gone and thought a lot about him. After her light was out and she lay staring into the darkness, exhausted but wakeful, she kept seeing Peter's face as she had first seen it half in shadow outside the front door. She thought:

'Oh, Chris—he *was* like you—oh, Chris, where are you—I'm so lonely!' And suddenly she turned her face to the pillow and for the first time for long months began to cry. She, who had thought that the well of tears had dried up because she had wept so long and so much for him.

But in the morning she was composed again and a little ashamed of her emotionalism. There was much to do—first and foremost a letter to poor Patty. The post brought one from the child—the usually badly spelt pathetic scrawl jumping childishly and irrelevantly from one thing to another:

'My darling Angelest Snoochiest Helen, I am longing for you to come down and see me again. Yesterday I played senter forward in the hockey match and I got a broose on my shin. Is Mummy back from Paris yet? I am growing things in my garden for the Spring. We all have a garden and have to put bulbs in it. Please can I have extra money for bulbs . . .'

and so on—and more mention of Mummy and the hope that she would see her but of course, by now, Patty would have had that wire postponing their visit. Helen went out early to post a letter to Patty but not before she had telephoned through to the clinic to hear Rita's appendix was out and 'the patient doing well'.

After that Helen hurried round to see Rita. There she was told by a sister that Mrs. Wade ought not really to have visitors yet, but kept asking to see Miss Shaw so she could go in just for a few moments.

Outside it was a dismal day. The fog of last night had turned to rain and it was very cold. But in Rita's room it was warm and dim and full of the flowers that had already been sent to her. (Helen had had orders to ring up everybody she knew last night and tell them about the sudden operation.)

She was quite sorry for Rita today. The beautiful glamorous Mrs. Wade without make-up and obviously in pain, despite the drugs she had been given, wept miserably and clung to Helen's hand.

'Oh, Helen, I don't want to die . . .' she moaned.

Helen looked down at the white face and twisted unrouged lips and thought how very much older she looked like this. It was a good thing Peter Farrington could not see her now. But Helen could never bear the idea of

anybody in pain, so—gentle and sympathetic—
she held the long thin fingers and comforted
her. 'You're not going to die, Mrs. Wade,
don't be so silly! Everybody says you are doing
very well—you've got a lovely strong pulse.'

Rita's large dark feverish eyes gleamed up
at Helen.

'Has—Pierrot—come?' Her voice was a
whisper.

Helen nodded and told her of Peter's arrival
but omitted to describe faithfully her reception
of him, although her cheeks burned at the
memory. She then gave Rita Peter's message.

At that very moment a probationer tiptoed
into the room carrying a huge basket of
hothouse roses with trailing green fern. Rita,
not too ill to be flattered by attention, asked
Helen to look at the card and read it to her.

Helen's cheeks were even a deeper red as
she did so. She uttered the words in a cold
clear voice:

*'With all my love and sympathy. I love you.
Pierrot.'*

Rita drew a long breath and shut her eyes.
Even though her lips twisted with a sudden
convulsion of pain, she smiled.

'So he's said it at last, he *does love me*—oh,
Helen, now I'm going to get better!'

The girl sitting by the beside looked down at
the pink roses and then back at the woman in
the bed and felt that same sick scorn which she
had felt last night. It wasn't that she minded

Rita Wade being besotted by a boy of twenty-six. It was the thought of Patty which detracted sympathy so completely from the affair. She was glad when the sister came in and told her that she must go, and give Mrs. Wade's last hypodermic a chance to take effect. Rita clutched Helen's arm and made her promise to see Peter and tell him how pleased she was with the roses and that she would write when she was strong enough.

'But I won't see him for a week!' she panted. 'I won't let him see me till I'm looking young and beautiful again. *Don't* let him know what a wreck this has made of me. And be careful about Patty and Nigel.'

Helen walked out of the clinic with those words ringing in her ears. About Nigel she had no feelings. He was a detestable man anyhow, and had helped to make Patty's life miserable in his time. But she really did not want to go on meeting Peter Farrington knowing that every time they met she must not mention the child. It was somehow so *degrading*.

But it was not her affair. And she had to take orders from her employer and as long as they were doing no harm to Patty, she would continue to carry them out. And in all conscience it couldn't matter to Patty one way or the other whether Peter knew of her existence or not.

Helen went to Harrods to do some of the shopping Rita had ordered . . . a new

61

swansdown cape to wear when she sat up in bed . . . a bottle of cognac . . . some handcream. She got back to the flat to find Peter Farrington, himself, waiting for her on the doorstep.

He took off his hat as he saw her and smiled—and once more the sight of that attractive face and chestnut head of hair pulled at her heartstrings. But she was getting used to it now. She greeted him quite serenely. He had, of course, come for first-hand news of Rita. She asked him in for a drink and a cigarette. He followed her, taking off a rainwet mackintosh, complaining about the English climate in one breath and in the other begging for details of 'poor sweet Rita'.

Gravely she gave him all the news he asked for and assured him that Rita was in no danger and that he would be able to see her at the end of the week.

CHAPTER FOUR

In the nursing-home, Rita Wade was having an argument with her nurse. The latter bent over the bed trying to induce Mrs. Wade to lie still and give herself a chance to get better. It was only a week since her operation. She was by no means strong yet. But she insisted upon behaving as though she were perfectly well—

fussing about her appearance (she had already spent an hour doing her hair, making up her face, lacquering her nails) changing first of all from a blue swansdown cape into a peach satin jacket, then back to the cape again. She was the most difficult patient the young nurse had ever had. And just because she was trying to do her duty, Mrs. Wade was being disagreeable and telling her to go away.

Of course nurse knew this was all because the 'boy friend' was arriving. So far he had not been allowed to see her. Nobody had, except a Miss Shaw, who seemed to be a kind of confidential lady housekeeper, and who came every day. Nurse pitied her. A sweet-faced girl, nurse thought, and Mrs. Wade always wanting something new, sending her on countless errands.

The so-called boy friend called to inquire every day—twice a day at first. The room was like a garden, full of expensive flowers, mostly from him. Anybody would think they were engaged, the way they were going on. Nurse herself had cast an eye at Mr. Farrington—he was very handsome and had the most engaging smile, and in her opinion he was too young for Mrs. Wade. She could do what she liked about beautifying herself, and certainly she was lovely, but nurse knew how old she was. She wasn't to be hoodwinked. Mrs. Wade was thirty-five if a day. Massage and make-up could do a lot but it couldn't hold back the remorseless march of Time.

With a resentful glance at her patient, nurse left the room. Rita, left alone, put the finishing touches to her eyelashes, then sank back on her pillows with a sigh. She felt weak and depressed and she had suffered agonies. But thank heavens she would be out of this clinic early next week, then she could do what she liked. And she would convalesce at the flat, and Pierrot could see her all day and every day if he wished. Helen wouldn't worry them. She was discretion itself.

Rita lay with closed eyes, confident that she looked very fragile and appealing which would make Pierrot more than ever in love. She turned over many things in her mind while she waited for him. The situation was difficult but not uncontrollable, she reflected. Of course this business of Patty was a curse. Rita did not really like behaving as though she had no child and deceiving Pierrot about her daughter. He was bound to find out in the end. Then she would just have to choose a propitious hour in which to make her confession. She would do it casually as though it didn't matter.

'By the way,' she would say, 'I have got a young daughter—a little schoolgirl, who is an angel—you don't mind, do you, Pierrot?'

Then she would produce Patty and just trust to luck that it would not strike Pierrot too horribly that Patty was nearly twelve and that she, Rita, was a good deal older than he had been led to believe.

The whole thing was rather shameful and she grew hot when she allowed herself to think about it. The good was always warring with the evil with Rita Wade. It was her supreme vanity and egoism, her sensual love of the good things of this life which generally conquered. Rita had fallen desperately in love with this handsome young man from Kenya—she loved him as she had never loved anybody before. And she had fancied herself in love a dozen times since she was a young girl. Her extraordinary beauty and magnetism had attracted and held men so continually that she was used to being admired and pursued. Now she could not do without the thrill of conquest. And Peter Farrington was more thrilling than any of her former admirers.

She had married Patty's father soon after she left school. That had been a mistake which she soon realized. Poor little Patty had been even more than a mistake. Rita had never been cut out to be a mother. But Tom had wanted children and there it was! Tom had been a slave to her but his work as a successful doctor had taken up a good deal of his time and left her free to make other conquests. She imagined she had been clever all through her married life and managed both husband and admirers with consummate skill. Whether poor old Tom went to his grave believing that she had never looked to the right or the left, she really did not know. But she was glad that he had lavished a great deal of affection on his small daughter. Personally Rita had found her husband a bore. But then everything with her eventually became a bore. Like having to look after a child.

Her one wish once she was free was to find another husband who must be both attractive and rich.

She lay thinking about Nigel Cressland for a moment and that particular thought made her uneasy. Those magnificent carnations by the window had come from Nigel and with them a card which simply said: *'Get well quickly. I must see you.'*

She had torn the card to pieces and would have thrown the carnations away except that it would cause comment. She did not wish to be reminded of Nigel. Why, oh why, had she ever started that affair with him? The money, of course. She had been so hard up when he came on the scene. He had never been her type physically. He was smart and quite an amusing companion and had introduced her to a lot of rich racy people. But as a lover she had never really cared for him. He was *not* an artist. And the soft, languorous side of Rita liked a man to be an artist in love.

She had found everything in Pierrot. She had never met a more talented young man. He was an amazing mixture—he had a sound business head and had come over to Europe as representative of a big East African Bank. He seemed to have plenty of money although he was very modest about it (Nigel was always blatantly rich). In course of conversation and without boasting he spoke of his lovely home in Nairobi—where he had a widowed mother and a young sister who might, he said, be coming to London quite soon to study music. The Farrington family were all musical, it seemed. Pierrot's love of the classics was a bit of a setback for Rita—but she was clever enough not to let him know how it made her yawn, and thank goodness he had another side—he liked theatres, cinemas, and gay parties. And he danced divinely. In fact he had been an enormous success with Rita the moment they had met in Paris at that dinner given by an old friend of Rita's who was married to a man in the Legation out there.

The next morning, after the party, Margot had rung Rita up at her hotel to tell her what a tremendous hit she had made with Peter Farrington. It had been Margot, a selfish, worldly wise young woman with no love for children, who had said:

'I shouldn't tell him about Patty if I were you. He's crazy about you, my dear, and a positive "catch". You keep Patty's existence dark until you have got him.'

At first the idea had revolted Rita then become a temptation to which she finally succumbed. And so Peter was not told about

Patty.

She tried to tell herself that she would alter and become really good and faithful for Pierrot's sake if only he would marry her. She would put men like Nigel and the frantic search for empty pleasure right out of her life. She would go back to Nairobi with Pierrot and be the perfect wife of his dreams.

That was how she felt at the moment and how she was feeling when a probationer ushered Peter into the room.

Her heart beat quickly when she saw him. A becoming pink tinged the marble pallor of the oval face which had haunted Peter Farrington's imagination ever since he last saw Rita in Paris.

He laid a huge bunch of roses on the bed, sat down at her side, took one of her long thin hands and held it as though it were made of Dresden china, and looked with eloquent pity at the invalid—down into the big dark eyes— at the wonderful red hair curling today down the snowy neck (he had never seen it like that before and it made her look very young and even more glamorous).

'My poor sweet Rita are you better?' he asked in a hushed voice. 'What a terrible fright you gave me.'

Her long pointed fingers curled around his which were hard, brown and strong.

'Pierrot!' she whispered.

He bent and kissed the white fingers.

'I have been frantically worried about you,'

68

he said, and took off his coat and put it over the back of his chair. Rita lay looking at him with her melting eyes. Her quick censorious brain was registering little odd notes—for instance, she must tactfully lead him to that wonderful tailor in Conduit Street who made Nigel's suits. But in spite of the suit which she didn't like, he was still wonderful with that rich, brown face, the supple lean figure, and very wide shoulders. Not an ounce of superfluous fat on him. And he was so sensitive—she could see him flush under his tan as she pressed his hand and she drank in, thirstily, the eager adoration in eyes that were a curiously light grey in that sun-browned face.

'Dear Pierrot!' she whispered. 'I'm much better and you don't need to worry about me any more. They are going to let me come home next week. It was a horrid appendix but they say the operation was most successful.'

'Thank the Lord!' said Peter.

During the next few moments they discussed her health and her recovery; he told her a dozen times how beautiful she was looking, then harked back to their meeting in Paris; said that he was profoundly grateful for all that she had done for him, it had been a revelation seeing Paris through her eyes and turned this business trip into something too wonderful for words. He said that it was tremendously lucky that the remainder of his work now lay in London and laughingly added

69

that he would see to it that the work was indefinitely delayed so he need not leave England for some time.

'My uncle is at the head of the show and I shall just cable to the old boy and tell him that he must let me stay until I want to go back,' finished Peter.

'Don't you want to go back?' she asked softly.

'You know that I don't. You know that I want to get to know you and you to know me,' he said gravely.

She bit hard at her lips. He had said that before, in Paris. And it was not at all what she wanted. She would have liked him to sweep her off her feet and cart her straight to a Registry Office—and marry her before Christmas—and before Patty came home. But he had a cautious streak—or was it just a wise one which was allied to his business training. He was impulsive but not stupidly so. He had hinted that it was his considered opinion that two people should never jump into matrimony after a brief association. In fact, he had told her in Paris that he knew that he was in love with her and hoped she loved him, but did not want 'to rush things'.

'You've had one marriage which you say was very unhappy, you poor darling—you must be quite sure that the next one is the right one,' he had said.

She found that definitely trying, but knew

that she must control her own ardour and conform to his principles and beliefs. She realized that he was an idealist. If she wanted him, she must retain the ideal and not let him think her too easily conquered. But certainly it was trying!

They continued to talk. He wanted to know what she meant to do when she came out of the clinic. He had just bought a car for his use whilst in England. Would she like him to drive her about in the country?

She shook her head. She was about to say that she hated the country at this time of year but refrained, hastily recalling that he had once mentioned that he was fond of country life—used to hunting, shooting and fishing out in Kenya. She knew that he meant that one day she should do all these things with him, so she must not disillusion him. It was easy to explain that on a foggy autumn day like this, for instance, it would be cold and dreary in the country, and she would be better in her own warm flat.

'I've got my nice kind Helen to look after me, too,' she murmured.

Peter crossed one leg over the other and sat back, his hazel eyes thoughtful.

'Ah! yes, Helen! . . .' he said.

Rita looked at him through her silky lashes.

'You've met her, of course.'

'Yes,' he said, and gave a short rather embarrassed laugh.

He found it slightly embarrassing to discuss Helen at all. What with business and the memory of the beautiful girl who had flashed like a meteor across his sky in Paris, his thoughts should have been fully occupied. And yet he had found himself thinking quite a lot about the young paid 'help', or whatever Helen called herself. Indeed, it was impossible to forget that strange first encounter with her on the night of his arrival in London.

He found her a sweet friendly person and he was glad that he had gone back to see her. The initial idea, of course, was to get first-hand news of Rita. But it had also been a blessing for him to find such a nice girl to talk to. A girl who knew as much about music as he did and was in fact better read than himself. He had also—being a friendly soul himself— thoroughly enjoyed taking her to that concert, it was something for him to do and he saw what a lot it meant to her.

With a frankness which was an intrinsic part of his nature, he told Rita now about the concert and how much he had enjoyed it.

'Of course, I meant to take *you*. I wired our firm over here as soon as I read in Paris that Yehudi Menuhin was playing in London and it was a pity to waste the tickets especially as your little Helen Shaw is so fond of music. I knew you would be glad I could take her.'

A frozen look came over Rita's beautiful face.

CHAPTER FIVE

Peter saw that look. It troubled him. He was too inexperienced with women to give it the ugly name it deserved—jealousy—cold stark jealousy. But he could see that she was not as pleased about Helen Shaw having been taken to the Menuhin concert as he had imagined she would be. He endowed his Rita with all the qualities of warmth and generosity which she always showed towards himself. He took it for granted that she was warm and generous towards others.

Rita's brain was working rapidly.

'So he's started to take Helen out—I won't have that—I've never heard of such a thing—what awful cheek on her part, going. *I won't have him taking any other woman out . . .*'

Then as rapidly she saw the other side of it. Peter had been lonely—had had the tickets-why waste them? And why should *she* demean herself by being jealous of a nondescript girl like Helen Shaw? Rita recovered her sense of humour. Before Peter could speak again, she said:

'What a wonderful idea, Pierrot, my sweet. I didn't know Helen liked music—at least I didn't think she had any particular taste. But it seems a pity because *I adore* hearing Yehudi play.'

'Oh, but Helen's most musical,' explained Peter with naïve frankness, 'quite astonishingly so. She's altogether a very educated sort of girl. Surprising to find someone like that doing your domestic work.'

Rita's eyes half closed and she looked at Peter's brown, boyish face through her long glistening lashes. Once more she was furiously jealous, but once more she smiled with perfect tact and replied:

'Yes, I'm very lucky to have her. She is so dependable. A little school-marmy perhaps and without much *savoir-faire*, but then what can one expect? The girl's had no background. I'm so sorry for her. When she asked me for the job, I felt I must give it to her—do what I could for the poor girl.'

Peter failed to see the sharp claws behind the velvet glove. He raised one of Rita's long, thin, beautiful hands and kissed it.

'You're awfully good to people. And I'm sure she must appreciate working for the most angelic person in London.'

Rita forgot to be jealous of Helen. In her chameleon-like fashion she swiftly took on the colours of a sublime benefactress.

'Poor Helen! I'd do anything for her. She has nothing and I have so much.'

Peter laughed a little, the red blood mounting to the high cheekbones which Rita found so singularly attractive.

'You certainly have everything,' he said

74

significantly.

She gave a luxurious little laugh and squeezed his hand in response. He was quite content with that and forgot Helen and the concert. She said that she would hurry up and get well and return to the flat so that they could see each other every day.

Rita was furious when a sister came in and said that 'her friend' must not stay too long. Rita wanted no interruptions. But once again she had to show off for Peter, and with her loveliest smile she begged the nurse for just 'another few moments'; then, when the woman had gone, sighed and shook her head at Peter.

'One gets so bullied in nursing-homes. Oh, Pierrot, I'm *longing* to get home!'

His enraptured gaze strayed over the lovely pale face with the flaming coronet of hair and he drowned, yet again, in the dangerous depth of those large velvety brown eyes. Before he left the clinic he was, if anything, a little more in love with Rita.

Long after he had gone, Rita's crazily infatuated mind circled around the memory of him, and ways and means of retaining the exquisite homage which he was paying her. At the same time the horrible memory of Nigel Cressland pushed its way through the fabric of her imagination, tearing it to pieces.

There was only one hope and she was gambling on it—that Pierrot would marry her before Nigel did anything desperate. She was also gambling, a little, on the belief that Nigel would never actually 'do her down'.

Worrying about Nigel and how to tackle him, her temperature went up. That frightened her. Whatever happened she *must* get well and go home so that she could settle things with Pierrot. She *must* break through that wall of caution which prevented him from rushing her into marriage at a moment's notice.

Before that evening was over, Rita had her surgeon and her doctor each in turn at her bedside, and implored them to effect a rapid cure. She looked pathetic and lovely, flushed with fever, dark eyes swimming. The surgeon had no time for neurotic women and told her bluntly that she would only get well if she relaxed and gave her nerves a chance. But the physician, younger and more impressionable, fell completely under the spell of the beautiful Mrs. Wade. He soothed and pacified her and was full of promises that she should be up and out of the clinic by the end of the next week.

Rita tried to compose herself; to look forward to Pierrot's visit tomorrow and to forget Nigel. As for Helen—her jealousy of the girl had only been temporary. She depended on Helen now. Helen was the buffer between herself and Nigel—and Patty.

When Helen came next day Rita told her how 'wonderful' Peter had been when he came to see her yesterday, Then, with half an eye on the younger girl, she added:

'By the way, you didn't tell me he had taken you to hear Menuhin . . .'

Helen coloured.

'It slipped my memory, Mrs. Wade. And I didn't think you'd be interested.'

'I'm interested in everything connected with Pierrot.'

'It didn't seem important about me going to the concert.'

'Oh, it's of no importance, of course.'

'Quite so,' said Helen rather coldly.

'How often does Pierrot call at the flat?'

Helen answered without hesitation.

'Every day. He comes to inquire after you and to talk about you.'

A pleased satisfied look replaced the wary expression on Rita's face.

'How sweet! He *is* rather sweet, isn't he?'

Helen's lips twisted a little. That was a term she disliked as applied to a man. And she would not really have called Peter Farrington 'sweet'. He had a lot of charm but he was such a forthright masculine determined person. In a way he was more masculine than Christopher who had had a lot of so-called 'sweetness' in his nature. But then Chris had been an artist. Peter was a business man—a banker—and a sportsman. His love for music was a queer angle, an interesting sidelight on his character.

Helen fell to thinking how much she had enjoyed that Menuhin concert at Peter's side and what warm happy memories it had

77

brought of the old days of companionship with Chris. In fact it had been rather too nostalgic, and she had go home with an aching heart.

She dragged her thoughts back to her employer again. Rita with an ugly little pout of the lips was mentioning the name *Nigel*.

'I suppose *he's* been around.'

'I've seem him once, and he telephones regularly,' said Helen.

'Yes, he comes here, too, but they have strict instructions not to send him up to my room unless they want to kill me,' said Rita.

Helen looked at Rita with her steady grey eyes.

'I don't quite see how you can always avoid seeing him, Mrs. Wade.'

Rita chewed her lower lip.

'For the moment it must be manoeuvred—it's of the utmost importance.'

'I'll do what I can. When will you be home, Mrs. Wade?'

'Oh, stop calling me "Mrs. Wade",' exclaimed Rita pettishly, 'it makes me sound like an old lady. I'm not much older you are.'

Helen had an inclination to laugh but remained studiously grave.

'You employ me—I can scarcely call you by your Christian name . . .' she began.

But Rita with one of her whims bluntly argued:

'I want you to call me "Rita".'

'Just as you wish.'

Rita's wondering mind came to rest an instant on the girl sitting beside her bed. She looked at the calm serious young face with the beautifully marked brows and that touch of even austerity about the lips. Helen wore a tweed suit and a blue cloth coat. A round blue beret was crushed down on the ash-blonde head. The gloves she held in her hand were shabby leather, with rabbit-fur gauntlets. Her bag was shabby—bulging with all the paraphernalia of a housewife. In Rita's opinion she was the very reverse of 'smart'. And yet when she chose about it, Rita could not fail to admit that there was a subtle attraction about Helen and that in a well-cut suit and with good make-up—a bit more glamour—she might even be called beautiful.

It was a thought for which Rita had no liking so she avoided it. Helen was, for the moment, invaluable. But what *did* the girl think about? How could she possibly enjoy life, just running the flat, shopping or mothering Patty? Were there behind that calm virginal mask no yearnings for a full exciting life—for all the fever and rapture of a love affair? Would she never replace her dead Christopher? How queer, thought Rita, and how unmodern. Not for the first time she labelled Helen as a Brontë character straight out of a book such as *Jane Eyre* or *Wuthering Heights*. There were moments when that touch of severity in the girl made Rita a little scared of Helen—and even annoyed her. She was not going to have anybody in her employ being critical. Although of course she knew perfectly well that Helen criticized her sharply for her denial of Patty.

And now, of course, up came the subject of the Christmas holidays. Helen never liked discussing the subject of Rita's child with her because it made her too angry deep down inside her, but she was forced to inquire what plans Rita had for the holidays.

Rita frowned and said that she 'had not made up her mind and she would let Helen know.'

'It depends of course on Pierrot's plans,' she added with that dewy look in her eyes that somehow never won Helen's romantic sympathy. Helen said:

'We were talking about you coming home when you asked me not to call you "Mrs. Wade" any more.'

'Oh, yes. Well, my nice doctor thinks I shall be able to leave here in about six days' time, so you can make preparations for that.'

Helen opened her notebook and looked at the dates.

'It'll be mid-term at the school, two days after that, Mrs.—er—Rita. You won't be well enough to go down, of course, so I will if you wish.'

'Oh, that'll be wonderful of you!' exclaimed Rita absently. Her mind was not on the mid-term but on Christmas which would be here in six weeks' time. By hook or by crook she must marry Peter before Christmas—*before Patty came home for the holidays.*

She heard Helen's cool measured voice:

'Patty was telling me that some of the parents go and stay a week-end down there so the children can go out all the time . . . Some of course go home.'

'Patty can't come home—I shall not be well enough to cope,' said Rita sharply.

Helen thought of the little girl who, with snub nose pressed against a school window, would watch so many of her companions being fetched away by doting mothers and fathers. She knew what an agony of envy and longing can smite a child over a thing like that. Once, Helen had been left at her school for the holidays and she had never forgotten the awfulness of it. She would not let Patty suffer that pain even for a short mid-term week-end. Eagerly she said:

'Do you think I might be spared to go and spend the weekend at Bexhill and be with Patty?'

For a moment Rita hesitated, her first thoughts for herself and how ill she could spare Helen in the flat. Then she considered alternatively how wonderful it would be if she were quite alone—Pierrot would come in and find her still weak and a little shaky, struggling to prepare a special supper for him. He would be touched and grateful. It would enhance her in his eyes. That thought afforded her a childish pleasure. She told Helen that she might certainly go to Bexhill:

'Of course! I couldn't *bear* poor little Patty not to have *someone* to give her a good time. I'll pay your expenses. You book yourself a room for the week-end. Miss Ponting knows an hotel where a lot of parents stay. I went there once and thought it the end! Afterwards I always used to go to Cooden Beach . . .'

'Of course,' thought Helen, 'Rita *would* go to one of the most beautiful hotels in the district and be comfortable even if she had to be bored by maternal duties.'

Nothing between them was said about Christmas. Sweetly Rita smiled at Helen and even pressed her hand at parting.

'I simply couldn't exist without you, Helen, you're *too* angelic, my dear. And Helen, don't be too cross with me about Patty, just for the moment keep my secret from Peter . . .'

That made Helen want to snatch her hand away. Her flush of bright scarlet was of shame—for Rita, not herself. Somehow she managed to renew her promise about Patty. Then, when she was about to open the door and leave the room, Rita called to her softly but significantly:

'Oh, Hel-en . . .!'

'Yes, Rita?' the name came with some difficulty from Helen who never found it easy to be on intimate terms with anybody before she really knew and liked them.

'Helen—you needn't give up any nice things that you want, to do just to entertain my Pierrot. If he asks you out again, tell him you haven't time. I know how busy you are. And he's very naughty, expecting you to amuse him.'

Helen's clear grey eyes looked straight into the dark ones tha held such a mixture of honey and gall. She understood perfectly well what Rita was driving at. And that faint scorn with which she always regarded Patty's mother rose in her now. So she was jealous because Peter Farrington had taken her to that concert and because he came to the flat every day! Without turning a hair, Helen said:

'Very well, thank you, Rita. I'll let Mr. Farrington know how busy I am if he should be kind enough to issue any more invitations.'

'Of course, if you *want* to go out—and if you have time—' began Rita sweetly. But Helen cut in:

'I haven't the slightest wish to go out with Mr. Farrington—or anybody else.'

Rita said in her honeyed voice:

'*Poor* Helen—I really *must* try and find you a nice boy friend once I'm better.'

Helen flushed but, tightly compressing her lips, made no answer. When Rita said things like that—kindly things on the surface—she could *feel* the scratch below it. She thought it best to keep silence. She walked quietly out of the room. Rita—left alone—nestled back against her pillows and shrugged her graceful shoulders. Helen Shaw was rather ungracious, and at times disconcertingly silent, she thought. Then a nurse came into the room with a note and some flowers from Peter. Thoughts of Helen vanished. Soothed and flattered, Rita read a charmingly worded card, inhaled the perfume of the roses her Pierrot had sent and was once more pleased with herself.

CHAPTER SIX

Two days later:

Helen had intended going out to see her aunt and uncle that night. But suddenly, during the afternoon, a wild storm of rain and wind swept London. And what with the deluge and the gale-force of the wind Helen decided that it was best to stay at home. She telephoned to her old home and put off the arranged evening.

Mrs. Shaw spoke to her.

'How are the eyes tonight, Aunt Mary . . .?' Helen asked. Mrs. Shaw was suffering from a painful form of rheumatism which affected her eyes and had been unable to read or sew for weeks.

'A little better, dear. How are you?'

'Oh, I'm fine,' said Helen cheerfully.

'Still liking your job?'

'Yes, very much.'

'Sometimes,' came Mrs. Shaw's rather soft melancholy voice, 'your uncle and I feel it such a tragic waste—you being a domestic for that Mrs. Wade when you have all those artistic gifts ...'

'Oh, Aunt Mary, dear, we've been into all that and I *assure* you I don't mind the domestic work. I'm left pretty much alone to manage things and I enjoy it. Besides, it's Patty I'm interested in. She'll be home in six weeks' time. I saw her yesterday and she was so pleased. Poor little thing.'

'Oh. well—if you're happy, dear ...'

Helen sighed without replying. Happy? Where was happiness? *What* was it? It seemed, for the time being, buried with Christopher.

Quickly, treading on that thought, she spoke for a few more minutes to her aunt giving her the latest news. She had had a sweet letter from Christopher's mother—this morning. She was expecting Mrs. Wade back at the flat next Friday, and then was going down to Bexhill for Patty's mid-term.

'You seem to be taking the mother's place to that little girl.'

Helen laughed.

'That's why I'm here, Aunty ...'

The front door bell rang. Helen said good

night, and put down the receiver.

Opening the door, she saw the tall figure of Peter Farrington. He was taking off a Burberry which was wet from the heavy rain. His hair was rough and damp. He grinned at her in that disarmingly friendly fashion which always made it so difficult for her to be formal with him.

'Ye gods, what a night! You folks over here need some of our golden Kenya climate. I'm half-drowned. Do I dare come in, or shall I take off my shoes?'

Helen eyed him doubtfully.

'I—I'm alone—I mean—I've had supper and—'

'So have I,' he cut in cheerfully. 'I meant to take you out for coffee. But look at the night. What I'd love is a pipe by your fire and to sit and listed to some good records.'

Helen opened the door wide and stepped back. It was a silent invitation to him to come in. She found herself unaccountably pleased to see him. Aunt Mary was right about one thing. She was too much alone, although she wouldn't admit it. And Peter was a charming companion—one after her own heart. At the same time she could not feel happy about entertaining him here, after Rita's remarks at the clinic this morning. Obviously Rita did *not* wish her to see much of her Pierrot.

Yet, as Helen watched Peter shake the raindrops from his dripping hat, wipe his feet on the mat and walk into the drawing-room. smoothing his hair back with both hands, her main feeling was of intense pleasure. It seemed so *right* to see that gesture (Christopher's very one)—to look at the roughened red-brown head—watch for that swift happy smile. Somehow they belonged to *her*—an intrinsic part of her—and not to Rita Wade. It was always difficult if not impossible for her to feel that Peter Farrington was the Pierrot—her infatuated lover—about whom Rita raved.

'It will be a good thing when she comes back,' Helen thought suddenly.

Peter sat down by the fire which Helen switched on. The central heating had taken the chill off the room already. He looked with pleasure round the luxurious room, then at the pale quiet girl before him. She was wearing a dark grey tailored skirt tonight and a pale yellow jersey. Her hair was not drawn into the usual demure bun. It was combed up on top of her head, Edwardian fashion. He saw, suddenly, what an attractive head it was and how the fair curls grew, in a touchingly childish way, on the nape of her slender neck. Really, sometimes Rita's 'right—hand girl' was almost a beauty, he thought. He wished she did not always look so sad. Still immersed in the past, of course.

He pulled out his pipe and lit it. She sat opposite him and smoked the cigarette he gave her. He did not often see her smoke. Tonight, for the first time also he noticed her hands. They were much smaller but broader than Rita's. Not so pointed, and she used alight coral nail polish. They looked capable, well-shaped hands. She was, of course, a very capable girl. Invaluable to Rita. Thinking of Rita, Peter began to discuss the patient's health. He talked at length and Helen listened and answered in monosyllables. It jarred, as usual, to hear him rhapsodizing about Patty's mother.

The atmosphere was better once the subject of Rita was dropped and Helen put a Sibelius symphony on the radio-gramophone which Peter wanted to hear.

Then she relaxed and enjoyed every moment, appreciating openly and enthusiastically, with him, the various movements as they were played. It was only when the symphony was over and Helen went to fetch some beer for him, that Peter remembered that frozen look on his beautiful Rita's face when he had told her that he had taken Helen out. He felt a trifle uneasy. He had thoroughly enjoyed this hour of music with the girl here. During the past week (when he had been here several times) he had felt happy and normal about it. Now, suddenly, he was made to feel conscience—stricken. 'How absurd,' he thought. 'Rita can't really mind— and Helen is so much alone—and I can't stand too many formal parties with business friends. Would Rita really mind me being here tonight like this?'

There was no answer to that, so Peter—happy-go-lucky by nature—forgot that he required an answer and asked Helen to play more music.

She, too, was enjoying herself. He saw the change in her. The pale statue of grief became an animated girl with bright smiling eyes and flushed cheeks. Lord, she was pretty like this, Peter reflected. One could hardly recognize Rita's silent, reserved 'domestic help' this evening. He felt warmly glad, because he had helped to make her happy.

They got up simultaneously to put on the other side of a record that had finished, and collided by the gramophone. Laughingly they apologized to one another. Peter put out a hand and brushed her shoulder.

'I've covered you with ash, my dear—sorry . . .'

My dear—how naturally he said that. How heartbreakingly like Christopher were his wide, sunny smile and those handsome brilliant eyes. The touch of his hand seemed suddenly to squeeze her very heart—until she winced with pain—with the longing for the yesterday that had been hers. But Chris would have caught her in his arms—held her close—whispered all his love and appreciation of her and the music against her hair—her lips.

Abruptly she moved away from Peter Farrington. Her pulses were racing and he saw that she had grown pale. He said, not understanding:

'Are you all right? What's the matter?'

She gave a short laugh, her face averted.

'Perfectly all right. Have some more beer.'

'No thanks. I ought to be going. It's ten o'clock.'

'Yes . . .'

He cleared his throat, feeling suddenly awkward and unhappy without knowing why. He glanced at her with anxious eyes.

'I haven't done anything to upset you?'

'Oh, no—no, of course not . . .'

'Are you sure—look here, Helen—I have offended you something I said—or did . . .'

Tense with her wrought—up emotions, Helen's control snapped for the fraction of a moment. She swung round to face him with furious eyes, hands clenched at her sides.

'Oh, stop apologizing. Go away. Don't come here—go and see Rita—I—oh . . .'

She broke off, horrified at herself, struggling to gird herself once more in the lost armour of ice-cold reserve. Peter stared at her, his lean brown face reddening. Then he understood.

He had just touched the automatic starter of the gramophone. The haunting strains of the slow movement from the Tchaikovsky Piano Concerto No. 2 filled the room. For Helen it was a room full of ghosts; but the man was reminded of musical evenings at home in Nairobi with his mother and sister. For that split second there was no place in either of their thoughts for Rita. But Peter knew that he could not let Helen struggle with her pain in this isolated dreadful fashion—and was conscious, also, of his own part in it—his likeness to the man who had died.

Years back when he first left college and began to learn banking, he had formed a friendship with a young doctor who was studying psychology. He had scoffed at first at Guy's psychiatry and then, despite himself, listened and learned a little. Some of that learning returned to him now. If one had a gnawing grief or fear it should not be bottled up—it should be uprooted and exposed to the naked light even though the uprooting be excessively painful to the sufferer. Only by exposition would the thing wither away and the person recover.

It was with deliberate intent of helping Helen that Peter acted now. He came toward her, took both her arms in a firm grip and said:

'Look at me, Helen. Look at me! I'm like your Christopher, am I not? Every time you see me you think of him, don't you? It worries you. And it hurts you, but you won't say anything about it. You just escape from it, and think about it after I've gone. Don't you. *Don't you,* Helen?'

Aghast she stared up at him, unwilling to believe that he could so rudely and insensibly open the wound like this. All her mechanism was suddenly jarred, set quivering. She gasped:

'Let me go.'

'No. I want you to face up to facts. I'm like this man and it upsets you. It shouldn't. You shouldn't allow it to. You shouldn't allow the loss of any one human being to affect the rest of *your* life, at your age. There are other things and other men. Other men who may remind you of him, too. One day you'll meet somebody who may mean everything to you and bring you happiness again. But not if you don't steel yourself to face up to your grief. You can't just nourish it, and starve yourself of comfort. You *are* starving. You won't try and be comforted. You won't even be happy because I look like Christopher and enjoy music with you, as he did. You're a coward, Helen.'

'Oh, don't, don't,' she moaned. And now he felt her trembling in his grasp and saw the wild tears pouring down her cheeks. He was physically as well as mentally disturbed by those tears. Yet he was glad of them. It was better for her to cry, to be true to herself, rather than go on building up that futile wall of reticence, of bitterness.

Gently, he added:

'Cry for him if you want to. But laugh, too. He'd want to hear you laughing. If I were

92

Christopher and I died and could see you like this, it would be a horror to me. I would not rest in peace—to think of you suffering like this, so long after my death. Your spirit is in chains, Helen. Release it, my dear. Come, and tell me about Christopher. *Really* tell me. Show me his photographs, which you have never done. Show me his work—his writing—his paintings. Let me learn to know him and talk to you about him. And then, when you see it does not always hurt, you'll be happy again. Please, Helen, do as I say. I know what I'm talking about.'

She stayed still a moment, her arms in the vice of his fingers. Gradually her trembling ceased and the tears dried up. She looked into the eyes that were Christopher's and yet not Christopher's and felt a strange compelling power emanating from him to her. He was not Rita's Pierrot. He was nothing to do with Rita. In this moment he was a complete stranger and yet somebody she, Helen, had known all her life—somebody who was opening the gate to liberation and trying to guide her stumbling footsteps towards it.

Quite suddenly she did not want to fight Peter any more nor hide from him her spiritual despair. She dragged away her fingers, turned and ran into her bedroom. She unlocked a case and took from it all her photographs of Christopher, one or two letters and some small sketches and paintings which he had done specially for her.

Peter stood where she had left him lighting his pipe again. He was a little nervous of this thing he had done. To psycho-analyse anybody, let alone this beautiful girl, would have been so much more in Guy's line than his, he thought. He wished Guy were over here at the moment to help Helen. And he began to wonder why he had meddled, for it was none of his business except for this unfortunate resemblance which he bore to the man she had been going to marry.

For a moment he thought that she would not come back and that he had made a blunder. Then he experienced a sense of genuine pleasure and relief when he saw her come quickly back with her arms full. She had not bothered to powder her nose, or worry about her tear—stained face.

She spread them on the sofa.

'These are Christopher's,' she said. 'I want you to see them. And look, this is his photograph—you can see how like you are to him, can't you . . .?'

She knelt by the sofa, sorting her treasures. He sat on the arm and looked at everything she gave him, one by one. And sure enough, examining the pictured face of the young dead artist he was profoundly moved by the extraordinary resemblance to himself despite small disparities of build and feature. He *was* Christopher. Christopher was *him*. The handwriting, of course, was totally different. The paintings he found slight, without genius, but charming. (Peter himself had not the slightest idea how to paint.) Now Helen was sitting crouched on the floor, sitting back on her heels like a small girl, reading aloud—a letter Christopher had written about that very Sibelius symphony which had just been played. And as Peter listened, he could imagine himself making a similar criticism of the pianist concerned—uttering the same appreciation of the great emotional work.

He said:

'Yes—your Christopher loved music, didn't he.'

Helen looked up at him, face flushed, eyes sparkling, and tossed back a stray fair wave of hair which had escaped from its pins.

'Oh, he did—we both did! Here's another letter about the Tchaikovsky which we just played . . .'

Silently smoking his pipe, Peter watched and listened. Time flew by now. The quiet demure little Helen seemed not to be able to stop talking—pouring out one reminiscence after another. It was as though a dam had been demolished and a torrent was pouring through—he could sense the relief that it was affording her.

He let her talk on. It was she who at last looked at her wristwatch and gave a cry.

'Heavens! It's half past eleven.'

He smiled down at her:

'That doesn't matter. Go on talking, my dear.'

But she jumped up.

'It's terribly late. Do forgive me. I was just losing myself. You've been so—so kind and patient. I can't tell you what it's meant to me to be able to talk like this to someone.'

He slid off the arm of the chair, put his pipe in his pocket and smiled again. He thought how very sweet she was. He thought:

'That poor devil Christopher. He missed a very wonderful wife, a very charming girl.'

And he thought how well he knew her suddenly. It was as though tonight he had been allowed a glimpse into Helen's very soul.

He had never known any girl as well as that before. (Not even Rita . . .!)

It was almost a shock to him to remember Rita; the beautiful and alluring creature whom he had made up his mind to marry. She was still a mystery to him in so many ways. Maybe that was half her fascination. Yet he hoped that the day might come when she would sit as Helen had sat just now, so naturally and candidly pouring out her heart, making herself known and endearing.

It was the first conscious comparison he made between the two women.

Helen, with a shy grateful look at him, was saying:

'Thank you for doing what you did tonight.

Thank you very much, Peter. You were quite right. I *have* been a coward, locking everything away. It's been wonderful showing you all these things . . .' She pointed to the papers and paintings.

'I'd like to think you will talk to me and show me things whenever you feel like it,' he said, 'and I'd *very* much like to think that you won't, in future, be hurt or troubled every time you look at me.'

Impulsively she exclaimed:

'I don't think I will be hurt any more after tonight. It's as though . . . as though . . .' she broke off, her face a warm pink.

'What, Helen?'

The ash—blonde head drooped.

'Oh, I don't know, as though you brought *him* into this room tonight to tell me to stop living in the past and to face up to the future.'

Peter held out a hand.

'I'm so very glad.'

'So am I . . .'

Their fingers met and clasped. Then, as she reached a pinnacle of new contentment, feeling nothing for Peter but friendship and gratitude, one word, one name from him put back the wall of constraint.

'Rita,' he said, 'Rita is very musical, isn't she? These are her records. It will be wonderful when she comes back and we can all three listen to them.'

Back came her slight feeling of disdain for

97

Peter, the poor dupe!—hopelessly deluded, utterly ignorant of Rita Wade's real character. But Peter had done with psychology for the moment and was continuing to refer to his *inamorata*.

'Rita said only this morning what a tremendous help and comfort you are to her, which I can well believe, and you must love looking after her. She's such a heavenly person if one might use that word.'

Silence from Helen. But her eyes strayed towards Rita's bureau. On the top of it there used to rest a silver—framed photograph of Patty in a party dress—a pretty frilly photo taken when the child was four. That photo had gone. Rita had not dared leave it there. But Patty remained, and none of Rita's cowardly scheming could wipe out her existence any more than Rita could put back the clock and make herself as young as she wished to be.

At that moment the telephone rang. Helen sighed and, walking across to the ivory instrument, picked up the receiver. At this hour who could it be? Nigel Cressland, perhaps. He had a habit of ringing up late, hoping to catch Rita.

But to Helen's dismay the voice that came over the wire in answer to her 'hallo' was Rita's own. The patient, in another of her moods, with the telephone by her bedside, had called up her flat to speak to Helen, caring little whether she roused the girl from sleep or not.

'I cant sleep tonight,' came the petulant voice, 'and they won't give me another tablet. It drives me mad lying here like this. I want to know what's been happening in the flat. Who have you seen today?'

Helen, hot, embarrassed, horribly conscious of the late hour and of Peter's presence, flung him a quick look then stammered:

'N-nothing—n—nobody much.'

'Were you in bed?'

'N-no.'

'What's the matter with you, Helen?' Rita demanded sharply. 'Are you in the drawing-room? Is anybody with you?'

Then Peter with a glorious disregard for the hour, fancying he heard his Rita's voice amplified by the microphone and with a totally wrong slant on her character, leapt to Helen's side, and put out a hand for the receiver.

'Oh, if that's Rita, *do* let me say good night to her!'

Speechlessly, Helen handed him the instrument.

CHAPTER SEVEN

With the frank naïvety which was essentially Peter's he seized the telephone and spoke to Rita.

'Good night, angel. Or ought I to introduce myself? This is Peter Donald Farrington speaking. Skip the Donald. It was a name given to me in honour of a Scottish grandfather. Did I ever tell you I had Highland blood in me? I must show you our tartan. You'd look wonderful, with your red hair streaming in the wind and my plaid flung over your shoulders . . .'

He broke off with a laugh. Helen turned away, rolling her eyes heavenwards.

'Ye gods!' she mentally ejaculated, 'no wonder they say that love is blind. Rita—with a plaid over her shoulder and her hair streaming in the wind—He's got her all wrong! Poor Peter Donald of the Highlands!'

Could either of them have seen Rita at that moment it would have been a rather ugly woman whose glorious hair was tied up in a chiffon scarf, whose face was shining with the cream which she had patted into it before settling down for the night—and whose lips were drawn into a grimace of ill-temper and jealousy. She could hardly take in any of the words Peter uttered, and she did *not* share his sense of humour. All she knew was that he was there, at eleven p.m. in her flat alone with Helen.

Peter said:

'Hallo, darling, are you there?'

Then with an effort Rita forced a cordial note into her voice and replied:

100

'Yes, I'm here, Pierrot.'

'How wonderful to be able to say good night to you, Rita. How are you?'

'Better, thank you.'

Peter cocked an eyebrow and wondered a little that she was not more herself—the Rita with a husky note of warmth in her voice whom he always found so seductive.

'Really better, darling?' he said.

'Yes, thank you. And you're speaking from my flat—I presume Helen's been entertaining you?'

'Yes. We've had some grand music together,' said Peter, with the same tactless candour which at least showed the woman in the nursing—home one thing—that he was guiltless of wrong-doing. Her wonderful Pierrot was without guile in this, and it was stupid of her to be jealous. But she felt an inordinate dislike of Helen for having him there in the flat. How *dared* she enjoy hours alone—hours of 'marvellous music' with Peter?

With a further effort Rita infused some warmth into her voice, and turned on the ready charm.

'But how lovely for you, Pierrot, darling. Tell me what you've been hearing—which of my beautiful records did you play?'

The conversation which followed was long and—so far as Helen was concerned—not to be tolerated, because she could judge from the things Peter said how far Rita was going with her lies and affectations. She was bent on deceiving the boy into thinking her everything that she was not.

Helen slipped from the room, moved into the small kitchen and automatically began to prepare a breakfast tray for herself just for something to do. But she felt tired and years older than her age. As though she were a woman having to stand by and watch an evil child playing a game. For there was something childish—and certainly evil—in the way Rita Wade was playing with Peter Farrington's emotions. If only he could see through her! Realize that she was merely 'shooting a line' and that all this love of music and art was sheer pretence in order to lure and impress him. Really, Helen thought, men were, on the whole, creatures lacking in perspicacity—men of Peter's type. He was so easy to hoodwink, ensnared as he was by Rita's looks and magnetism. It took an experienced, equally scheming creature like Nigel Cressland to see through her.

For a moment Helen stopped moving around the kitchen and stood holding her tired head between her hands. When that telephone bell rang just now it had put an end to an important emotional crisis in her life. She had been as though under a spell with Peter's warmth and kindliness and understanding blunting the edge of the old aching pain. She had begun to feel almost happy. As she had told him, it was as though he had brought Christopher into the room to give her courage and enable her to carry on. Then Rita's voice had shattered the peace rudely and sharply. No words had been said on the subject, but she *knew* how bitterly Rita resented finding Peter in this flat tonight.

Why should she, Helen, care? Rita Wade and Peter Farrington were of no importance in her life. Why should it matter to her what they did or said? She had come here to be of help to little Patty. She should not allow it to distress her because Peter Farrington was heading for disaster. And yet she knew in this moment that it did—it mattered quite a lot; because he was nice and because he was like Christopher.

The telephone conversation in the other room seemed to be lasting a long time. Then Helen heard the bell tinkle and an instant later came Peter's voice:

'Where are you, Helen?'

She went back into the sitting-room. Peter looked pleased with himself. Helen felt suddenly cross as well as tired. He was a fool to be so misled. She had no patience with him. Abruptly she said:

'I'm afraid we must break up our musical evening. It's late.'

'It is, too,' he said cheerfully, 'and I do apologize for having kept you up.'

She lifted her sad grey eyes and looked at

him a moment, compassionately again—without scorn. Poor deluded Peter! That alert tanned young face of his looked so happy and satisfied. How long would the bubble last before it exploded? she wondered.

He smiled at Helen but thought of Rita.

'I think she seems better tonight.'

Helen forced a mundane answer:

'That's good, isn't it?'

'I told her how much we enjoyed the music and what grand taste she has in records.'

A faint ironic smile appeared on Helen's lips. She remembered buying those records at H.M.V. in Oxford Street.

'Well, good night, Helen,' said Peter and focused his full attention upon the girl again. They had had an awfully good evening, he thought. So very nice and friendly and—once he had broken through that reserve of hers—he had thoroughly enjoyed the intellectual harmony and basic understanding between them. She really was a nice girl, this Helen—and he wished she didn't look so lost and lonely.

He had told Rita over the phone that it would be nice when they could all three have some good music in the flat. He remembered now that she had not answered. Why? Surely she hadn't *minded*. He really did feel that he wanted to do something for Helen.

'Good night, Helen,' he said again.

Now all her efforts at being harsh and

critical about Peter, and her indifference to her own life, were swept away. The inevitable tenderness which Peter roused in her when he looked at her with that sweetness, that suggestion that *she* mattered a little to him, stole back into place in her heart.

She said in a low voice:

'Good night and thank you again for what you did tonight.'

'Don't despair, Helen,' he said gently, 'never despair, you know . . .'

She nodded mutely, swallowed and—afraid of herself—shut the front door upon him rather hurriedly. She returned to her room, and began to cry. But they were not morbid tears. They seemed to bring her release, even hope. It was without hurt at last that she looked at the familiar photographs of Chris, balancing them against her mirror, smiling at them through her tears.

'Good night, darling,' she said. 'I wonder if you enjoyed the Tchaikovsky when Peter and I played it tonight. I know you were there. And he's rather nice, poor Peter, isn't he, Chris? So like and so unlike you, my dear. I wish he wasn't going to marry Rita. It's an awful thought. She isn't nice, Chris. What a muddle it all is! Sometimes I feel I'd like to run out of this flat and never come back into it.'

But she couldn't and she wouldn't because of Patty. As she settled down in her bed to sleep, another thought suddenly struck her.

Rather a disturbing one.

If she ran away from this *ménage* it would mean never seeing Peter Farrington again. She wouldn't really like that—no, not at all. How could he bear such an uncanny resemblance to her dead love and mean nothing!

She turned her face to her pillow. Quite humanly and insidiously there crept into her mind a thought—*a mere* fantasy, of course—about Peter and herself. Supposing she had met him and he had been free—unknown to Rita—a friend of hers, Helen's . . .? Might that not have opened up a new world? He was the only man she had met, since Christopher's death, toward whom she had felt in the least bit drawn, or whose friendship she desired.

But if there had been no Rita—she lay wakeful, remembering not only the comradeship that had come into being between them this evening, but the strong soothing clasp of Peter's fingers on her arm and the urgency of his voice when he had said:

'Your spirit is in chains, Helen. Release it, my dear . . .'

With him and through him she had achieved the miracle. After long months of being imprisoned in her own egoistical despair, she had come out into the light and lived again. Sitting at Peter's feet, talking of the past and even laughing over the things she had laughed at with Christopher.

It had been really wonderful—until Rita's

telephone call.

Suddenly Helen set her teeth and dug two small clenched hands into her pillow.

'Oh damn, *damn!*' she said, in a fierce whisper.

And she tried to stop thinking and wishing and regretting.

But it was a long time before she could stop tossing and turning and abstracting her mind from either past or present. As for the future, there just didn't seem any for her. She told herself that the best thing for her to do was to make her mind a blank except for the thought of Patty and all that she meant to do for the child.

All the same she was in a more natural, liberated mental state that next morning when she went round to pay her usual duty call on Rita at the clinic.

She was not prepared for the unattractive reception which Rita gave her.

The invalid was sitting up in a chair, half—dressed, having taken a few steps round the room on the arm of her nurse. She felt physically weak and correspondingly bad-tempered, and she still bore a deep grudge against Helen.

Without answering Helen's polite inquiries as to her state of health, Rita snapped:

'In my absence I think it a little untoward of you to entertain men alone so late at night in the flat.'

107

Helen stared, then went crimson. Of course she had known that Rita was displeased at finding Peter at the flat last night but did not expect her to be quite so crude about it.

Rita regarded the younger girl resentfully through her long lashes.

'Well?'

Helen stammered:

'Really, Mrs—Rita—there is no question of me "entertaining men late at night" in the way you put it.'

'It was well after eleven when I phoned you and if I hadn't done so, I presume your party with Peter would have gone on till midnight.'

Indignantly Helen replied:

'I can't help it if your friends call and insist on coming into the flat and then don't leave early. It doesn't much matter whether it's Peter Farrington or the Lord Chamberlain himself, I could hardly be rude to either.'

'Nonsense,' said Rita, in her sharpest voice, 'you could quite easily have told him to go away.'

'But why—' began Helen, then stopped, indignation subsiding, replaced by a cold anger. How dared Rita speak to her like this. All that was proud and independent in the girl rose to the fore, superseding even her desire to succour the unfortunate Patty.

'If my conduct doesn't satisfy you, you have only to say so and I'll go,' she said. 'I'll go at once.'

But now Rita's jealous anger, having had an outlet, was cooling. She controlled herself. She knew that Helen was a very valuable ally and that she would be a fool to risk her walking out. But she had been unable to resist a dig at the girl. Peter, over the phone, had certainly convinced Rita that the evening had been an innocent one. All the same it annoyed her intensely to think of him there enjoying that music alone with the girl. As for his repeated suggestions that they would make a 'nice trio' listening to classical music, that was preposterous and she would soon let him see that it was not to be part of her convalescence.

Helen had risen to her feet.

'I'd better go back and pack,' she said icily.

Then Rita climbed down.

'Don't be such an idiot, Helen. Sit down at once.'

Again Helen coloured to the roots of her hair. Rather nervously she flicked a stray fair strand of hair back from her forehead.

'No, I'd much rather go. I don't like the way you spoke about me entertaining men in your flat. Peter insisted on coming in and we—we heard some records and I didn't realize how the time was passing—neither of us did.'

Rita winced. She had no particular wish to be reminded of the fact that the time had passed so pleasantly for her Pierrot that he had lost count of time. But she did remind herself that it suited her book for the moment to retain Helen's services.

'Don't be such a little idiot, my dear. *Do* sit down,' she said, and gave Helen one of her most charming looks of entreaty and friendliness. 'I know I'm a jealous hag. I'd have cut my tongue out rather than say anything really to insult you. You've been perfectly sweet to me and Pierrot has appreciated your efforts to entertain him while I'm laid up. I'm just jealous! Not of you, silly girl, of course not. But envious of the hours spent with him. You do understand, don't you? Sit down, darling, and stop glaring at me. I've just had my first walk and I feel as weak as a kitten.'

Only half mollified, Helen took the chair again but her heart beat fast and her sense of outrage had not gone. Rita continued to talk—cajoling—flattering—whilst making it very clear, Helen thought cynically, that she wished her to know that she could never in a thousand years be jealous of *her.* But at the same time apologizing for her outburst.

Rita finished:

'You know I couldn't do without you and you must learn to know me a bit better. You know I'm a creature of moods—' she sighed—'Oh, it would be so wonderful to find somebody who would understand me and take no notice when I'm horrid . . .!'

Helen put her tongue in her cheek. One couldn't argue with Rita Wade when she behaved this way, although she, Helen, hardly

110

believed a word Rita said. But Rita could always play a trump card by the mention of Patty.

'I had such an amusing letter from my Patty this morning,' Rita was adding, swerving now on to a new subject and completely ignoring the fact that she had been so disgustingly rude to Helen. Helen sat down again. Rita had got her way. She was not going to lose the girl. As for being annoyed about Peter in the flat, she was a fool to let the thing worry her for an instant. Pierrot was madly in love with *her.* She had him where she wanted him.

She read Patty's letter aloud to Helen. It was the child's description of a hockey match in which she had played goalkeeper, followed by a rapturous account of Helen's last visit.

'. . . *Oh, Mummy, I do love Helen . .*' was one line on which Rita deliberately put emphasis and with a honeyed smile at the girl, 'There you see! Neither Patty nor I could do without you.'

Helen bit her lip. Really, it was useless trying to deal with Rita Wade as though she were a normal woman. Everything she did and said was so exaggerated. But Helen felt better now, warmly glad that little Patty had so much enjoyed her visit to St. Cyprian's the other day.

Then somebody knocked at the door.

'Oh, these probationers! They fuss in and out all the time!' said Rita pettishly. 'I wanted to talk to you about my coming home. I think

I've persuaded my doctor to let me go back this week-end.'

Again the knocking . . .

'Come in!' sang out Rita.

The door opened cautiously, then a man walked into the room. A big man wearing a smart dark blue coat, carrying a felt hat in one hand, and a bunch of carnations in the other.

It was Nigel Cressland.

Helen, thinking rapidly, came to the correct conclusion that Nigel must have slipped past the usual guard of nurses and, at long last, forced an entry into Rita's room.

CHAPTER EIGHT

Rita looked so ghastly that Helen decided upon prompt action. Rather like an avenging angel she placed herself between her patient and the man who had so boldly walked into her room.

'I'm very sorry, Mr. Cressland, but Mrs. Wade is not fit to see anybody at the moment,' she said.

Rita dared not look at Nigel. Deliberately she leaned back against her cushion, closing her eyes and letting her arms hang limply on either side, as though she were in the last stages of exhaustion, but she could feel rather than see the cynical unbelief on the man's heavy handsome face. She heard him say:

'That's too bad. But surely—er—she must be a little better today as she is up? I particularly asked a young nurse just now if Mrs. Wade had been seeing visitors and I was told that they queued up daily for admittance into the royal presence. So I didn't see why an old pal like myself shouldn't be granted an audience.'

Rita shivered a little at the sound of that familiar, sneering voice. What a brute Nigel was! A dangerous brute, too. It must have been that new probationer—little fool—who let him in. So far, the sister in charge of her case had frustrated the previous attempts of the unwanted visitor to come in here—at Rita's express command.

'I really don't think you ought . . .' Helen began.

But Nigel dropped all pretence of being amiable or friendly. His smile gave place to an ugly twist of his lips. He flung the carnations on the bed, deliberately unbuttoned his coat and flung that after the flowers.

'I have had enough of this nonsense,' he cut in, 'and I would be obliged if you would leave me alone with Rita.'

Then turning to the shrinking woman in the chair who was still trying to stage a 'faint', huddled in her feathered cape, trembling under the fleecy camel-hair rug, he said:

'Come along, Rita, snap out of it and ask

your charming confidential housekeeper, or whatever she is, to get out.'

Helen, flushed and resentful, looked to Rita for her orders. Rita opened her eyes and looked back at Helen with an expression of fear which Helen found a trifle puzzling. Why should she be so afraid to meet her ex-fiancé? Was it only because she feared that he would make trouble between her and Peter Farrington? Whatever it was, Rita seemed to become cowed into submission by Nigel's presence and his peremptory orders. She said faintly:

'Yes—you'd better leave us, Helen. But don't—go right away—stay outside if you will and make sure nobody else comes in.'

Nigel Cressland put his hands into his pockets and glanced from one woman to the other, with a freezing smile.

'Yes, make quite sure that the latest boy friend, who is such a success with Rita, does not come face to face with *me*,' he said—with so much menace—such a sinister quality in this effort of flippancy on Nigel's part—that Helen felt rather sick. Hateful man—she thought, as she closed the door behind her. And if it had not been for the business of Patty, which always detracted her sympathies from Rita, she would have pitied the woman she left in there to face Nigel and his bitter malevolent tongue.

There was a bench in the long white

114

corridor with its faint odour of antiseptics and the hot, rubbery smell of the lino and central heating. Helen sat down and thought, rather grimly:

'Let's hope to goodness Peter does not choose this exact moment to call!'

And she kept an anxious eye on the door which bore the printed card marked MRS. WADE.

Inside that room, Nigel stood with his hands in his pockets before Rita's chair, rocking a little on his feet. The thin, selfish mouth under the black moustache still wore that cold, sinister smile. Rita felt quite genuinely ill when she looked up at him, but she had realized that she could not avert this moment any longer and that she must see Nigel.

His gaze travelled over her curiously and without pity, although his sensual side, which had always been stirred by Rita, acknowledged that her illness had in no way lessened her attractions. In fact because of her added pallor, that transparent look, the faint lilac stains under the big dark eyes and the girlish method of letting the beautiful red hair float down to her shoulders, she was more than ever an artistic triumph. But for the moment her physical appeal left him unmoved. He was too filled with ice-cold rage against her.

'And now, my dear Rita,' he said softly, 'I want an explanation of the way you have been stalling me—all these countless snubs

115

delivered by yourself and your excellent Helen who has obviously acted on your orders.'

Rita, panting a little, put her hands up to her throat as though she were choking. She stammered:

'Nigel, don't be so horrible—really—to barge into my room and bully me like this when I've just had a dangerous operation—it's inhuman—and most ungentlemanly.'

He flung back his head and burst out laughing.

'My God! That's rich! That line in any West End play, coming from a character like yourself, would get the biggest laugh of the show. Poor little Rita, being bullied! Poor, gentle, *ladylike* little Rita, who likes her boy friends to be *gentlemen*. And likes the gentlemen to have fat bank balances as well as good manners. Really, my sweet, it doesn't suit you to do the swooning, delicate—minded Victorian! And it just won't wash with me. I know you too well.'

She went scarlet and now she, too, was angry, with a resentful anger, a sense of outrage which superseded her fear of the man.

'You d—d swine!' she said between her teeth.

'That's better,' he said, dryly, and seated himself on the edge of her bed and pulled a cigarette case from his pocket. 'Have one—and calm down. Let's have a rational conversation.'

'I won't,' she said hysterically, 'I won't have anything to do with you.'

The gold case bearing Nigel's initials was far too reminiscent of the past that she wanted to wipe out. She hated the sight of it. She pushed his hand violently away. The case clattered to the floor.

Nigel picked it up, his lips curling. He knew his Rita in this state. They had had rows before.

'Now, now, temper!' he drawled. 'Lovely women with red hair should learn to control themselves. But you were always a *leetle* out of control when you couldn't get your own way, weren't you, my sweet? Only I'd rather you didn't chuck my one and only gold case on the floor and dent it. It may have to be offered to a pawnbroker shortly.'

She glowered at him through her lashes, her long fingers clenching and unclenching spasmodically, her breast heaving.

'Oh, go to hell!' she said.

'All in good time,' he smiled. 'Hell will no doubt be my final address, and you may live there with me. But not just yet. I hope and believe we both yet have to unravel our tangled lives in *this* world. Well—it looks like being a very pleasant world with so much effort on the part of the Government to rob us of our little pleasures. Plus the fact that *I*, personally, don't look like being able to pay for such pleasures, unless my luck changes.'

Fresh words of abuse which Rita had prepared died on her lips. Nervously she passed her handkerchief across those lips smearing it with rouge. She began to try and fathom his meaning.

Nigel—suggesting that he was hard up—saying that he might have to sell his gold cigarette case—heavens!

Nigel lit a cigarette and blew a cloud of smoke in the air.

'I trust this won't bring on a relapse,' he said.

'A lot you seem to care whether I live or die!' she muttered.

'I cared very much once, but you died on me in that hotel in Paris, didn't you? Quite frankly, my dear Rita, although I am very glad your appendix operation was a success, I don't feel in a very sympathetic frame of mind about you. You used me and my money for as long as seemed necessary, then you chucked me aside without any conscience just because you fell for something newer and more attractive. Isn't that so?'

She moistened her lips with the tip of her tongue. Her gaze wavered before his.

'What if it is? As I told you at the time, one has a right to break an engagement, that's what it's for—or should be—a period of time during which one finds out whether a person is suited to one or not.'

He snapped:

'Don't sit there moralizing to me. I never heard such tripe. When you left me to go to Paris you were quite determined to marry me. We fixed the date—and the honeymoon. What's more, you little gold-digger, you got a cheque out of me to spend on a trousseau in the Rue de la Paix. Then, when I turn up at your hotel, you coolly tell me the whole thing's off.'

Rita's expression was murderous. She was afraid of Nigel but for the moment she was fortified by her knowledge that a very wealthy young banker—far more attractive than Nigel—was in love with her. She was fighting for her Pierrot.

'Well, I changed my mind at the last moment—that's all,' she said sullenly.

'But I don't happen to have changed mine. I haven't the slightest respect for you, my dear girl, but I still want to marry you.'

Rita's lips curled. Her inordinate sense of vanity was barely flattered. She threw him a scornful look.

'If you're broke, Nigel dear, why not try and find yourself a wealthy widow? I should have thought—'

'Well, stop thinking!' he broke in rudely 'and get this straight. You belong to me. I *bought* you. Yes, it's no good looking hurt or shocked. You owe me thousands, Rita, and you're not going to sneak out on me just because some young puppy in Paris fell for your beautiful white skin and red hair and all that Hollywood film—star glamour.'

'I know I've behaved rather badly, Nigel, but I'll pay you back—if you'll just wait—'

'Till you're married to the other fellow and can fleece him? No thanks. If there's to be any payment it's to be when and how I want. And I want *you* as soon as you can arrange our wedding.'

Rita groaned and clutched at her heart.

'Fetch a nurse, Nigel please! I think I'm going to faint . . .'

He remembered suddenly that she *had* just got out of bed after an operation. He saw the sweat on her forehead, her laboured breathing, and a new appeal of fragility, defencelessness in her. He forgot the other man and his own rancour. Hastily he flung away his cigarette, leapt to her side and took her hand.

'Rita darling. I've been an awful brute—I ought to be shot—Rita, are you all right? Look, precious, it's all because I'm so crazy about you. And if you'll only give *me* another chance, I'll wipe out all those debts. I'm not so broke really. I hope to pull off a very big deal in the City this week. Rita—open your eyes—speak to me!'

Despite her swimming senses she heard what he said and took heart. She realized that she *must* conciliate Nigel—play for time—time in which to consolidate her position with her

East African banker.

She responded to Nigel by a feeble pressure of the fingers, gave him a wan smile and whispered—

'Dear—Nigel—you're very sporting. I know I'm the *end*. But don't be cross. Just wait till I'm home again—out of the clinic—then we'll talk it all over.'

He promised to wait; covered her hand with kisses and told her that he wasn't cross any more and that he would overlook her little 'lapse' in Paris and that whatever he made out of his new deal would be his wedding present to her.

Those were his last words after which Rita recovered and he took himself off, knowing that he was a fool and feeling one. That *he*, Nigel Cressland, the cynic, so experienced with women, should let a woman like Rita get the better of him even for a single moment! It was monstrous. As he passed Helen, who was still sitting outside on her bench, he flung her an unpleasant little nod and smile.

'Faithful unto death,' he sneered. 'Well, well! If I ever need any help, I shall send for you, dear Helen. How old-fashioned you are. Most touching! You can go in to our Rita now. She's feeling a little faint, poor sweet. But *please* don't try and ward me off with a lot of silly excuses if I happen to ring up or come to the flat again, which I shall be doing very shortly!'

Helen looked after Nigel's departing figure, her lips tightening. That man made her squirm. And *that* was to have been poor Patty's stepfather, poor little mite! At least she hoped that Rita would no longer consider such a thing.

She went back into the invalid's room to find Rita with her face buried in her hands, sobbing.

Round the corner of the corridor Nigel, hat in hand, gloomily awaited the lift which would take him down to the front hall.

When it came up, there was only one occupant, a very young girl wearing a short skirt, a beaver jacket and beaver beret at a jaunty angle on rich brown curls. She carried a basket of roses and some journals. She looked to Nigel about sixteen, as fresh and tanned and glowing as though she had just come out of the sun. And not the sort of sun that women get in beauty parlours, he thought. Always a Don Juan in his own estimation, he gave the girl the full benefit of his handsome blue eyes, removed his horn-rims and said:

'Can I direct you to any room in this maze of corridors?'

The liftman, chewing gum, gave the pair a meaning look, clanged the doors, and took his lift down again. The young girl smiled at Nigel, then glanced at a piece of paper in her hand.

'Mrs. Wade, Room No. 7,' she read.

Nigel's face brightened.

'Ah yes. The lady I've just been visiting, as a matter of fact. First to the left, second to the right and the last door on the right. But I doubt if they'll let you in. She isn't too well today.'

The tanned young face clouded.

'Oh dear, Pierrot said she was so much better and that I was certain to be allowed in. That's why he left me at the entrance and said he'd come back for me.'

Nigel grew interested.

'Pierrot?'

'My brother,' said the girl. 'Peter Farrington. Do you know him?'

'Peter Farrington?' repeated Nigel slowly, 'no, I don't think I do know him.'

'Well, I'm Glenise Farrington—I'm called Glen . . .'

Nigel bowed.

'How do you do, Glen? I'm Nigel Cressland.'

'How do you do, Nigel?' She was deliciously naïve and charming, he thought, although he was as a rule bored by young girls.

Then she added:

'As a matter of fact, my brother is sort of engaged to Mrs. Wade. At least he's going to be. Mum and I have had heaps of letters already about her. I hear she's absolutely too beautiful and heavenly for words, and I'm *dying* to see her.'

Nigel stiffened in every limb. He felt an ice-

123

cold anger and, at the same time, a burning curiosity. In a flash he placed this 'brother' whom Glen called *Pierrot*, as Rita's new boy friend. About to be engaged to her, was he? That was indeed interesting.

The girl prattled on.

'It's terribly exciting as I only landed by plane early this morning from Nairobi. Mum let me come to see Pierrot because a cousin of ours was coming over and it was a last moment affair, so we didn't warn Pierrot. I just rang up his hotel from the airport and he nearly passed out with astonishment. He had a very important business date at midday so he told me to come along here and introduce myself to his Rita. By the way, are you sure you haven't met my brother?'

'No,' said Nigel softly. 'But if he is going to—er—become engaged to Mrs. Wade, I would like to have that pleasure. Are you expecting him to come on here later in the morning?'

CHAPTER NINE

Glen answered at once:

'Yes I am—just before twelve.'

Nigel's glance narrowed. He took a silk handkerchief from his pocket, polished his

124

glasses and replaced them. His lips smirked a little.

'I may perhaps look in and get you to introduce us. I am most interested in Rita's—er—future husband. I am a very, *very* old friend of hers.'

Glenise Farrington was seventeen, young for her age, and with only one absorbing passion in her life—music. Already she had taken a medal for playing the violoncello in Johannesburg and her one ambition was to play in a big orchestra. Pretty and charming though she was, she was not particularly interested in men—or perhaps she had not yet reached that stage of development. And Nigel Cressland was so much older than she—so far as she was concerned he might have been her father. She had been told by Pierrot that Rita was still in her twenties, therefore it seemed to her quite in order that Rita should have an old family friend like Mr. Cressland. She beamed at him.

'Oh, yes, do come back and meet Pierrot. He's an angel. You'll like him awfully.'

Nigel pulled on a pair of leather gloves. The smirk vanished and for a moment his teeth dug into his lower lip. Little idiot, he thought, she little knew what she was saying! Rita had got as far as this, had she? Publicly announcing her relationship with this boy with whom she was infatuated. Well, he'd deal with her, all in good time. As casually as he could, he asked

Glenise where she was staying and she answered at once with her delightful frankness that both she and her brother were at the Hyde Park Hotel. Then he bade good-bye to Glenise and went down in the lift which had once more come up and opened its gates for him. As he walked out into the grey chill of the autumnal morning he felt a slow deadly anger consuming him. Just now, when Rita had nearly fainted, he had felt almost tenderly towards her, ashamed of his own heartlessness. But this chance coincidental meeting with her new flame's sister had killed all tenderness. Nothing remained but his passion for Rita which was in his blood—Rita, *damn* her, got under a fellow's skin! But he was going to make her marry him as she had promised, and throw up this other man, or ruin her—which he had it in his power to do.

As soon as Nigel reached his offices in the City, he sat down, wrote a note and sent it by hand direct to the clinic.

Glen Farrington, meanwhile, had knocked on Rita's door. Helen cautiously opened it and began to say that Mrs. Wade was too ill to see anybody, when the young girl broke in, in a high sweet voice:

'Oh, *can't* I even peep at her? I'm Glen—Glenise—Rita will know who that is.'

Sitting in her chair where Nigel had left her still weeping weakly, Rita heard that voice and the name, and sat upright, her tears drying like

126

magic.

She exclaimed:

'Good heavens! Pierrot's young sister! She must have arrived unexpectedly from East Africa—Helen—Helen, listen a moment . . .'

She whispered excitedly, beckoning to Helen who turned back to her with a little sigh. Already she had wasted half the morning in the clinic. And there was so much to do.

Rita was garbling a lot of instructions now. Glen was Pierrot's sister. She must be allowed in. Get that vanity case there on the bedside table—find her her comb—her mirror— quickly.

In the next moment, Rita looked as though she had never wept or been through a disagreeable scene with Nigel. Face carefully made up again. Wonderful hair falling in a shining cloud to her shoulders; hand outstretched; deep dark eyes glowing with welcome. (Helen thought: *I hand it to her—the world has missed a fine actress in our Rita. Doubtless it's her Italian temperament but I couldn't swing from one mood to another with such ease and brilliance.*)

'How perfectly *wonderful* to meet Pierrot's little sister—I am still not too strong but, of course, *you* can come in for a moment, Glenise, darling. When *did* you arrive? Pierrot didn't know you were coming, did he?'

Glen laid the flowers and magazines on the table. Helen would have made her escape now but Rita quickly bade her stay and arrange the flowers (Nigel's horrid carnations, too, abandoned there on the bed). Rita loved to see her room full of flowers. It soothed her vanity.

Now, almost with awe on her face, young Glen was introducing herself to her brother's 'girl friend' about whom he had written so much from Paris. She was at once dazzled and flattered. Rita came up to Glen's highest expectations. She was just *too* lovely, and so fragile-looking. And Glen was at once where Rita meant her to be—at her feet. Literally, she sat there, on a stool, her beret off, fur coat loosened, and told Rita all about her sudden flight, and how her mother had given her permission to stay with Pierrot in England as long as he cared to put up with her, and get herself fixed up at one of the Colleges of Music, for the coming term.

Glen, in her young and eager way, had a lot to say about her music and herself. And Rita listened, with a patronizing smile, taking in very little about the music, disinterested in the child's violoncello, but ready to be charming because Glen had Pierrot's brilliant attractive eyes and his trick of glancing sideways. Yes, there was a strong family likeness.

At the same time Rita was making rapid mental calculations. It was bad enough suffering Helen's presence in the flat, but it was going to be an awful nuisance having her future sister-in-law hanging around as well. Or was she going too far ahead by so labelling Glen? Pierrot hadn't even proposed to her yet. But Rita was relieved and soothed to note from every word Glen said, that Pierrot's letters home left little room for doubt that she was his Chosen Woman.

Helen, artistically arranging the lovely flowers, was forced to hear all the conversation. She listened, as usual, with a cold irony. How wonderful it would be if Patty's mother were the sweet young thing she liked to appear! And how she could act her part so conclusively with so much on her conscience, Helen could not imagine. Rita seemed a past-mistress of self-deception.

Then suddenly a bombshell—Helen started and turned round and looked at Rita as she heard Glen say:

'Oh, I met an old friend of yours by the lift, Rita. He was awfully nice. A big man with horn-rims. Nigel something or other. We had a long talk.'

Silence. Helen blinked. She saw Rita's face go scarlet and the long, thin hands grip the sides of her chair. Helen had to admire the admirable restraint with which Rita said:

'Oh, really?' Mr. Nigel Cressland, you mean?'

'Yes, that's it. I asked him the way to your room. Or rather, he told me.'

Rita lied glibly:

'Nigel Cressland is my lawyer. I don't much like him, but I have to suffer him. You know—wills and things—when one has an operation . . .' She smiled wanly.

Helen bent over her roses again, shaking her head. She had never known anyone get themselves more readily into a morass of lies and deceit! Really! It was almost as though Rita had a psychological dislike of the truth.

Then a louder bomb exploded in the sickroom.

'Mr. Cressland said he hadn't met Pierrot yet, but wanted to, so he might come back later when Pierrot's here,' announced young Glen ingenuously.

Again Helen glanced over her shoulder, wondering if Rita would stage another swoon. She was as white now as she had been red and really did look ghastly. Helen thought: *'One doesn't like to see even a snake tortured. I suppose I'll have to weigh in . . .'*

Quietly she came forward and suggested to the very nice girl who was Peter's sister that it might be better for her to go now and come back tomorrow because it was Mrs. Wade's first day up and she wasn't very strong.

Rita was grateful for this interference in what seemed a crucial moment but tried to control her rising hysteria. With laboured breathing, she bade a pretty apologetic farewell to Glen and added:

'Please tell the sister that I won't see

anybody else today but Pierrot. I couldn't bear my solicitor again. I shall get Helen to lock the door. Helen, you know, looks after my flat—and me—I don't believe I introduced you properly after you first came in. She's my right hand . . .'

Somehow Helen got Glenise away and shut the door behind her.

Then Rita turned eyes of despair upon Helen.

'That's finished it,' she said in a hoarse voice, 'of all the ghastly things to happen, Helen! *Why* did Fate have to bring Pierrot's sister into the clinic just at the moment Nigel was here. Now she'll tell Pierrot about him!'

Helen, chafing to be away from this nest of intrigue and get out into the fresh air again, spoke rather shortly:

'Well, you fixed that, didn't you? You said he was your lawyer.'

'Yes, but Nigel will soon *un*fix it. He knows now about Pierrot—he knows his name—and knowing this, I bet he got hold of the address, too. He's an absolute *swine*! Oh, Helen, this will be the *end*!'

Helen sighed and remained silent. How difficult to be sympathetic, with the thought of Patty tugging at her heart, wandering through her mind like a little accusing ghost—accusing her mother of being a traitor to her.

Rita, with shaking fingers, lit a cigarette.

'Everything is against me at the moment,'

131

she added through her teeth. 'You probably think I deserve this . . .'

Helen looked at Rita with those grey honest eyes which the older girl found so infuriatingly critical. She said:

'It's none of my business, really, and I don't want to be dragged into it nor do I think it my place to pass judgment on you or anybody else. Your conscience is your own private affair.'

'But you think I haven't got one—Yes, I know you do! You don't like me, Helen. You don't approve of all this!'

Helen squirmed. A direct attack on her emotions always made her feel uncomfortable. She said awkwardly:

'If I don't, it isn't anything to do with your love affairs. You can shelve all the Nigels in the world for all the Peters and I'll sympathize. You *know* what upsets me.'

Hot—eyed, miserable but still defiant, Rita muttered:

'Well, for God's sake don't mention Patty to me now. I've enough on my mind.'

'Quite,' said Helen coldly.

There was such quiet scorn behind that word that Rita flinched. There were moments when she could willingly have hit Helen. But the girl's help was more than ever necessary to her now. She struggled to regain her self—control, and conveniently dropped the delicate subject of Patty (who, of course, Rita knew, was Helen's *raison d'être* for the help she gave).

Now, Rita said urgently, Helen must make perfectly sure that Nigel did not get into this room again this morning. She would see him later, herself, and find out what harm had been done by this meeting with Glenise.

But she did not have to wait long to find out. A smiling probationer popped into the room with a note, and the moment Rita recognized the handwriting, she tore open the envelope. From Nigel himself! She began to shake as she read what he had written.

'So his name is Pierrot. How delightfully romantic and he is well off enough to stay with his baby sister at the Hyde Park Hotel. How convenient for you. And you are practically engaged to him. How revealing for me. Enjoy your convalescence, darling. I'll be seeing you.'
'NIGEL.'

The note, written on Nigel's office paper, shook in Rita's hand. When she raised her face to Helen again, her features were distorted with rage and fear. But she no longer cried. A cold loathing of her former lover crept over her. If he thought he could bully her, use that wretched money he had loaned her, and the bank business, as weapons, he was wrong! She would beat him at his own game. She would make Pierrot marry her—before the hammer fell (just when it would fall she hadn't any idea

133

at the moment). But the deadliness of her position cured her of her hysteria and suddenly made her icily determined.

She crushed Nigel's note in her fingers. The expression in her eyes rather shocked Helen.

'Helen,' she said, 'I've got to get out of this home before next Saturday. Go and ring my doctor. Tell him I want to see him at once. I'm coming home the day after tomorrow even if it's by ambulance. I'm not going to risk any more coincidental meetings between Nigel and my . . .' She stopped.

Somebody had knocked on the door. A man's charming eager voice called:

'May I come in, Rita?'

Rita drew a deep breath and relaxed her whole body again. 'Pierrot!' she whispered.

A look of supreme tenderness softened those big brown eyes which a moment ago had been black with rage. As usual, Helen marvelled at this woman. It seemed she really did care for Peter Farrington. A pity that she couldn't combine all that was best in her nature with her love. Or was it love? Wasn't it merely a mad infatuation?

'Let him in, Helen,' Rita said.

Helen opened the door. As she saw Peter's tall figure and caught his quick delightful smile, she thought of their evening in the flat—the wonderful music—the friendship and peace he had brought to her so unexpectedly. And now it was as though he and Christopher combined to smile and rend her heart, yet at the same time bring her a nameless joy.

'Hallo, Helen!' said Peter.

She answered shyly, conscious of Rita behind her:

'Hallo . . .'

Then with a faint colour in her cheeks, a tightening of the muscles in her throat, she turned back to Rita.

'I'll be getting along,' she said. 'You'll phone me if you alter your arrangements, won't you? I'll get everything ready for you if you come home the day after tomorrow.'

'What's this I hear?' said Peter, walking into the room. 'I've just seen Glen and she tells me you're not so fit. Surely you oughtn't to be up, let alone leaving the clinic, my sweet.'

Rita waved a hand in the air and gave him her most welcoming smile.

'Darling—heaven to see you! Come and sit down—I'm much better. I only told dear Glen I was giving it out to unwanted visitors that I wasn't so well. What a *delicious* person your little sister is, Pierrot. And what fun your getting her over so unexpectedly. I want to hear all about it . . .'

Helen left them alone and shut the door.

On her way home, her mind focused as usual on the all-important subject of Rita's daughter. She thought:

If that woman decides to come home this week—she'll be lying about on the sofa for

135

ages—she won't want me to go away and Patty will be disappointed again—about mid-term. I *promised* to stay down at Bexhill. I *promised*. I can't let her down!'

Then her thoughts switched back to Christopher's double—this new influence in her life. And it was beginning to be quite an influence—despite all her efforts to disregard the fact. She began to visualize what might be happening now in Rita's room. Peter, taking Rita in his arms—kissing that wide scarlet tempting mouth. Looking into those gorgeous eyes. Believing every word she said. And Helen felt nauseated. More than that, she felt suddenly angry and jealous.

She knew that she would like to be in Rita's shoes at this very moment. Because Rita was in Peter's arms.

CHAPTER TEN

The monitor's sharp voice pulled Patty with a jerk from her day-dreaming.

'Patricia Wade—stop sucking the end of your pen.'

Guiltily Patty drew the wooden penholder out of her mouth.

Somebody giggled. Patty giggled back out of sympathy. The monitor snapped:

'If you think I'm so funny, Patricia, you can

stay in for half an hour after the others have gone.'

Scarlet, heart thumping, Patty threw the senior girl at the mistress's desk a beseeching look. The half hour after 'prep' was supposed to be free and she had wanted to finish painting Mummy's Christmas card.

'Oh, *please*—Barbara . . .!'

'I don't want to hear any more from you,' cut in Barbara's cold voice.

Mortified Patty returned to her work. Tears magnified the French translation. One dropped on to the exercise book and made a blot. Then the classroom door opened. Another senior put in her head.

'Miss Ponting wants to speak to Patricia Wade in the study.'

Patty blinked. *The Head!* Oh, goodness, what had she done now? How awful!

She smoothed her creased green gym-slip, pulled up a crooked stocking, refixed the slide in her hair and walked out of the room. One of her friends whispered as she passed:

'Good luck, Patty.'

That was kind and cheered her. But she was a bundle of nerves as she knocked on the study door and was admitted. One so hated going into this room although it was warmer and cosier, because of its coal fire and thick carpet, than any other room in the school. But girls rarely entered it except when they were in for what they called a 'jaw'.

To Patty's surprise and relief, however, the Head greeted her affably.

'Oh, yes, Patricia, come in. I've just had a telephone call from your mother.'

Patty's cheeks flooded sensitively with colour.

'Oh, have you, Miss Ponting?'

Miss Ponting eyed Patty over her glasses. She was a big stout woman with bobbed grey hair. She wore a severe line in suits and a hand—knitted faded blue jumper which had been washed and stretched out of all recognition. She had no interest in Patricia Wade, whom she labelled one of the dull negative types in the school, added to which Miss Ponting disapproved of Mrs. Wade. She bore no particular animosity against Patty but would have been more interested if the child were a brilliant pupil or had influential parents.

What with Government interference, taxation and impoverished parents, St. Cyprian's wasn't doing so well. Miss Ponting had her old age to think of. Her chief interest lay in girls like Elizabeth Turner, whose father was Sir Manfred Turner. A new knight, of course, and—Miss Ponting knew it—a vulgarian, but the title was useful on the school brochure.

'I'm afraid, my dear, I've got a disappointment for you,' she said as brightly as though delivering words of praise.

138

Patty, whose brain never worked very fast, nervously unclasped those hot sweating little fingers of hers behind her back and blinked questioningly at Miss Ponting, who added:

'I believe that—er—Miss Shaw was coming down tomorrow to take you out for mid-term, was she not?'

Was coming—Patty's heart gave a horrible jolt—what did that mean?

Miss Ponting leaned over her blotter and gave a little cough.

'Well, I'm sorry, my dear child,' she continued, 'but you must be a good girl and face your disappointment bravely. Miss Shaw has had to cancel at the hotel because at a moment's notice she was called home where her uncle is lying dangerously ill.' (Miss Ponting unconsciously slipped into B.B.C. oratory.)

Silence except for the ticking of the clock on the desk and the hoarse snore of a very old pug lying in a basket beside Miss Ponting.

A blow of this kind always had the effect of first numbing Patty then of making her feel quite sick. For a moment she felt so sick because Helen wasn't coming down tomorrow after all that she ignored the reason and a cry broke from her:

'Oh, Miss *Ponting*!'

The head mistress cleared her throat and said unctuously:

'These little things are sent to try us, my

dear, and in accepting our disappointments well, we form our characters. Now you are going to be a good girl and just sit down and write a nice letter to Miss Shaw and another to your mother to thank her for the telephone call.'

Patty's breathing quickened. Her small face screwed up. No Helen—no going out. Mid—term here in school with the same awful food and supervision. No change—nothing—and six whole weeks more to Christmas!

And capping the bitterness, anguished pity for Helen whose uncle was 'lying dangerously ill'. Mummy was ill, too, and had no one to look after her. What would *she* do?

Miss Ponting's bright voice broke in:

'One nice thing, Patricia, your dear mother is home again and is much better.'

'Oh, Miss Ponting, then why can't I go home for mid-term?' burst from Patty's overflowing heart.

Miss Ponting hastily explained that it wouldn't be convenient, and that Mrs. Wade had said that someone else was in the flat helping her until Miss Shaw returned.

'Now run along, dear,' she dismissed the child, 'and tell Barbara—it is Barbara who is taking prep, is it not?—that you have special permission to write your letters now.'

Patty was too disciplined to dare stay and launch a further protest. She wheeled round and walked out of the study, half-blinded by the scorching tears that began to chase down her face.

In the corridor she bumped into somebody, looked up and was horrified to see her arch—enemy, Miss Eccles.

Miss Eccles was a tall, thin young woman who, on account of strong magnifying glasses, exceptional height and a long nose, looked more formidable than she really was. She did not really hate Patty. She rarely thought about her. In fact she was suffering in her way as badly as Patty, having been jilted during the summer holidays. In consequence her patience was strained. She snapped at the little girl:

'Do look where you are going Patricia. You walk so badly.'

Patty hurried on. Bad—everything was bad. Black as ink! And she would spend her mid-term in charge of *Miss Eccles*.

Oh, Helen. Oh, *Mummy!*

Unable to control herself any longer, Patty stumbled into a cold odorous little room where the lower class kept hockey-sticks and gum boots and hung their coats and hats. Here, at least, she could be alone. She buried her face against one of the coats and sobbed bitterly.

*   *   *

At about eleven o'clock that following morning, Rita Wade, having had a nice hot bath, put on a graceful almond-green two-piece with which she wore a heavy gold necklace and her gold crescent earrings.

She was looking and feeling altogether better and stronger. She sat down at her bureau in the well-heated drawing-room and tried to focus on a few accounts. But she soon found that too depressing and abandoned it. She retired to her sofa and picked up a new *Vogue*. In half an hour darling Pierrot would be here. Glenise had gone out to shop. Dear Glenise! Quite domesticated and willing to take Helen's place for a day or two, and tactful as well—always managed to leave her alone with Peter.

Rita smiled dreamily at her thoughts. Things were going well. The doctor had helped her get out of the clinic and she was once more her own mistress. So far Nigel had not been round to carry out his threats and she was positive that Pierrot would propose marriage at any moment. So well were things going, indeed, that she was not even annoyed because Helen had had to rush home to her aunt's assistance. The old uncle seemed to have had a stroke.

Suddenly she remembered her small daughter and had the grace to feel sorry about the child's mid-term. She bestirred herself to write a little note, full of love and sympathy, and drop a pound note into the envelope. She told poor Patty to find someone to take her out and buy something nice. That would cheer

142

her up. (Money compensated Rita for most things, so why not Patty?)

Remembering her telephone call to Miss Ponting, Rita frowned. She had forgotten to pass on Helen's frantic messages. It was really quite silly the way Helen had been so upset at having to let Patty down. And why foster the child's affection for Helen? Rita wanted it all ways; she wanted Patty to worship *her* despite the fact that she was ill-prepared to make any sacrifices for her.

She scribbled the words:

'Mummy misses you badly . . .'

The front door bell rang. Rita hastily put away her writing pad. Glen had her own key and it might be that Pierrot had come early. Or was it Nigel? Cautiously she peered through the frosted glass of the front door then with an exclamation swung it open.

For a moment, shocked beyond measure, she stared down at a small familiar figure in green school uniform and at a small white face with red-rimmed, anxious eyes. Rita gasped:

'Patty!'

An instant's silence. Then Patty rushed at her, clutched her mother as though she were drowning and said in a heartbreaking voice:

'I've run away—oh, Mummy, I've run away from school. Don't be cross. It was so awful! I just had enough in my money box for my ticket and I ran away when nobody was looking. The others were all going home. Mummy, let me stay with you till Monday, please!'

CHAPTER ELEVEN

Automatically Rita hugged her small daughter's quivering figure. She was not so inhuman as to be left cold by such an appeal, such an exhibition of genuine suffering. And in her selfish way she wanted Patty to be happy. Patty was her flesh and blood. The tie between them was too fundamental to be eliminated totally. But she liked to feel that Patty's happiness could be invoked by the odd present or treat, without disorganizing her own life. She was far too interested in herself and her pleasures to give serious thought to the psychological needs of her child or anybody else's. While she hugged Patty and began to question her as to why she had run away from school, her mind was frantically searching for a way out of this predicament.

She kept thinking:

'Pierrot will be here in a moment—oh, heavens! *Pierrot will be here in a moment . . . !*'

Quickly she shut the front door and drew the child into her bedroom, switched on an electric fire, sat down on the bed feeling weak and still shocked by the unexpected arrival of her daughter and stood Patty in front of her.

'Darling, what on earth has happened? I'm

absolutely staggered! You've done an awful thing running away like this. How *could* you.'

Patty struggled out of her school coat and hat, snuffling a little, drawing the back of her hand across her streaming eyes.

She began a garbled explanation—how awful it was at St. Cyprian's—how nobody loved or understood her—Miss Eccles and the Matron particularly hated her and no matter how hard she tried, she could never do right. Nearly all the other girls were either going home for mid-term or being taken out. When the Head told her Helen wasn't coming, she couldn't *bear* it. She had just enough pocket money with which to buy a single ticket to Victoria.

'I want you and Helen—I don't like anybody else—' sulked Patty desolately. 'I want to come home . . .'

Rita chewed her lower lip. Now she had a most uncomfortable recollection of Patty's father—a certain night when they had had 'a scene' because Rita had wanted to go away for week-ends and travel abroad and always be out, gay, social, utterly unlike Tom. *He* adored his own home and concentrated on her and the daughter who was then only a baby. She shuddered to see how alike they were—father and daughter—she could almost hear Tom saying:

'Why can't you understand me? I want just you—nobody else . . .'

145

'Oh, Mummy,' came Patty's imploring voice. 'You won't make me go back till Tuesday, will you? Please ring Miss Ponting up and tell her not to be angry and that I can stay. Only for the week-end like all the others.'

Rita looked and felt frantically anxious. It wasn't that she so much minded having Patty around but *this* week-end—with Glenise staying here and Pierrot to account to—it was a dénouement which she had never anticipated.

But no time now to start worrying as to why Patty was unhappy at boarding-school, or remind herself that Tom had always put his foot down on the subject and maintained that it was a crime to send sensitive children away from home—all she could think about was saving herself from disaster at Peter's hands, and at the same time behaving decently to her own child.

It was part of Rita's make-up that she should struggle to run with the hare and hunt with the hounds and that she had no active wish to be wicked or unkind but was just too weak and self-centred to make a real sacrifice.

Feverishly she tried to find a way out . . .

She dried Patty's tears, hastily found some sweets. Mournfully Patty sucked a toffee which temporarily silenced her, and regarded her mother with swollen eyes. Then waiting for sentence, turned over a page of a magazine, found a coloured plate with a funny picture and gave a little giggle. The sudden switch from tears to laughter would have gone to the heart of any woman but Rita, whose nerves were at fever-pitch.

'Don't stand there acting the idiot. Go and wash your face and hands. You're filthy,' she said frowning.

'Yes, Mummy,' said Patty meekly, and turned towards the bathroom. There, her spirits rose a little. It was so warm and nice and she sniffed with delight at the familiar odour of Mummy's bath salts, and felt a secret satisfaction at the thought of the staff at St. Cyprian's searching for her.

Of course, at any moment, the Head would ring Mummy—but she, Patty, was here, so it's *snubs* to her.

Rita walked up and down her bedroom, clenched hands beating against each other, brows knit anxiously. It was too late to get rid of Patty. For a moment she had thought of ringing Helen and saying 'come and take her' but even Rita could not do a thing like that. When she had telephoned the house earlier today to find out when Helen could come back, she had been told that the old uncle was expected to die at any moment and Mrs. Shaw was in a state of collapse. Obviously Helen couldn't leave them. If only she, Rita, had more time to act! But she felt too weak and ill herself to turn out on a cold day like this and conduct Patty to the Shaw's house, even if they would have her under the circumstances.

The front door bell rang. Rita felt the bedroom swim round her. She clutched at a chair for support, full of self—pity. It was awful that she should have to face a crisis like this so soon after her operation. She shook from head to foot with sheer fright.

It was Peter—or Glenise—and in either case she was lost. Peter would know at last that she had a daughter of eleven and that she must be years older than he had thought. He would also know that she had deceived him in the most cowardly fashion.

Before Rita went to open that front door she received what she afterwards imagined was a heaven-sent inspiration. Her brow cleared. Her eyes sparkled with delight in her own brilliant wit and imagination. Of *course!* That was one way out. *The only way!* Superb! And nobody else would know what she was going to say in confidence to Peter, so nobody could deny it.

She stopped trembling and grew calm again. She hurried to the bathroom, and spoke to Patty.

'Go into your own room and look at a book, dear, until I send for you,' she said hurriedly.

Patty, whose small face looked pale but clean now, gave her a beseeching look.

'Oh, Mummy, you won't send me back, will you?'

'We'll see, we'll see,' Rita soothed her, 'I'll

speak to Miss Ponting on the phone.'

'Oh, Mummy—' began Patty in an excited voice.

Rita shut the door upon the small figure. The front door bell was ringing again as though the visitor was impatient. Patty crammed a few more toffees into her mouth and walked into her bedroom, feeling much happier. She began to pull out a drawer in which she had left some treasures.

Then Rita let Peter into the flat.

For a moment the man noticed nothing, not even that Rita was looking a little flushed and harassed. But as he followed her into the sitting-room he said:

'You're not very strong yet, my dear. It's a pity there isn't someone here to answer the door. I got you off your sofa.'

'Oh, no, it's all right—I'm much better,' said Rita in a high voice. And then, contrary to her usual policy of 'never be the one to make the first move', came close to him and lifted her large, brown eyes with an appeal which he found impossible to resist. A look that awoke all his most passionate feelings as well as his wish to protect her. He caught and held her close. For a moment he looked down at that flawless face, thin, spiritualized by her recent illness, his senses swimming.

'Oh, my lovely adorable girl!' he said.

As his lips touched hers and clung, she surrendered herself with a warmth and

149

eagerness which she had only shown to him once before—on that night in Paris—for since then she had been cool and a little withdrawn which had often tantalized him. It seemed to him that in this kiss Rita was *asking* for his love and readily he gave it. And now—in a flash—in a moment which he had never anticipated—he said all the things she had been scheming and hoping for.

'I love you—I love you, darling adorable Rita. Rita, marry me—marry me soon—I don't think I can go on without you . . .'

With a long sigh the woman leaned back, eyes shut, the beautiful slim body relaxed and satisfied. He kept his arms around her. His lips touched the long, white throat.

'You will marry me, won't you? I know now that you're the right one for me—I've been waiting to speak—but I know now,' he said urgently.

'Pierrot, my darling,' she whispered and opened her eyes and gave him a dazzling smile.

'Will you?' he repeated.

She continued to smile, her gaze travelling over the young eager face. How handsome and vital he was! And what a lover. It would be a very different marriage from the old boring mistaken one with Tom Wade. He would take her to East Africa, and there, where he was known and money flowed, she could lead a wonderful luxurious life with him. His proposal of marriage, she thought feverishly, had come at a most propitious time. He could not, would not, back out of it no matter what she chose to tell him so long as he kept his illusions about her. And she was going to make quite certain that he kept them, no matter how much she lied—nor, she told herself dramatically, even if she imperilled her immortal soul.

After a moment she disengaged herself from his arms and allowed him to sit with her on the sofa, her head against his shoulder. Cheek to cheek they sat there. Pierrot said:

'You haven't answered my question, yet darling. Are you going to marry me? Or am I a conceited fool to imagine that you'd accept a chap like me?'

His humility did not touch her or awaken her remorse. It merely gave her a stronger sense of victory, of control over him. She said:

'Before I answer finally, Pierrot, my sweet, there's something very important which you must know.'

'Something about you?' he smiled in a way which suggested that nothing she could say could alter his own decision.

'Something connected with me . . .' she began.

Then she stopped. The drawing-room door was pushed open. Patty walked in. It was just like Patty, Rita thought, suddenly furiously angry with her small daughter, to come in at

151

the wrong moment—just as she was about to make her explanation. And so disobedient! Patty began:

'Mummy, can I have . . .?'

Then stopped shyly, eyeing the stranger on the sofa beside her mother. Peter rose to his feet. For a moment he was too thunderstruck to speak clearly. *Mummy.* Good Lord, what was all this. Rita hadn't got a child. Was he mad or dreaming?

Rita went scarlet then very pale. Well, she was in for it now and come what may must carry out the plan she had evolved. She said, as sweetly as she could:

'Patty darling, I'm busy just now. Run back to your bedroom.'

Patty gave Peter a timid little smile which revealed the band across her small irregular teeth, dropped a book, picked it up, flung her mother a penitent look and fled. She hadn't meant to annoy her but she wanted a pencil and there wasn't one in her bedroom.

Peter remained standing, looking down at Rita in the most puzzled fashion.

Of course that funny little girl in the green school uniform couldn't be Rita's *daughter.* She was far too old. Nearly ten or eleven, he judged. Rita must have a niece or someone. He hadn't heard aright. The child couldn't have used the name *'Mummy'.*

Rita patted the seat beside her.

'Sit down again, Pierrot. Now you see what

152

I've got to tell you before I accept your offer. You may not want to marry me when you know...'

He pulled the lobe of his ear, his brows knit.

'That is impossible. But who is the child?'

'My adopted daughter,' said Rita breathlessly.

'Adopted daughter?'

Peter's voice held an incredulous note. But he picked up one of Rita's long lovely hands, and stroked it.

'But why haven't you told me about her before?'

Her lashes flickered but she deliberately held his gaze, putting all her soul into her eyes as she answered:

'Well you see, Pierrot—it's all rather a muddle—I've so longed for my freedom since Tommy died and for a chance to be happy again and poor little Patty has been a bit of a burden and responsibility. I did mean to tell you in Paris and then let it slide because she wasn't really anything to do with us—I mean, she has no connection with our love for each other. But when you asked me to marry you just now, I realized that I *must* tell you at once.'

He was still a bit stunned. He said:

'But what on earth are you doing with an adopted daughter of that age. It isn't as if you were nearly old enough to be her mother . . . :'

Rita's heart gave a guilty leap and then with

triumph in her eyes she continued to explain—creating her story as she went along. Six years ago, when Patty was four, her parents had been killed together. The mother was Rita's cousin and greatest friend. Rita was Patty's godmother. The couple had no relations on either side except some very old aunts. Rita and her husband had adopted the orphan. Patty didn't remember her own parents and had grown up with them as though she were their own.

'She's been away at boarding-school ever since I met you,' said Rita hurriedly.

Peter continued to look at her in a puzzled way. He was making rapid calculations. Six years ago—why that was when Rita was in her early twenties. The first year of her marriage, presumably.

'I think it very wonderful of you,' he said, 'but I'm surprised your husband let you take on a child of four when you were still such a kid yourself.'

Now Rita's gaze dropped. She began to feel dreadful about this but having gone so far she carried on with the wild story. They had changed Patty's name to Wade, she said. They had not wanted the poor little thing ever to know that they were not her parents. Patty called her 'Mummy', and believed it to be true.

'But she'll have to know one day, darling—I mean, when she gets married, she'll have to produce her birth certificate,' put in Peter.

154

Rita's heart plunged. She was falling deeper and deeper into the morass, getting herself tied up in knots she would never be able to untie! But the future must take care of itself. All she wanted to do was to manage the present to her own satisfaction. Besides, she would see to it that Patty was in a different country by the time she was old enough to get married. *Peter must never see that birth certificate.* Hastily she piled more lies, one on top of another, giving Peter a histrionic account of the adoption of little Patty and how much they loved her. How, in recent years, she had become rather a handful, so that she, Rita, had at times regretted the adoption. That was one of the reasons why she had not mentioned it to Peter before.

'Though, of course, you would have to have known at Christmas when she was due home for the holidays,' added Rita glibly.

'Well, I think it's far too much for you,' said Peter slowly, 'although it's just the sort of kind, sweet thing you would do. Forgive me for a pertinent question, but did the parents leave you the means to support the child?'

'No, nothing. My cousin was always hard up,' muttered Rita.

'You poor little thing,' exclaimed Peter, 'what a burden for you. Just a slip of a girl, not only having to face widowhood but supporting a child at school. I call it positively noble.'

Rita had the grace to blush burning red. But

she had to admit that her story had met with tremendous success. She gave Peter a pathetic look:

'Perhaps I was stupid not to tell you about it at once.'

'It certainly wouldn't have made any difference to my feelings for you. In fact, now that I see what a grave struggle you've had, it makes me love you all the more.'

Rita's relief was so great that she burst into tears. Then had the pleasure of being comforted and petted and of hearing Peter say that the sooner she married him the better. And they'd take the poor kid out to East Africa with them and give her a chance. 'I'm very fond of kids, you know,' he said.

Rita released herself from his embrace, blew her nose, found her powder compact and lipstick and delicately repaired her face. Everything was turning out wonderfully well. As for Patty going abroad with them, well, she wasn't quite sure about *that*. But for the moment all was well and the sooner she rushed through this marriage the better. There was always the bogy of Nigel and her debts in the background.

Peter lit a cigarette, sat back and watched his beautiful Rita make up her face and run a comb through those glossy red curves of hair. He thought how young and sweet she looked, and how tenderly he had felt when she had wept just now in his arms. And then as he had time to collect his thoughts and review the whole affair, he began to wonder a little why she had kept the secret of the adopted child so closely hidden from him. She had not mentioned the child even during their most intimate talks. Helen Shaw hadn't mentioned her either. What funny creatures women were! He supposed he didn't understand them. His own mind and character were so straightforward. He couldn't quite comprehend the complexities of mind that could keep Rita from saying one word about her adopted daughter.

He was not fully aware just then—complete realization was to come later when he was alone with his thoughts—that Rita's confession raised the first faint doubt within him about her being a wholly truthful person. In fact, when he really started to think seriously about it all, he seemed to remember all kinds of things Rita had said, stories of her past and particularly of her 'utter loneliness' which could not strictly be called true. She had always had the child. It seemed a bit odd.

But here with her, body and brain still on fire with the memory of her passionate kisses and complete surrender to him, he was still completely at her feet.

Rita, anxious to embroider her story, was telling him now that she had asked Helen not to mention Patty.

'I wished to be the one to tell you about my

poor little adopted daughter,' she said.

Peter smiled tolerantly.

'There was no reason to keep it from me at all, angel. It was quite unnecessary.'

'And you still want me to marry you, Pierrot?'

'Of course,' he said.

Her heart leapt with triumph. She gave him her hand and he kissed it.

'I'll have to adopt her too,' he said, 'but I still think it's ridiculous—you at your age with a large schoolgirl. I should think everybody must know that she's adopted—I mean Helen . . .'

'Oh, of course, most of my old friends know she's adopted but nobody ever mentions the fact because I've asked them not to. And I don't want you to mention it, even to Helen. I've got a "thing" about it. I want that child to think I am her mother, and our future friends can be told if necessary.'

It was all a bit too complicated for Peter Farrington. The main thing seemed that Rita was being very unselfish and noble about it all. He promised not to talk about it except, he added, he would naturally have to tell the truth to his people.

'They know you're only twenty-six, darling, and that you couldn't have a kid that age. And besides, she doesn't bear the slightest resemblance to you.'

'Of course, her hair has a red tinge,' said

158

Rita, cleverly, 'because red hair is in the family and you must remember that she's my cousin's child.'

'Call her in and let me have another look at her,' said Peter with a laugh. 'I think we ought to get to know each other if I'm to be her stepfather.'

It went against the grain with Rita to follow up all the lies she had told by introducing Patty properly to Peter now. She knew she had really done a dreadful thing—it was yet another cowardly act of betrayal towards her child. But she argued with herself that the end justified the means and it would be all right in the end if Patty were happy. She, Rita, must marry Peter and get to Nairobi with him without letting him meet any of the friends who could give her away.

She knew that she was swimming in deeper waters than she had ever meant to swim in but there was no backing out now. She only hoped to 'get away with it'. As long as she remained Peter Farrington's 'ideal girl' that was all that mattered. Physically, she could cope—she knew that; she looked only twenty-six, whatever she felt like.

Already she was formulating in her ever—scheming brain the wording of an announcement which must go into the papers as soon as possible—the announcement of her engagement to the rich young banker which would enable her to borrow some money and pay back her own bank—and Nigel. Then he would no longer be able to threaten her and she would start a new life as Pierrot's wife and salve her conscience by being also a good mother to Patty. Peter wasn't like Nigel. He loved children. He would accept Patty. It was all going to be *wonderful*.

CHAPTER TWELVE

Helen's uncle, George Shaw, died that weekend.

It seemed to Helen that she was doomed to lose those whom she loved. With the passing of dear old Uncle George she lost a devoted relative and friend. Her frail invalid aunt was prostrate after the funeral. But fortunately, perhaps, for the girl, Mrs. Shaw did not ask her to remain longer in the house than was necessary for the immediate straightening of affairs. She had an old friend, a maiden lady of her own age, who lived alone in a small flat in Earl's Court. To this flat Mrs. Shaw retired, and let her own place furnished in order to make a few pounds extra for her needs. Helen, she said, must go back to her own life and under no circumstances would she be allowed to sacrifice herself to the service of an aging woman who spent most of her time in bed or on a couch. Isobel Brinkley, her friend, was of the same *genre* and had an even older but stronger woman friend—a domestic servant of a class quickly dying out—humble and devoted. Old Emily would look after both the delicate ladies.

So Helen left the old ladies in their flat and returned to Rita's where the whole atmosphere was so very different.

She had been away from her job for a fortnight.

During those two weeks, on top of the worry of her aunt's affairs, she had received one or two minor shocks connected with Rita. She had telephoned her employer one morning and had been amazed to hear Rita announce that little Patty was there. After hearing why— Helen had left her aunt's house for an hour and rushed round to see the child. Patty had received her rapturously.

'Mummy says I can stay for my mid-term, isn't it scrumptious?—and I'm going to have a new stepfather called "Uncle Peter". Oh, Helen, he's super! We have a marvellous game together and he can do card tricks—he showed me. He's heaps, *heaps* nicer than Uncle Nigel...'

That was the first shock. Then, bewildered, when the child was out of the room, Helen turned to Rita for an explanation, which Rita volunteered in a shamefaced fashion.

'Patty burst in on us—I couldn't avoid it— and so in the awful muddle I told Pierrot she was—my adopted child. He doesn't think me nearly old enough to be her mother. So that's that. Oh, don't looked so shocked, Helen . . .'

Rita's voice trailed off, her face had reddened and her brows knit angrily when she caught the look of utter scorn in the girl's clear eyes. Helen's first reaction had been to leave this woman's flat and never see her again. She was utterly disgusted. Such fantastic behaviour was beyond her understanding—or forgiveness. But in the next breath Rita was making it impossible for her to go.

'Patty and I will want you just as much—if not more now, as it looks as though I'll be married to Pierrot soon. Although he is willing for Patty to go with us, I shan't want to take her out to East Africa straight away—I must give my marriage a chance. I'll leave her in school—near you. If she isn't happy at St. Cyprian's we'll find another. But for our first six months together, we really must be alone . . .'

And so on—every word leaving Helen convinced that Rita's passion for Peter Farrington was almost a madness—making her not only unprincipled, but crazily oblivious to her fundamental duties.

Once again she had 'pulled the wool' over Peter's eyes. Poor ignorant Peter! Helen did not know whether to be sorry or angry about him. But the thought of him and the way he was being so shamefully deceived affected her.

162

She did know that. It had far too deep an effect on her, for her peace of mind. As for the child—after looking at the happy little face (happy because Patty was receiving a little affection and attention at last) Helen could not go her way and abandon the small, pathetic girl. Anything might happen in Rita's stormy life. Helen resolved to remain for the time being.

Patty returned to school and started the second half of term in a decidedly happier frame of mind. And Helen went back to her old job in the flat, releasing young Glen who, despite her youthful admiration for her future sister-in-law, found domestic duties a trifle irksome and looked forward to having that 'good time' in London that she had anticipated.

How had Glenise taken the sudden, rather startling innovation of Rita's 'adopted child', Helen wondered? She discovered by a chance phrase dropped from the girl's lips when Glen came to see Rita a few mornings after Helen had come back to the flat.

'You know, Helen,' she said in her nice friendly fashion, 'I do think it so noble of Rita to have taken on the upbringing of a child like little Patty—don't you? Even though she *is* a sort of relation.'

Helen avoided Glen's gaze.

'Patty is a very sweet child,' she said.

'But still an awful trouble for Rita. And in a

163

way it's rather hard on Pierrot. Having an eleven-year-old stepdaughter, don't you think?'

Helen dared not think. Her ears burned. She said bitterly:

'Has your brother—said so?'

'Oh, no, because he likes kids, but I bet he'd rather have Rita to himself,' said Glenise airily, and walked off, whistling in a blithe way, quite unconscious that she had given the older girl fresh food for thought.

For the rest of that day Helen brooded over Glen's remarks. It was so sickening—hearing Rita called 'noble' when she was one of the most ignoble of women. And as for the existence of Patty being 'hard on Pierrot'—yes, maybe it was. A young man of his age would normally fight shy of marrying a woman with a schoolgirl daughter like Patty. Had he been told she was Rita's real daughter, he might have deplored it, and instinctively, whatever he said, he would resent the adopted one—the intrusion on his privacy with a newly married wife.

No wonder Rita talked of 'leaving Patty behind' when she married Peter.

Would that marriage ever take place?

The more Helen thought about it—the more she dreaded it for *him*—the charming, Christopher-like Peter—the kindly, honest-to-God Peter—the crazy, foolish Peter, blindly in love with a woman who was no better than an adventuress.

Helen went about her duties in that flat, seeing Peter quite a lot these days—more than enough, now he came as Rita's acknowledged fiancé—though never alone. And her queer sense of bitterness, of regret over the affair, deepened rather than grew less.

The end of November found Rita in high spirits—her best mood. For some inexplicable reason, Nigel Cressland had not appeared on the scene to frighten or bother her. She had gone round trembling for a while after the engagement announcement appeared in the daily papers—wondering if it would evoke his immediate wrath. But he maintained a strange silence. At times Rita feared it to be a sinister one. But at least he was giving her time to consolidate her position and she feverishly sought to do so. Without appearing too eager, she manoeuvred Peter into fixing Christmas week for the wedding. She ran up fresh bills, foolishly and recklessly, in order to buy lovely clothes for her trousseau. And she had a long private talk with her bank manager about her overdraft.

Mr. Cressland might, she told him, withdraw his guarantee, but now she was about to marry Mr. Farrington (of the well-known East African bankers)—she could, herself, guarantee to pay back the loan immediately after her wedding. Her future husband was going to settle some money on her.

The bank manager, impressed by the name of Farrington and the engagement—and having assured himself that the affair was on solid ground—told Rita not to worry. With or without Mr. Cressland, the loan could continue for the present.

Rita returned home full of elation.

'I have a feeling my stars are shining brightly just now. My luck has turned,' she told Helen. 'And once I'm Peter's wife I'm going to turn over a new leaf—you'll see, Helen. I'll be a wonderful wife—and later I'll have Patty in Nairobi, too, and be a wonderful mother to her. And when I've got lots of money I shall remember *you*—you funny, quiet little thing . . .'

She laughed good-humouredly at Helen. The girl turned away.

'I don't want anything,' she said abruptly. 'Except to see Patty happy.'

Rita pouted. She was in one of her not infrequent moods when she wished to be the best of friends with everybody in the world—and particularly Helen—just because Helen was so difficult. It challenged Rita's inordinate vanity. She put out a hand and laid it on Helen's shoulder.

'Won't you forgive my cowardice about my age—and tell me you want to see me happily married to my beloved Pierrot?' she asked coaxingly.

Helen looked into the lovely, doe—like eyes which were in such contradiction to the

166

hardness of this woman's make—up, and somehow shrank from her touch and her attempts to draw near. *She knew that she did not want to see Rita married to Peter*: she loathed the idea of Peter being drawn, beyond recall, into the net which Rita was weaving—almost as much as she would have hated it had Christopher himself been involved.

She could not trust herself to answer Rita but walked from the room. Rita shrugged her shoulders. She picked up the exquisite sable tie which had been one of Peter's engagement presents, in addition to a magnificent diamond ring (Peter's mother had had the flawless stone flown especially from Johannesburg), and went out shopping.

That afternoon, while she was alone in the flat, Helen took an hour off from work and put on the Tchaikovsky *Romeo and Juliet* music which she loved—which Chris had loved—(and Peter, too.)

Peter called unexpectedly to see his fiancée. He had told her he had a business appointment but it had been cancelled, so he came straight round, hoping to find her in.

It was a bitterly cold winter's afternoon. A few snowflakes were whirling down from a leaden sky. It was dark in the flat already. Helen opened the front door to Peter and at once his ear caught the strains of the lovely music.

'Oh—one of my favourites. How nice,

Helen!' he exclaimed.

Quickly she turned and led the way into the sitting-room. In silence they both sat and heard the music through until it was finished. Then Peter smiled at the girl.

'That was glorious. D'you know I haven't heard any good stuff for weeks. I *needed* that . . .'

She smiled back. The old sense of comradeship reviving—she felt suddenly happy—happier than she had been since her uncle died.

'Shall I put on some more?'

'I'd love it!' he said and sat back and began to fill his pipe. Then remembered suddenly that Rita hated pipes, the smoke in her sitting-room so put it away and lit a cigarette. Thoughtfully he watched Helens slender figure—the pale, thin young face with its hint of tragic sadness. She was a sweet person, he thought—so restful to be with—a very sympathetic personality.

Suddenly, rather guiltily, he found himself reflecting upon how, during the month since his engagement, he had led a most hectic existence. Rather too hectic, for his liking. And he didn't feel fit. He was a man who liked a lot of fresh air and exercise and he was used to freedom from worry. Now he was always worrying—deep down inside himself; about Rita and their future life. He found her every bit as disturbingly beautiful and attractive as ever. But it had seeped into his consciousness, slowly, but insidiously, that he did not altogether want the life *she* was planning. He could do with the odd theatre and cinema and gay party. But not continual ones. Since Rita had recovered from her operation, she seemed strong enough for perpetual excitement (she slept late, of course—he had wanted her to ride with him in the mornings but she was never up before eleven); and she kept this place at a terrific temperature and always with lights on— Peter found it all a bit too artificial—like the gaieties which seemed necessary to *her.* Sometimes he wondered if she would ever want a country life—to walk with him or ride, for instance, in the lovely open country to which he belonged. Or would she plunge him into the same feverish life of pleasures which one could lead, if one wanted, in Nairobi—there even more so than in post-war London.

When he allowed himself to think seriously about it—Peter Farrington was definitely troubled.

As for her supposed love of music—that seemed so odd—that she had said she liked good music—bought the records—but never wanted to play them.

Most certainly she was not a genuine musician like this girl, Helen. Nor was it easy ever to induce Rita to share with him his occasional love of repose, of serious thinking. Rita seemed to alternate between hectic pleasure—seeking or hours alone with him of passionate love—making.

Peter was tolerant of these differences between them so long as he was with Rita and under her spell. It was only when he was away and had time to reflect—or with a kindred spirit, like Helen—that he made any kind of comparison.

He was making one now. He would hate to admit it—but he knew that he wanted to go on sitting here quietly by the fire, listening to Tchaikovsky—watching the responsive light in Helen's grey eyes. He did not want any outside disturbance—none at all. He was perfectly happy like this. And as he looked at Helen he began to wonder how things were with *her*. For he had not spoken to her alone since their evening when she had told him about Christopher.

The front door bell rang—a harsh interruption of the flowing, beautiful music. Peter frowned.

'Must you go?'

Helen sighed. She, too, had been relaxed and happy. Now, once more, the mask of weariness, remoteness, fell across her face.

'It must be Rita—she sometimes forgets her key.'

'I'll let her in . . .' Peter said.

And before Helen could move, he traversed the room with that easy stride of his and went out into the hall. She turned the gramophone

170

down to a murmur, and listened. No doubt it *was* Rita. Glen was at a cinema with a South African girl friend whom she had found in London. Nobody else was expected, Helen thought.

Then her heart gave a most uncomfortable jerk.

She could not hear the visitor's voice, only Peter's, courteous and friendly:

'Oh, yes, I've heard my sister mention your name. Do come in, of course,' he said.

Then he thrust his head in the doorway and added in an undertone to Helen:

'Bang goes our Tchaikovsky! It's Rita's solicitor, Mr. Cressland. I had to say "come in"—he's just taking off his things.'

CHAPTER THIRTEEN

Helen stood speechless. It was too late to regret that she had not insisted upon opening the door herself and dealing with Nigel. Ever since Rita left the clinic there had been a fear in Rita's mind that Nigel would come and start trouble, but somehow in the last few days she seemed to have cast off that particular worry, and the name had not even been mentioned.

Helen, far from being naturally an *intrigante* like Rita, was now quite incapable of dealing with the situation. Dismayed, she watched

171

Nigel's heavy figure stroll into the sitting-room. What would Rita say to this, heaven only knew! It was frightful, she thought. Her wide grey eyes stared at Nigel who in return eyed her over the rims of his spectacles with malicious humour.

'Ah! My dear Miss Shaw, and how are you?' he asked and extended a hand.

Helen went scarlet and compressed her lips angrily. She knew that Peter was watching them. Once again, despite her loathing of deception and lies, she had to be a party to both. There was a time when she might have felt some sympathy for Rita's discarded lover, but not now. He had proved himself far too unpleasant and undeserving of anyone's pity. Added to which she could never forgive him for the many hours, days, and perhaps weeks, of childish misery that he had caused Patty.

She barely touched Nigel's fingers. He was, she could see, bent on playing a role at the moment—aping the solicitor he was supposed to be. No doubt it afforded him a certain twisted amusement. He turned from Helen and addressed Peter quite affably.

'Charming little flat this and so agreeably warm on a chilly day like this,' he said briskly, rubbing his hands together and then spreading them out to the glow of the electric fire.

'Is it still snowing?' Peter asked by way of making polite conversation, but he gave Helen a look which plainly suggested that he was annoyed by the interruption of their music.

Nigel seated himself in a chair and grinned at Helen whose face remained expressionless, then, with that malicious look, gave close attention to the tall, gracefully built young man at her side.

So this was Rita's new boy friend, he thought darkly. Very young. The sort of build and looks to appeal to a woman. Much too young for *her*. The foot would never be able to hold her. Too nice. Rita did not want anything as nice as that. She needed an experienced hand, *damn* her—he swore at her in his thoughts, sudden violent jealousy for Peter Farrington wiping the smile off his face.

For a moment the two men talked at random, exchanging comments about the weather, the Government, and finally East Africa.

'You're lucky to live in a place like Nairobi. In fact, I hear East Africa is *the* country to go to these days,' he added.

'Of course I think there is nothing like it,' said Peter; opened his cigarette case and added: 'Oh Lord, I seem to have smoked all mine . . .'

'That's all right,' said Nigel and rose and walked to the table on which stood Rita's transparent nylon box—one of the many toys he had given her at some time or another. It struck Peter then and there that Rita's lawyer knew his way very well about her flat, whilst

173

Helen looked on with trepidation wondering when Rita would arrive.

After a moment Peter said:

'Rita has told you, of course, Mr. Cressland, that she and I hope to be getting married before Christmas.'

Helen caught her breath. She saw Nigel's eyes narrow and the hands on his knee clench but he smiled.

'Rita, herself, hasn't actually told me anything about it,' he said, after a pause. 'I think it was your sister at the clinic who first gave me the information.'

An instant's silence. Peter frowned. He had noticed the use of Rita's Christian name. Presumably this fellow was an old friend of Rita's, as well as her solicitor. Peter was not sure that he liked Mr. Cressland. There was something about his manner, the fleshy, self—indulgent face—the smart suit, carefully chosen tie and socks and rather pointed suède shoes which somehow jarred on Peter. He had an uncomfortable recollection, suddenly, of a morning when he and Rita had been walking down Bond Street and she had sweetly but quite plainly implied that *he* needed a London tailor. She had even looked a little shocked when he had laughed and told her that in his opinion as long as the chap wore a clean shirt, old clothes were much the nicest, and that he disliked ultra—smartness in a man.

Helen wanted to go out and prepare tea but

174

dared not leave the two men alone. She was terrified of what Nigel might do or say. And she was on the *qui vive* for the sound of Rita's footsteps outside the front door.

Nigel said:

'Of course I haven't seen Rita for a few weeks. First of all she was laid up and then I was; went down with the 'flu, then had a week in the country recuperating. But I expect Rita has told you that she expected me to come and see her.'

Peter gave a slight laugh.

'As a matter of fact, she didn't,' he said.

Nigel raised his brows.

Peter frowned again. There was something about this chap that he definitely disliked, although he told himself it was unfair to form a too speedy impression about anybody. But thinking things over, it struck him that in none of the talks he had had with Rita about their future—or her past—had she ever mentioned her lawyer's name.

Then Rita came back.

She did not ring the bell. She had her key with her this time, let herself into the flat and rushed into the sitting-room in her usual tempestuous fashion. She was feeling slightly annoyed. She had seen Peter's car down in the courtyard and realized that he had made an unexpected call, and that she had missed being here to receive him.

'Why, hallo—' she began; then stopped

dead and stood on the threshold staring at Nigel's all-too familiar figure as he rose in his chair. Every drop of blood receded from her face. But the man thought he had never seen her look more beautiful—so much better than when he had last seen her at the clinic. She was exquisitely tailored in a dark violet—blue corduroy velvet suit with lace ruffles at the throat and her beautiful sable tie frosted with snowflakes. Diamond drops of melted snow glittered on the little violet—blue velvet hat with its curled feather, upon the Titian head. He had never seen anyone to match her, he decided mentally, and despite his anger, his resentment because she had dared to jilt him, he knew that he still fiercely desired her.

At the same time, with a cruelty born of anger, he resolved to play cat—and—mouse with Rita.

He crossed the room and held out a hand.

'My *dear!* how are you?' he asked in a hearty voice.

Helen watched breathlessly. She feared for a moment that Rita was going to faint. She dropped the parcel she was carrying. Nigel stooped and picked it up. Helen noted the expression in Rita's eyes as she took the parcel from Nigel's fingers. It was one of mingled terror and loathing.

Then, as ever, Rita controlled herself and became mistress of the situation. She was a born actress, Helen thought, with unwilling admiration, as Rita broke into a theatrical welcome.

'What a *wonderful* surprise, my dear Nigel! How *are* you? Why, it's quite a little gathering. I didn't expect *you*, either,' she added, turning to Peter.

He, too, had been thinking what a picture of grace and fashionable beauty she made. Yet as he came forward to relieve her of her parcels and take her furs, he looked a moment down into those wonderful eyes, so full of passionate love for him and felt inexplicably disgruntled, none of the usual eager delight welling up in him. A few moments ago he had been at peace, listening to the music he loved with Helen. Now the flat was once more charged with excitement, with that feverish restlessness which Rita always managed to bring with her.

Nigel was the next to speak.

'I have been introducing myself to your— er—fiancé,' he murmured to Rita.

She bit her lip, trembling a little with nerves. She knew Nigel well enough to be aware of the mockery behind his smile and those words. A sinister mockery. So, she thought, as she crossed the room towards the fire, the hour had come—Nigel had turned up and meant to make his presence felt. Just how far he intended to go, she had no idea. She could not guess whether he meant to ruin her now, at once, or not. She felt no security just because, for the moment, the conversation became

177

general and Nigel somewhat surprisingly allowed himself to be thought her lawyer. She gritted her teeth with annoyance at herself for ever having invented that story to young Glen (among all the other dangerous stories). It was like an evil ball that she started rolling and now even she could not stop it.

'Make some tea, Helen,' she spoke rather sharply to the girl in her agitation. Helen, glad to escape from the tense atmosphere hurried into the little kitchen and switched on the electric kettle.

Rita took off her coat, seated herself on the sofa and reached for a cigarette. The box was empty. Peter said:

'Oh, heck, and I haven't got one.'

Nigel moved forward, regarding Rita through narrowed eyelids.

'I have a box of Rita's favourites in my overcoat pocket. I'll fetch them,' he said.

'Good,' said Peter, coldly.

Rita's favourites, eh? The fellow was very familiar, he thought. A trifle moodily, he walked to the window, drew aside the filmy net, and looked down at Knightsbridge. It was snowing hard now. In the darkness the flakes looked grey and dirty. An icy draught came through the window. He drew in a breath of the air gratefully. He felt a sudden dislike of London and the English climate and a longing for the clearness, the sunlight, the blue skies of his native country. He never felt really at ease in Rita's perfumed, hothouse flat. And he definitely did not like her lawyer.

Rita looked with dismay at Peter's back. She saw resentment in the hunch of his wide shoulders. Hurriedly she slipped to his side.

'Darling, I'm so sorry—Nigel is the last person I wanted—'

Peter muttered:

'If he has only come on business, why can't he see you in office hours, darling, or is it an excuse for a social visit?'

Rita swallowed hard.

'I—yes—I dare say it is.'

Nigel came back with the cigarettes. He snapped on the little gold lighter and held the flame to Rita's cigarette as he had done hundreds of times before. She had to put a firm restraint upon herself; she wanted to tell him, hysterically, to get out of the flat and never come back into it.

Peter, hands in his pockets, intercepted what he thought a most peculiar look between his fiancée and her solicitor during the lighting of that cigarette. Why the hell couldn't the fellow stop smiling in that smug way? Peter was not a jealous man, nor one who looked for ulterior motives or intrigues of any kind. He, himself, was far too frank and healthy minded. But he was not insensitive to atmosphere and he sensed a very definite one in this room at the moment. Added to which, he was still in love with Rita and going to marry her, so he was closely aware of her merest gesture or implication. Despite the way she laughed and talked, he was quite sure that *she* did not like her lawyer, either. She had no real welcome for him—Peter imagined he had learned to differentiate between Rita's sincere moments and artificial ones. But he never liked her when she was artificial.

They all three sat down again. Nigel said:

'Would it be impertinent of me to ask when you propose to get married, you two?'

Rita stammered the answer.

'Just before Christmas.'

'I see,' he said. His lips twisted and he put his tongue in his cheek.

Rita hastily added:

'I know there are one or two things we have to talk over. I must come to your office and see you, Nigel.'

'Do by all means,' he said, with a meaning look. 'I have been expecting you.'

She made no answer but smoked her cigarette in silence, conscious of impotent rage and fear. Why did Peter look so cross? What was he thinking and feeling? Oh, why in *heaven's* name had that fool, Helen, let Nigel in here like this?

Peter was a little nettled by the obvious intimacy which existed between Nigel Cressland and his future wife. He said abruptly:

'If you don't mind Rita, I think I'll take the

180

car along to the Odeon and meet Glen. Se and her friend are there, I know. The afternoon show comes out about five, I believe. I'll collect them and bring Glen back here later. You might perhaps like the chance of a talk with—er—Mr. Cressland.'

Nigel smiled.

'That would be delightful.'

Rita also rose. She gave Peter an appealing look. She could not bear the thought of his going, especially as he did not seem very pleased with her. On the other hand it was better that he should go—safer—she was so terrified of what Nigel would do or say in front of him.

Nigel gave her a horrid jolt by his next remark addressed to Peter:

'By the way—I suppose you have met the youngest member of the family—your future stepdaughter?'

'Oh, yes,' said Peter coldly, 'you mean Patty . . .'

Feeling sick in the pit of the stomach, Rita hurriedly intervened.

'You'll have to hurry, Pierrot, or you'll miss Glen . . .'

And firmly she shut the sitting-room door upon him and then stood leaning against it facing Nigel, her eyes blazing.

'You—you devil, Nigel . . .'

He gave an evil chuckle.

'*Pierrot*? How charming—how whimsical! Is

181

it your rendering of the name "Peter", my dear? You are a little given to whims and fancies, aren't you?'

She ignored the point. She did not waste time in telling him that Peter's own mother had nicknamed him Pierrot when he was a small boy. She said:

'What do you want here? What are you trying to do?'

'My dear girl—please don't upset yourself. I'm sure, even though you are contemplating an early marriage, you still have not totally recovered your strength.'

'Oh yes I have. Now tell me why you have come . . . ?'

'To see you—isn't that the privilege of an old friend?'

Her dark eyes glittered up at him.

'You aren't my friend anymore, and you haven't come here in friendship.'

He shrugged his shoulders.

'Very well. Then let us drop this farce of the lawyer and his client and face up to home truths—that is, if you are capable of truth, my sweet. We have such a lot to say to each other. And you know you can't bamboozle me as you do our good-looking young hero from East Africa. By the way, how delightful he is! Such *youth!* Makes me feel quite an old roué. But isn't he a trifle too young for you my dear?'

'That's my business.'

'Also mine,' he bowed and then added:

'Don't stand there glaring at me, sweet; come and sit down.'

Her breath came very fast. The points of her long nails dug into her palms in the effort not to scream at him. So far she had been talking in a low voice, waiting for the sound of the front door to shut upon Peter.

Peter had just put his head into the kitchen and told Helen that he was going to pick up Glen.

'By the way, I may be wrong, Helen,' he added, 'but I don't like that chap, Rita's lawyer.'

Helen thought:

'You're dead right! I wish all your instincts were as right. I wish you could realize what *she* is like, too!'

Peter paused a moment, hat in hand, to look at the girl's pale, shadowed face and it seemed to him, suddenly, that Rita kept Helen cooped up far too much in this central—heated flat. Helen never seemed to go out and enjoy herself, and when she did get away, it was only to somewhere like her aunt's house, to help in a crisis. For the second time that afternoon, he was somewhat disturbed to find himself criticizing his future wife—reflecting uneasily that the longer he knew her, the less did he find her wag of thinking and living in line with his own. It was a disagreeable discovery. Yet— she was still the beautiful goddess, the siren, who had bewitched him in Paris. Possibly, he told himself, his ruffled feelings were due to jealousy of men like that chap in there next door who treated her so familiarly.

He switched his mind back to Helen.

'Get on your hat and come with me in the car to fetch Glen,' he said.

Her grey eyes looked at him wistfully. That was so like Chistopher—the boyish impulsiveness of the invitation! But she smiled and shook her head.

'I couldn't possibly—thanks all the same. I've got the tea to make.'

'Oh, bother the tea! I'm sure Rita would make it for once. You need a breath of fresh air, Helen.'

Now she felt the impulse to burst out laughing; to laugh with him and be gay and lighthearted for once. Nothing would have been nicer than a drive through the snow in Peter's beautifi car, she thought.

'I'm quite sure Rita would get the tea for once,' he repeated.

'No, I can't possibly ask her to,' Helen exclaimed.

'You're much too conscientious, I shall ask her—' he began and turned to the door.

Helen was horrified by such ingenuous and tactless behaviour; even though she felt a warm wholehearted pleasure because he made the suggestion. She caught his arm.

'Peter, no—of *course* I can't go. You *mustn't* ask!' she said breathlessly.

He looked disappointed.

'Well, one of these days I'm going to speak to Rita about you. Sometimes I wonder if she realizes how much you do for her—what a lot you do for everybody, in fact. That child, Patty, worships you. When I talked to her the other day, it struck me that you were more like her adopted mother than Rita.'

Helen's heart beat quickly and her cheeks felt warm. His praise, his interest in her, seemed surprisingly sweet and desirable. But the subject of Patty was one she dared not begin to discuss with him. She turned back to the kitchen.

'You ought to go or you'll miss Glen,' she said under her breath.

'O.K. But I'll tell you something,' he said seriously, 'the Bach choir is doing Christmas Carols at the Albert Hall next month, and I'm going to buy some tickets and you have got to come with Rita and me to hear them. You'd enjoy that, wouldn't you?'

A quick sigh escaped Helen.

'Oh, I would *adore* it!' she said longingly.

The Bach choir singing Christmas Carols!— a grand, wonderful experience which she had already had with Christopher and never forgotten. But it was the last thing on earth Rita would want to hear, and she would see that Helen didn't get the chance either—with Peter!

But Helen was glad that Peter had asked

185

her. After he had gone she arranged the tea tray and thought, wistfully:

'He's very sweet—so much too sweet for Rita Wade.'

And following that thought came another, unrestrained, right from the heart.

'Oh God, I hope he doesn't marry her!'

CHAPTER FOURTEEN

The battle that ensued between Rita and her discarded lover was hot and bitter, with a good many unpleasant recriminations on both sides.

Nigel Cressland laid his cards on the table there and then.

He told Rita that he was not going to let her go; that he had no intention of being flaunted by her in this easy fashion. Whether she hated him now or not, he still wanted *her*. He was violently jealous of the young man she had chosen to put in his place, and it was useless, he told her, for her to imagine she could get away with such behaviour.

'It's an outrage on me,' he said, 'after all I have done for you.'

Rita tried to laugh this off. She had arranged with her bank to give her breathing space even if Nigel should withdraw his guarantee, she told him. And as for all his other presents and cheques—bit by bit she would pay them back.

But Nigel was not accepting this. He made it quite plain, and with deadly precision, that he did not believe her—that he knew that she intended to vanish to Kenya with young Farrington, leaving her debts unpaid, and that in his opinion she had behaved so atrociously she should not be allowed to get off scot free. What was more he, Nigel, intended to tell Peter Farrington the facts.

For a time Rita tried to call Nigel's bluff. She told him that she was not afraid of anything he might do and that Peter knew everything about her—even, she added, triumphantly— that she had a child of Patty's age. He still wanted her.

To which Nigel, with narrowed eyes, said softly:

'Are you sure you have told him *everything?*'

Rita, sitting in a chair shivering by the fire, felt sick with fear for a moment as she remembered all the things Peter did *not* know—the absolute truth for instance, about Patty, and her own age—about her former association with Nigel—the wild parties— Nigel's paying Patty's school bills—and a good deal more besides.

She was beginning to feel cornered. But when she asked Nigel why he still wished her to remain in his life, since he so obviously despised her, he laughed, and gave her one of the old possessive looks.

'You are still the most beautiful woman in London, my dear, and you would still make the best type of hostess to help me entertain my various European contacts. You remember Lemberg, don't you?'

A brief nod from Rita; yes, she remembered the Swedish stockbroker whom she and Nigel had entertained in London last winter. She had hated him because he was fat and bald and far too interested in *her.* But Nigel went on to explain that Lemberg had asked Nigel to bring the beautiful Mrs. Wade to Stockholm and was going to pay their expenses and entertain them royally when they got there; which also meant that Nigel would bring off a big business deal which he badly needed to do.

In the end, he broke down her defences. She was forced to climb down, to ask him what he wanted her to do. He said:

'Break your engagement with your young man in the same abrupt way you broke ours, my dear.'

He wanted no less from her. When first she refused, he threatened to expose her, and then she pleaded for time. At length he said:

'Very well, one week my dear, just one little week to readjust your plans. After that— finish! You come back to me.'

He left the flat before tea. He was no longer in the mood to act the benevolent lawyer in front of her new boy friend, he said.

Helen, bringing in tea, found Rita in one of

188

her 'states', weeping with rage and fear. Without pity Helen listened to a hysterical version of the row with Nigel. In the end, Helen said:

'I don't think you can expect anything else. Nigel Cressland is obviously a man who wants what he has paid for.'

Rita winced and then began to weep again.

'I will not let him ruin my life. I will *not* give Pierrot up. I shall tell him my side of the story—what a hard struggle I have had and how I was forced to accept help. He'll forgive me.'

'And does Nigel know the story you have told Peter about Patty?' Helen asked dryly.

'No,' Rita muttered. 'Thank heavens he doesn't. I avoided it.'

'*That*, of course, is the one thing Peter wouldn't forgive,' Helen said more to herself than to the woman huddled in the chair.

Rita heard but made no comment. She didn't care what Helen thought or said. Helen was only a pawn in the game she was playing. Her mind was busy seeking a way out of her maze of difficulties.

She cried herself into such a state that she dared not allow Peter to see her. She told Helen to explain to him, when he returned, that she had a bad headache and that she was lying down but would meet him for dinner later tonight. They were going to see a new film.

Then Peter and Glen came back.

They both looked so charmingly youthful, gay and happy, laughing together over a shared joke, it warmed Helen's heart to see them. Brother and sister were really delightful, so refreshing after the sinister atmosphere created by Nigel and Rita.

Of course, Peter was distressed to hear that his Rita had retired with a headache. But he was glad to find that Rita's 'solicitor' had gone. He couldn't stand the fellow, he said frankly.

The three of them had a happy tea— curiously happy, Helen thought ironically, considering that the hostess was absent. She knew how different she, personally, always felt in Rita's presence. Rita as a rule reduced her to silence and the nervous wish to get away. But now Helen sparkled—joked and talked with Peter and young Glen. Glen giggled over a funny film she had just seen. And finally upset her tea on Rita's beautiful green carpet, so Helen rushed for a cloth and hot water, and Peter, chiding his young sister with mock severity, went down on hands and knees and insisted upon helping Helen mop up.

Peter had never been in a more hilarious mood. Somehow, with Rita, he was never able to give rein to that natural sense of fun within him. He felt that she would think it undignified to see him sprawling on the floor. She, herself, was always so careful to adopt the most striking and beautiful pose. It struck him suddenly that he was never *really* at ease with Rita. But he thoroughly enjoyed this foolish tea party with his sister and Helen. Helen, who looked as he had never seen her before, kneeling on the floor beside him, a strand of fair silky hair falling across her eyes, her cheeks flushed, white teeth glistening as she laughed with Glen and himself. How sweet and amusing she could be, he thought. Here was a Helen who had very much come out of her shell.

Finally Peter got up and accidentally trod on Helen's hand. Her cry of pain dismayed him. Glen said:

'Oh, you clumsy old thing, Pierrot. *Poor Helen!*'

'My dear, I'm frightfully sorry,' exclaimed Peter, and stooped and helped Helen on to her feet.

She laughed and put the injured hand behind her back.

'It's nothing at all.'

'Glen's right, I'm a clumsy idiot. Let me see,' he said, and drew the hand out for inspection. He could see that he had trodden heavily on two of the slim fingers. A pink mark was visible. He cursed himself.

'My full weight! Poor Helen, indeed.'

She laughed again.

'Honestly it's nothing.'

'Kiss the place and make it well,' young Glen sang cheerfully.

Peter grinned at his sister and then turned back to Helen.

'O.K. here goes,' he said, and raised her hand to his lips.

It was an entirely innocent and insignificant action but Helen felt the blood scorch her face, her very throat, and for a moment she could only look blindly up into the laughing hazel eyes which so closely resembled Christopher's. Peter looked back at her, a little startled by the obvious emotion on her face. But he thought he understood. Gently he dropped her hand and turned away, his heart going out to her in sympathy, in more than that—the strange tenderness that this girl somehow always managed to stir in him.

Helen recovered herself. They all laughed again.

But Helen did not forget the touch of Peter's lips on her hand for a very long time. And he forgot it until much later that night, after he had taken Rita home from the cinema. Then he remembered it and the hot sensitive blush that had swept across Helen's charming face.

Rita looked ravishingly beautiful in one of her smartest dresses when he took her out that evening. There was no trace of the frightened weeping woman whom Helen had seen this afternoon. Deliberately she used her old wiles to captivate Peter afresh, as though she wished to reassure herself that she still held him in the hollow of her hand. It was hard for any man to resist her in such a melting mood and when Peter left her at the flat, he still believed that she was the most fascinating creature he had met and that he wanted her for his wife. He walked back through the cold night to his hotel, his senses swimming at the memory of her in his arms, of her intoxicating loveliness as she lifted her lips for his good night kiss.

But later, when he lay in bed smoking and thinking before he turned out his lights, the memory of Helen Shaw returned—of that deep emotional look in her dark grey eyes—of the ruffled fair head—the soft crushed fingers which he had lifted to his lips.

Yes, very definitely, he remembered Helen as well as Rita. Two such different women, two such different kisses! And he found them both rather disturbing.

Rita, that next morning, when Helen took her breakfast to her, flung Helen a letter bearing the Bexhill postmark. She said:

'That's from Pattykins. She seems to have got some good marks this week, for a change.'

'She was happy, when she went back after mid-term,' said Helen. 'And a happy child usually works harder than a miserable one.'

'Oh, you and your child psychology!' jeered Rita.

Helen said nothing but walked to the window, pulled the curtains aside and looked down at the street.

'Yesterday's snow hasn't "lain",' she said. 'It's wet and slushy—rather a beastly morning.'

Rita yawned and dug the point of her knife into the apple that Helen had brought her.

'It's going to be a beastly week,' she muttered.

The one week of grace that Nigel had given her! She knew that he would come again and threaten her afresh. She must resort to desperate measures. She had realized that last night. She must put Pierrot's love to a considerable test. In fact she must make every effort to speed up their marriage. His hungry arms and lips last night had told her that he was still madly in love with her. She could still sway him. She must persuade him to get a special licence and marry her without delay. Once she was Mrs. Farrington, Nigel could do his worst. Peter would stand by his wife. She *must* achieve that somehow.

Almost as soon as breakfast was over, young Glen came round to the flat. Helen had grown fond of Peter's sister, but Rita was beginning to find the girl a bore, always in the way. She wanted nobody there to distract Peter's attention from herself, even his own sister. But she greeted Glen with her usual affectation of goodwill.

'Lovely to see you, darling.'

But Glen had no answering smile. She looked crestfallen.

'Something awful has happened, Rita,' she

said, 'Pierrot is coming round in a moment to see you.'

'What?' Rita asked sharply. 'What's happened?'

'Oh, it's nothing *really* dreadful, I suppose,' said Glen with a little laugh, 'except that it means your wedding will have to be postponed.'

Helen glanced at Rita; saw her go white, and her eyes widen.

'Why?' she demanded breathlessly. '*Why* will it have to be postponed?'

'Because,' said Glen, 'there is some trouble going on at home—a lawsuit for the bank or something and our uncle wants Pierrot as a witness. He may have to fly home for a few weeks, and put the wedding off until the New Year.'

Silence a moment. Helen felt her heart beating strangely fast. Then Rita said in a queer suffocated voice:

'Unless, of course, we arrange to get married—before he goes.'

CHAPTER FIFTEEN

Glenise looked worried.

'Yes, of course. I suppose that could be arranged but I rather think Pierrot has other plans.'

'What plans?' Rita asked so sharply that the young girl stared. Rita bit her lip. She had to exert all her control. She added more calmly:

'Never mind, darling! I'll see Pierrot about it when he comes.'

Glen glaced at Helen, whose expressionless face did not betray her own conflicting sentiments. Rita got out of bed, slid into a dressing—gown and turned to the window, clenching her hands spasmodically. What a thing to have happened! If Peter went to Kenya now and left her alone and still unmarried, it might be fatal—it would put all the weapons into Nigel's hands. She felt distracted. It seemed as though fate were against her; impotently, silently, she raged against this new development which was taking Peter so far away from her.

Helen walked away and into her own little room, meaning to get her hat and coat and go out on a shopping errand for Rita. Peter's young sister followed. She watched Helen combing a strand of smooth, fair hair into place. She had become very fond of Helen. As far as she knew, Rita was still in her twenties, but she seemed to Glen so much older in her ways than Helen, who was simple and unaffected and although serious-minded more ready to talk and laugh about simple and ordinary things than Rita. In fact, Glen was secretly growing fonder of Helen than of the glamorous Rita. At their first meeting, her romantic young heart had gone out in a rush to the girl of her brother's choice. But something had happened—Glen could not really put a name to it—to stem that impulsive tide. Little by little she had become antipathetic to Rita, who still seemed to her beautiful and clever and, quite often, fascinating—but there was something about her now and again which almost repelled the young girl (not that she would dream of letting Peter know it); she adored her brother and if he loved Rita that was enough for her. But Glen could never love Rita like a real sister. She did not understand those lightning—like changes of mood, or the occasional signs of irritability and even bad temper which Rita could not always conceal.

It had even arisen within Glen to wish that Helen, who was so sweet and kind and utterly unselfish, were going to be her sister-in-law, although she dismissed this thought as nonsense.

Now she said:

'Rita is in an awful hurry to marry Pierrot, isn't she, Helen?'

Helen did not answer for a moment. Her face coloured slightly. The child's naïve remark hit home. And somehow—whenever Helen talked to young Glen—or Peter—she had a strange feeling of personal guilt because she *knew* how unworthy Rita Wade was of either of them. Yet her lips were sealed. It was not her affair. Time and time again, she wanted to run away from it all. She stayed only because of the unfortunate Patty.

Glen added:

'As a matter of fact I think Pierrot has got some bright scheme for bringing our mother back with him from Nairobi because Mum wants to see her one and only son married, so I am sure he won't rush the wedding through now.'

Helen sighed. How complicated it all was! She could find it in her heart to be sorry for Peter's mother, if the poor woman expected to find Rita Wade a fine decent sort of girl whom any woman would want her son to marry. As though reading those thoughts Glen ingenuously continued:

'It may be awful of me to say so, Helen, but I have been thinking things over; I have often wanted to confide in you; but, *honestly*, I don't think Mummy will care much for Rita.'

The colour in Helen's cheeks deepened. She gave Glen a quick look and then turned back to the mirror and put on her hat.

'Why don't you think so, Glen?'

Glenise studied her finger—nails, her own cheeks a trifle hot.

'Oh, I don't know!' she said in an embarrassed way, 'Rita just isn't Mummy's type. I know she is marvellous to look at and you can't help being fascinated by her and all that, but do *you* really like her, Helen? I have often thought you don't.'

Now it was Helen's turn to feel embarrassed. But she dared not voice her genuine sentiments. Not that she was astonished that Glen had begun to feel disillusioned in Rita. It was only a question of time before Peter must share in that disillusion—it was just that a woman, even as young as Glen, had a quicker and surer instinct about another woman. Men, inexperienced like Peter, were more easily deceived.

She stammered a reply to Glen.

'Oh, I don't know—you mustn't delve too deeply into things. I mean, if Peter loves Rita, that's all that matters, isn't it?'

Glen walked up to Helen and put an arm around her waist with a show of schoolgirl affection.

'All the same, I wish Pierrot had fallen in love with *you*.'

That was rather too much for Helen, who drew away from Glen in a startled fashion.

'Oh, what—what rubbish you talk, you silly!' she stuttered.

An imp of mischief suddenly entered Glenise who gave a searching look at Helen's face.

'I believe *you've* got a soft spot for my brother!'

Hastily Helen turned away from Glen and dived into the wardrobe for a coat. Her hands shook. She was surprised and not a little upset to find how those lightly spoken words affected her. She tried to make a flippant reply.

'Of course I have. Haven't we all?'

Glen sighed.

'Oh, I think he is wonderful. My mother and I both adore him. You have no idea how sweet and kind he is and how popular with everybody in Nairobi. I couldn't bear it if he didn't marry the right person. Oh, Helen, tell me truly, *do* you think Rita will make him happy?'

It was not possible for Helen to lie about that to this girl who was looking at her with such a clear honest gaze. She murmured something about 'being late, and mustn't stop to natter' and fled from the bedroom, feeling profoundly miserable and depressed about the whole affair. As she hurried downstairs with her shopping basket on her arm, she was haunted by the memory of those words that Glen had so guilelessly spoken: *'I wish Pierrot had fallen in love with you.'*

And suddenly she wished it, too. Madly, desperately, she wished it! That Peter, who was so like her lost love Christopher, had met and fallen in love with *her* before Rita Wade, who was nothing short of an adventuress, had ever crossed his path.

She had a crazy desire to go to him—tell him all that she knew and warn him against the woman he proposed to marry. She could not.

200

She had no right to do so. Peter Farrington was a grown man with a mind of his own and he must work out his own destiny. *It was not her business.*

As she went out of the front door and into the courtyard, where an icy wind pierced through her, she met Peter hurrying into the building. He took off his hat and stopped.

'Good morning, Helen. Is Glen there?'

'Yes.'

'Then you know the news.'

'That you have got to fly home at once? Yes,' she said.

He stood for a moment looking down at her, a slight frown on his face.

'It's a bit tricky, but I have got to go because I'm an important witness in the case and the cable my uncle sent is urgent. It is a matter of big finance, otherwise I wouldn't dream of leaving London now, just before the wedding.'

She looked up at him silently, her heart beating fast (as it must always beat, she told herself, to see Christopher's eyes looking down at her from Peter's attractive face).

'However, it will have to be postponed now,' he added without hesitance.

She felt an almost terrible joy surge through her as he spoke those words. She was alarmed by the very violence of her emotions. And terrified that her expression had betrayed her, she said nothing.

He had, in fact, caught that strange glow in

the dark grey eyes raised to his and wondered at it. Without understanding, it made him feel uneasy. In a quieter, less harassed moment, he remembered it again and asked himself if it were possible that Helen was *glad* that his marriage with Rita must be postponed?

But he was too busy to stop and talk longer to her now. He told her quickly that he hoped to fly to Nairobi at the end of the week. The director of the bank here, in London, was doing his best to get him an air passage, because the matter was one of such urgency. Peter added that he intended to send Glen down to Devonshire tomorrow. While he was away, he wished her to stay with their cousins the Fletchers who had been asking her down there ever since she arrived in England.

'They have a farm near Hartland Point,' he said, 'and a young daughter, of Glen's age. It will be better for her to be there than gadding around town alone while I'm away, and in any case, Rita's flat is full and will be fuller when little Patty comes back from school.'

Helen said:

'Then you don't expect to get back before Christmas?'

'Possibly not. I shall try, but I shan't know until I'm home.'

Then adding that he hoped to see her again during the day, he went on into the building.

Helen walked down Knightsbridge, feeling very unsettled. What was going to happen

202

now? The situation was becoming critical. An unspeakable real-life drama with Rita and Peter playing the leading parts and herself, Helen, as a helpless onlooker.

She loved Peter Farrington. Of that now she had no doubt. Try as she would, she could not stop herself from loving him, and there was just nothing she could do about it.

Rita, as usual, kept an impatient Peter waiting half an hour before she was dressed and ready to join him. She was a study in black and white—one of her most attractive tailored suits. Her red hair was swept to one side of her head. She wore jet earrings, which gleamed as she moved her head and which she had bought in Paris. They had always charmed her young lover.

But she found him in a difficult and incomprehensible mood this morning. He was a Peter weighed down by business worries and responsibility, producing that practical sensible side which was far from agreeable to her. She had found it much easier to deal with the tempestuous lover of Paris days. After their first kiss, he paced up and down her room, hands in his pockets, cigarette between his lips, talking about the bank, lawsuits, the difficulties of getting a seat on a plane at a moment's notice these days, and every subject, it seemed to her, but their wedding. Her magnificent eyes looked at him resentfully through the long, darkened lashes. When he paused for breath, she said:

'I'm sorry about your worries but you don't seem to see how dreadful this is for me, with our wedding date fixed and everything.'

Peter's thoughts were, in fact, so much on business and so far removed from weddings, that he had to readjust them hastily in order to reply to Rita's reproach. He took his cigarette from his mouth and gave her a faint apologetic smile; holding out a hand.

'My darling—I'm dreadfully sorry! It is the most damnable thing to have happened. I couldn't be more sorry. That goes without saying, surely.'

She stifled the anger rising in her. She could not bear it when Peter thought about anybody or anything except herself. And whilst dressing, she had quite convinced herself of the extreme necessity to pin him down to an immediate marriage. With the threat of Nigel hanging over her she could not, must not, let Peter go, before binding him to her irrevocably. At the same time she had resolved to be calm—to manage the situation cleverly, without losing her head. She let Peter talk for a moment longer and then suddenly put her arms around his neck and hid her eyes against his shoulder.

'Oh, Pierrot,' she said in a muffled voice, *'Pierrot!'*

His arms closed around the beautiful form. He breathed in the familiar and intoxicating perfume of her hair. He did not think of business now, only of how much he had wanted her from the first moment they had met.

'It's quite damnable,' he repeated hugging her close to him, 'but it will only be for a few weeks at the most, angel. You can be quite sure I'll rush back as soon as I possibly can. I'll be back in London the moment this case is over, and it's bound to be heard before Christmas.'

She raised her head and looked at him in horror.

'You mean you won't be back until the New Year!'

He kissed the top of her head with a tenderness which suddenly irritated rather than soothed her in her present state of suppressed agitation.

'I'm afraid so, darling,' he said. 'We must just both be patient. After all, a few weeks is not much in a lifetime, is it?'

She set her teeth. She had never been more irritated. If only he knew what even a week's delay meant to *her!* She was driven now to fight for her cause. She gave a long sigh, and reaching up on tip—toe, pressed her cheek against his hard, brown face.

'Pierrot,' she breathed, 'why should we wait even those few weeks? Why shouldn't we be married by special licence before you go?'

He looked at her with astonishment then

gave a little laugh and released her.

'My sweet, that's quite out of the question. My name is down for a flight and I may have to go at any moment, even tomorrow. Besides, I don't know whether Glen told you, but I had a letter from my mother yesterday, suggesting that she should come to England for our wedding. She so hates the idea of not seeing me married. So I thought that this would be a good chance to bring her back with me.'

Rita stood speechless and appalled. It was almost as though she tottered, in that moment, on the brink of ruin. This was worse than she had anticipated. Nothing could be less agreeable to her than the idea of an inquisitive future mother—in—law arriving on the scene—a woman capable of prying, discerning and finding out all sorts of things. What *could* be worse than the doting mother of an only son? Rita was driven to desperate measures. She went back to Peter and caught his arms with both her long pointed hands.

'Pierrot—darling—I love you so terribly much. I can't bear to send you away knowing that I'm still not your wife. Pierrot, why don't we risk it—risk you not getting on the plane today or tomorrow? One can get a special licence within forty—eight hours . . .' she stopped, breathing hard, eyes glittering up at him.

He looked down at her, embarrassed and tongue-tied. It was so unlike his ideal of

206

Rita—that she should behave in this fashion—without that delicate reticence and understanding which was necessary in a moment like this. It hurt him suddenly to watch her coming down from the pedestal on which he had put her; cheapening herself. His ears burned; but gently he took her back into his arms.

'Darling,' he said, 'it's very, very sweet of you to want this, and I want it, too. But I do think, out of respect for my mother's wishes, we ought to delay our wedding, in view of what has happened; especially as I can now arrange to bring her back to London with me.'

Rita ground her teeth. She had to exert tremendous control to fight down the hysteria rising in her. Large tears welled into her eyes and glistened on her lashes.

'Then you can't love me—as much as I love you,' she stammered under her breath and pushed him back from her.

He was horrified and deeply embarrassed. Once again he felt as though a cold wind blew across his warm, idealistic love for Rita, chilling it. Yet he could not bear to see tears in her eyes nor hear that note of pain, of bitterness in her voice.

'Darling,' he said, 'darling, that isn't true. It is not because I don't love you that I am postponing our wedding. It isn't fair of you to suggest such a thing.'

She gave a wild little laugh.

'And suppose I feel so strongly about it that I say I won't marry you at all if I don't marry you *now*?'

He stared again. That seemed to him such a monstrous thing to have said that he could hardly believe he had heard it. Then he laughed.

'Of course you must be joking,' he said.

Already she had regretted the challenge she had flung at him, aware that it weakened her arguments and could only humiliate her in his eyes. Despair settled upon her. She gave a shuddering sigh and hid her face in her hands.

'Yes—I was joking,' she whispered.

He was perplexed by her attitude and could not begin to understand it.

In a way, her eagerness to marry him was flattering and yet, faintly, it cooled his own ardour. He felt that she had made things awkward and even unpleasant for him and he was resentful because she did not wish to consider his mother's point of view. He had always been devoted to his mother. Besides, he could not see the necessity for a rush—marriage, much though he loved and wanted Rita. He was taking a sane sensible outlook and he would have liked Rita to be reasonable.

He began to talk to her, to discuss his mother's point of view, to comfort her as best he could, enlarging on what a wonderful wedding it would be with his family here, as well as Rita's friends and how much better it would be for Glen, too, to have her mother with her at the start of her musical training.

Rita listened without hearing a word he said, completely bound up in her own difficulties and misfortunes. She only knew that she had lost . . . that she could not, in decency, go on suggesting an immediate marriage and that she hated this practical Peter just as much as she adored the poetic fervent young lover whom she could twist around her little finger. When at length she dissolved into tears, he became wholly loverlike, held her in his arms, kissed and caressed her, and begged her not to be so upset. After a while, he thought that he had succeeded in convincing her that it was for the best that the marriage should be put off.

Once more in control of herself, Rita sat beside him on the sofa, holding his hands, letting him tell her all his plans, trying to give him the impression that she understood and was in complete agreement with him now. And he could not begin to guess at the hell of anxiety and fear into which he had unconsciously flung her.

But later on, when he left her to keep an appointment with her dressmaker, it was not so much the sweet and sympathetic Rita that he remembered, but the wild and unreasonable one who had startled and distressed him, and who had revealed a side that he had never seen before. Frankly, it troubled him. He could not reconcile it with his first boyishly ardent ideal of Rita. When he left her it was with a strangely heavy heart.

The next thing to be done was to send a wire to Devonshire and arrange for Glen to travel down there tomorrow. He had promised to take Rita out to lunch, later on, and spend the afternoon with her.

For the first time since he had fallen so madly in love with her that afternoon did not appear so much in the light of a pleasure as a duty. He shrank from further misunderstandings. He felt suddenly that he could not endure another long session of emotional debate in Rita's over—heated sitting-room. He wanted to laugh with her . . . be gay and normal, and intoxicated with life as they used to be during those rapturous days of their early love affair. He wanted to feel at peace with her and with himself, and not go back to Kenya in this state of mind, which was worrying. For he did not feel at all how a man, confident of his future wife, should be feeling, and he was forced to admit it.

There was an amusing comedy on at one of the big theatres and, without consulting Rita, he went in and took a couple of stalls for the matinée. Two cancellations had at that moment come through.

When he met Rita, he told her about the show.

Rita had had a bad morning—almost frantic

with mental worry and the chagrin of knowing that she had 'lost face' with her fiancé. She had determined to be her sweetest and most amiable when she met him again. But things had not been made any easier by a telephone call from Nigel which came through after Peter had left the flat. It was important that he should see her directly after lunch, he said. Lemberg had wired from Stockholm. He was telephoning Nigel's office at three o'clock. It was about the proposed trip to Sweden.

'I insist on seeing you and making a definite arrangement with you, before that call from Lemberg comes through,' Nigel declared.

No amount of argument from Rita would make him change his mind. Neither did she dare tell him that Peter was on the point of going abroad, in case Nigel did any damage before he left. She had wanted passionately to spend the afternoon with Peter—every moment was precious now—but she dared not anger Nigel. She promised to go to his office at half past two.

She announced casually over the lunch table that she had an appointment with her lawyer, and could not manage the matinée. (Besides, she added, she hated 'funny shows'!)

Peter looked disappointed. Rita had been charming and at her best while they were drinking a cocktail at the 'Caprice' before going to their table, and he had looked forward to taking her to the theatre, and told her so.

'I can't bear that lawyer of yours,' he grumbled, 'besides—surely you'll have plenty of time to see him when I'm gone.'

She managed to give him a brilliant smile which masked the despair in her heart. She was beginning to feel that if ever a woman was being called upon to pay for her sins, it was she.

The long and short of it was that she dared not give way to Peter. She must mark time with Nigel. So the lunch ended not too successfully, and in the end, Rita was driven to suggest that Peter should take someone else to the matinée.

'Take Glen,' she said with the same bright, hard smile.

But Peter looked moodily into the big dark eyes.

'Glen has already got a date—no—I think I shall ask Helen. She seems to do a lot of work and get very little fun. Don't you think it would be a good idea if I took her?'

Rita shrugged her shoulders. She was beyond feeling petty jealousy today.

If you wish,' she said indifferently, but could not resist adding: 'But surely you can think of someone more exciting?'

Peter did not want anybody more exciting. He had had enough excitement for the moment. He wanted a girl who would be cool, calm, and companionable. He felt he would enjoy seeing a witty comedy with Helen.

He excused himself from the table and went out to telephone to her and ask her if she would meet him at the theatre.

At first Helen refused. She echoed Rita's words:

'Surely if Rita or Glen can't go, you can find somebody more exciting than me to take to a show ...?'

He said brusquely:

'I shall expect you in the foyer in half an hour. That is if you would like to come ...'

An instant's silence. Then her answer came with a strangely vibrant note in that usually cool voice.

'I'd love to come, Peter. Thank you very much.'

Who was it, Helen asked herself as she came out of the theatre with Peter that winter's afternoon, who wrote the words, *'One Moment in Annihilation's Waste ...'* For her this was it, this moment with Peter; a few hours of sheer happiness—the sort of fun she used to have with Chris, and which she had thought for ever lost to her.

She had not known Peter could be so amusing. Of course it was an amusing play and they shared the jokes and admired the first-rate acting. For Helen it was a great treat—the first show of its kind that she had seen since Christopher died. Cares and woes and all the anxiety of her invidious position in the Wade household were laid aside. She thoroughly enjoyed the festive atmosphere in the theatre. It was such fun, too, to hear Peter laughing loudly like a schoolboy, and to join in the laughter with him.

He gave her tea in the interval. There was only one difficult moment; when he brought up the name of little Patty.

'I can't quite understand,' he said, 'why Rita didn't tell me about her adopted daughter when I first met her. I suppose she thought I wouldn't like having a kid around. But I do. She needn't have worried. I want some of my own . . .'

And he had laughed a trifle self—consciously. Helen had thought how nice he was—so very much nicer than Nigel Cressland who wanted Patty out of the way.

But she swerved from the dangerous subject of Rita's child and felt her cheeks grow hot when she thought of the lies, the hideous conspiracy against Peter, fabricated by a woman who was too much of a coward to admit her real age. She hated herself for the part she, personally, was forced to play in it all. She quickly turned the conversation to something else, and Peter made no further allusion to Patty.

But the very fact that Peter was so nice, full of the charm of simplicity—of humour and a very real integrity—made her all the more concerned for him. She could not bear the thought that he intended to marry Rita. But at least she could be glad that he was going back to Kenya. Much water might roll under the bridge before he came back, she thought.

Peter, too, had enjoyed the matinée in Helen's company. Not for the first time it struck him that he could never really be as much at ease with Rita as he was with Helen. In actual looks, this girl could not compare with Rita who was so strikingly lovely. But while he was out with Helen today, he noticed quite a lot of delightful things about her, her looks 'grew on one', he told himself. He noticed that she had an exquisite skin, almost untouched by cosmetics and a calm beauty of her own, with that smooth, pale gold head and smoke-grey, expressive eyes. They were not such sad eyes today. They had danced with mirth in response to his own. It was with regret that he drove her back to the flat. And it was with some perturbation that he realized he would like the afternoon to continue; that he had no great desire to hurry back to the woman he was going to marry.

He was alarmed by such feelings. Was he so fickle that he could be madly in love with one girl, and charmed by the company of another? he asked himself. It was not in keeping with the man he believed himself to be. During the drive from the Strand back to Knightsbridge, once or twice, he caught the thoughtful glance of Helen's grey eyes and was moved suddenly to question her about herself.

'How are you feeling these days, Helen? Things any easier?'

Her heart beat quickly. She was grateful for his kindliness. Her memory flashed back to that evening when, in his determined way, Peter had broken through the wall which she had built around her heartbreak and despair.

From that night onwards, she had begun to feel so much better and more normal—more sensible about poor Chris. She owed it to Peter, to what he had done for her. It struck her, now, sitting beside him, driving through the darkness of the November night, that she was not so much conscious of the dead man's memory as of the presence of the living one. That thought at once frightened and fascinated her.

She answered his questions:

'Yes, things are easier, thank you, Peter.'

He smiled.

'That's good. You know, Helen, when one door shuts, another always opens. That is, if one doesn't turn the key in the lock too firmly.'

She turned from the brightness of the eyes that were Christopher's—and looked out at the stark leafless trees in the park through which they were now passing It was very cold and there was a hard frost. The wheels skidded slightly as they turned around the big fountain facing Buckingham Palace. She said:

'I think the old door is unlocked for me

but whether another opens or not is problematical.'

'You should get out and about more, Helen,' he said, 'you're too much alone and—too much a slave to other people.'

Her heart was warmed by the praise behind those words. She smiled and shook her head.

'It's better to work than to think too much.'

'All the same you work too hard,' he repeated, 'and I think you have been too long in London without a break. I wish I could waft you to Nairobi while I'm over there. You'd love the sunshine, the blue skies—that's what you need for a bit.'

Her heart leapt and she closed her eyes for a moment, mentally luxuriating in the picture he drew for her. And she drew intense pleasure from the fact that he wished her to be out there with him—that he had mentioned *her* and not Rita. Though quickly she reminded herself that such words, lightly spoken, were not the least important. He might have said them to anyone.

Peter continued:

'You would like my mother and my home. We have a beautiful house and a very lovely garden, just outside the town. My mother is devoted to her garden. I think I shall have a hard task persuading her to leave it even for a month or two. But she wants to be at my wedding, so I hope she comes back with me.'

'I hope so, too,' said Helen.

217

Yet her heart sank at the idea—dreading all the awful complications that might ensue if Mrs. Farrington saw through Rita and did not like her.

As though in answer to that unspoken fear came Peter's next words:

'Speaking in confidence, Helen, I'm not quite sure what my mother will think of my marriage. You know what mothers are'—he gave a brief laugh—'they always have a particular idea of the girls their sons should marry. The fact that Rita is a widow, with an adopted daughter, won't exactly please her.'

Helen said in a low voice:

'Your little sister made that same remark this morning.'

'Glen? Did she now?' said Peter reflectively, and pulled a packet of cigarettes from his pocket and lit one, brows knit. Then as though conscious of disloyalty, he made haste to add:

'But we'll get over that. Rita charms everybody she meets.'

'Yes,' said Helen and stared out of the window again. She was thinking:

'In a few seconds we shall be back at the flat and my Moment will be over. I may never have another one with him. He is so sweet—so very nice. And I love him—*oh, God, I don't want to love him but I do!*'

Peter continued on the subject of Rita.

'Look after her while I'm away, Helen, and try to get her into a better state of nerves.

Make her go to bed early—get away from town and get some country air or something—she's terribly nervy.'

Helen nodded. She felt that there was nothing that she could say. She did not need to be told that Peter was worried deep down within him about his engagement and no longer quite so blindly in love. But she knew that his sense of loyalty would be as strong in him as his passions. It would take far more than a show of nerves or a difficult mood to shatter his original conception of Rita. If, in fact, there were doubts in his mind, he would step on them. Having once given a promise, he would not easily break it—to Rita or any woman.

Then he said:

'I'm glad you are with her. It's always good to know you are around. You're a wonderful friend. *My* friend, as well as Rita's—I hope.'

She gave a swift upward glance. For a moment her heart surged towards him in a great rush of emotion, and a longing which had to be sternly controlled. He looked back at her. Several times, those beautiful eyes of Helen's had spoken volumes, perplexing him and giving him something to think about. In this particular moment, with the memory of Rita swept aside, he experienced what he imagined to be a rather unworthy desire to gather Helen up in his arms and kiss her. Not for the first time, he was conscious of her

219

astonishing sweetness, that lost, lonely side of her which silently asked for tenderness and comfort. He leaned towards her, and then ashamedly drew back and laughed unsteadily.

'What a darling you are, Helen!' he murmured.

She sat rigid, speechless, the pulse in her throat beating—her heart on fire. It was as well, she thought grimly, that this drive came to an end and the car slowed down and turned from Knightsbridge into the courtyard of the big block of flats wherein Rita lived.

As they stopped, Peter made only one more remark whict Helen hugged to herself when she thought about it afterwards.

'I'll look forward to introducing my mother to you in the New Year. And you'll help me take care of her, won't you?'

'I'd love that,' she said.

And suddenly she was conscious of how much she was going to miss him. There would be a blank when he had gone. For there was something in Peter—something akin to Chris, which belonged to her—and her alone—which could never be Rita's. She knew that—she felt it—and the knowledge was both sweet and bitter.

But now she had to come down to earth again and remind herself that he was still Rita's future husband. When they go up to the flat, they found Rita standing by her fire smoking a cigarette in a long amber holder.

She was looking extremely pleased with herself. She had changed from her suit into a attractive housecoat of olive—green velvet which had delicat lace at throat and wrists. She wore her hair as Peter liked it best curving in a satin red helmet down to her shoulders. She had seldom looked more entrancing.

Somehow Helen's heart sank as she saw her. How could any man withstand such as Rita? Helen was quick to note the expression of admiration and excitement darken Peter's pupils. He went towards Rita quickly.

'So my glamour girl is home first! And, say—does she look glamorous?'

Rita surrendered both hands to him. Without looking at Helen, she said:

'You're very late, you two. Get some drinks, Helen—quickly—I want a cocktail and I'm sure Peter does.'

Helen left the room. Her ears burned. There had been something rather unpleasant in that command—so peremptorily dismissing her. She stood a moment in the hall, drawing off coat and hat, rubbing the back of her hand against her cold cheek. Suddenly all the elation of the gay afternoon with Peter vanished. It was as though she had been flung out into a desert waste. She was once more terribly alone, and with all her heart she hated the thought of Peter, in there, with Rita in his arms. Rita's wicked crimson mouth upturned for his kisses. The siren drawing him back into the net—drowning him—obliterating all his better impulses; blunting the fine edge of his perception. And she had thought he had begun to see the light. Vain hope, she told herself miserably.

Not for the first time, she wished that he had never come into her life, never pierced that stern armour in which she had encased her emotions. She had loved Christopher very deeply and he had died. Now she loved Peter and in another way he, too, must die, to her.

How applicable were those poignant words written by the great poet Heine, she thought bitterly.

> Twice have I loved unhappily,
> Twice has love passed me by.
> Oh sun and moon and stars laugh on!
> I laugh with you and die!

She could not, would not, suffer again, die again, she told herself in sudden wild panic. She must not love Peter Farrington. And with that panic fluttering at her heart, like blind moths beating their wings against the fire that burns them, she rushed into her bedroom and shut the door. She would not get the drinks for Rita. She would not look at Peter again tonight—a Peter coming straight from Rita's arms, foolishly infatuated once more.

A moment later she heard Rita calling. Then an angry voice outside her door.

'Helen, where the devil are those drinks?'

Helen answered in a suffocated voice.

'I don't feel very well—would you please excuse me . . .'

Rita shrugged her shoulders and went into the kitchen to fetch a tray for herself. It was a nuisance, but she could not be bothered to find out what was wrong with the girl. She had been too annoyed all the afternoon by the thought of Helen at the theatre with Peter. And she didn't want Helen in the room while they were drinking their cocktails either. All too soon Glen would be arriving. That was bad enough. Rita wished to be alone with her fiancé.

Their embrace, just now, had been passionate enough to satisfy even Rita. She thought she had got Peter right back where she wanted him. There were moments when she was not analytical, and quite incapable of probing under a moment of sensuousness. She could not dream that when Peter held her close to him just now, it had been with the deliberate intent to avoid mental analysis within himself; subdue that faintly stirring doubt as to whether she was the right woman for him and allow the very force of her appeal to his senses to triumph.

None of this was apparent to Rita. And she was in a gay mood because she thought she had managed Nigel very cleverly, too.

He had been difficult at first. Then she had

told him that Peter was going back to Kenya on business and that as soon as he was gone, she would take the opportunity of cabling him and breaking their engagement. She had also promised to travel to Stockholm with Nigel before Christmas.

She had, in fact, made herself so agreeable that she had successfully wooed him into an amiable frame of mind. He seemed prepared to believe all she said.

Of course, in her complicated, intriguing mind, she had already made up her mind to double—cross him. She meant to work things so that he did not find out when Peter came back. And between now and then, she would vanish right out of Nigel's life. She had decided to let the flat and go into the country, to some quiet hotel in which he would never find her. There, instead of in London, she would receive Peter and his mother. Peter was always talking about country life and deploring this artificial existence which she led. Very well, for him she would turn herself into a 'country girl'. She would make a good impression on Mrs. Farrington. She would learn golf. In beautifully cut tweeds and brogues she would go for long healthy walks, play games and lead the simple life. She would make quite sure that Nigel never traced her. She had also reached another conclusion. *Helen was a danger.* She knew too much, and there was a quiet accusation in those grey eyes of her; which constantly made Rita squirm. She was not going to let Helen meet Mrs. Farrington or see any more of Peter. She would give her a week's notice. That was another thing she intended to do, the moment Peter left the country. *There would be no Helen* when Peter came back. And Patty—well, Patty would just have to put up with it.

CHAPTER SIXTEEN

It was early that next morning that Peter rushed to Rita's flat to tell her that he would be flying at midday. There had been a sudden cancellation and he had been given the seat.

Helen received him—and the news—before Rita was even awake. Peter, despite his hurry, found time to think how nice she looked in that fresh green overall, with a green scarf to match, tying up the fair hair. Helen, arrayed for housework was, in his opinion, quite charming. He followed her into the sitting-room, where she hastily drew the curtains and let in the grey winter's light, then he blew on his hands and spread them out to the glow of the electric fire she switched on.

'It's a dickens of a cold morning! Won't it be grand to have some sunshine at home for a few weeks!' he exclaimed.

Helen smiled at him, hands in the pockets

225

of her overall.

'Yes, you'll love it.'

But her smoke-grey eyes were not smiling. They were strangely wistful. She had grown so used to the sight of Peter coming in and out of this flat all day, every day. Heartache though it gave her at times, it had also made her happy. And every time she saw him now, she loved him more. He and her dead love were incorporated into one. When she thought about Christopher—she thought about Peter. She could no longer separate the two.

And bitterly she disliked and envied the woman next door. Though she was sure that she would never have felt like that had Rita been a nice person—a girl who was in the least calculated to make him happy.

Peter said:

'You must look after yourself, as well as Rita, while I am away. You're a bit thin in the face, and Glen and I are rather fond of you—we don't want you to fade away!'

The words were carelessly uttered and the affection with which he regarded her was more brotherly than anything else, but it set her heart and cheeks on fire. She turned away.

'I smell coffee boiling over,' she stammered and vanished.

Once having put the coffee aside, and wiped the top of the electric cooker, she had to make those heartbeats slow down and tell herself not to be an idiot. It was as well that Peter was going away, she thought bitterly. Her feelings for him were growing altogether too strong. Quickly she went along to Rita's bedroom, knocked on the door and entered.

She wrinkled her nose, disliking the over—scented, stale atmosphere. How Rita could sleep with windows shut, and central heating full on, she could not think. A peevish voice from the pillow:

'I told you not to wake me until I rang—'

'Very well,' said Helen coldly, 'then I'll tell Peter you are still asleep.'

Instantly Rita was sitting bolt upright; she switched on the lamp beside her, yawned, looked at her little clock which said half past eight, then blinked at Helen.

'What the devil is Peter doing here at this ungodly hour?'

'He's just had word from B.O.A.C. that he's flying at midday. He's come to say good-bye.'

Rita muttered an imprecation, flung off the bedclothes, and reached for her satin dressing-gown which she folded quickly around her, shivering in her sheer chiffon nightgown.

'How infernal! What a time to say good-bye to anyone! He must wait. I must have a bath and dress. He can't see me like this . . .'

Helen eyed the woman on the bed, wondering what Peter would say if he could see his 'glamour girl', with red hair tied up in a net, her face greasy with cream, dark lines under her eyes, rouged lips an ugly smear. There was no denying Rita's age at this time of the morning, and in this dishevelled state. A very human wish surged in Helen's breast to call Peter in and say:

'Look at her! Look at what you think is young and fresh and good, you fool, oh, Peter, my *darling*, you fool!'

She half-listened to the spate of orders Rita shot at her—tell Pierrot to wait—make him stay to breakfast—put the fire on—(all the things Helen had already thought of doing— and done!)

While Rita bathed and dressed, Helen laid the breakfast table, made the thin brittle toast that Rita liked, and cooked an egg and bacon for Peter. He came into the little kitchen and watched, sitting at the end of the table, pipe in the corner of his mouth.

'Aren't we domesticated!' he jeered, grinning at her. 'Umm! It smells good. And I'm going to eat it all. Men are selfish guys!'

'Women can be just as selfish!' Helen said, basting the frying egg with a spoonful of bacon fat. And she was not going to tell him how dearly she loved this moment—so unexpected and sweet—cooking his breakfast for him.

'Oh, I think women are rather *un*selfish on the whole,' he said, 'my mother is. She used to give up everything for us in the early days, before my father made so much money. We didn't always have so much of this world's

228

goods, you know. Fathei had brains and guts and some influential friends, and there you are! But I can remember my mother doing the cooking in a little farm we had up country because our boys were such poor cooks and she wanted us children to have the best of everything. I was only six or seven but I can remember it—'

'Tell me more,' said Helen wistfully, while her ears strained for the sound of the bathroom door opening. It was so nice to hear about Peter when he was a little boy in Kenya. Why, *why*, must Rita come in and spoil it all?

Finally, Peter insisted upon carrying the tray bearing the breakfast, through to the sitting-room.

'I shall think of this when I am in Nairobi,' he said, 'I couldn't be more glad Rita has you here with her. *You* are another of the unselfish ones. And I think Rita is, too, in her way. I can never get over her goodness in adopting that kid, and looking after her all these years . . .'

Helen's hand, trembling a little, knocked a cup over then set it straight again. It was terrible to hear Peter say things like that, terrible to know the *truth*. She was almost thankful that Rita chose this moment to join them.

A little astonished, Helen looked at Rita, who this morning was putting on a new act. She wore one of her newer, most simple dresses—a soft grey-blue wool with a tight bodice and long full skirt, and her gorgeous long hair tied back with a girlish bow. She had applied the faintest and most delicate make—up to her face and in the dim morning light she managed to look even younger than usual and very appealing. With a sad wan look in her big, dark eyes, she approached Peter.

'Oh, Pierrot,' she said, 'what an awful blow! I never thought you would go so quickly.'

Ignoring Helen, who was already pouring out coffee, she put up her face to be kissed. Peter was charmed by her appearance—her physical appeal could never fail to stir his youthful admiration—but somehow he felt awkward, embracing Rita with Helen in the room. He gave her only a brief kiss, took her hand and led her to the breakfast table.

'Never mind, my sweet. We will make the best of it and I'll soon be back. Now listen, I have only one hour to spare before I report to the Air Centre. Come and help me eat the superb breakfast Helen has cooked. Glen will be here, too, in a second.'

Rita flung Helen a moody look but forced a smile.

'Isn't the egg too hard? I ought to have cooked it for you myself—'

'It's exactly as he asked for it,' Helen found herself snapping, and with heightened colour walked out of the room to refill the coffee pot. She really could not stand the sight of Rita with her girlish bow, holding Peter's hand, taking up that 'Sweet young thing' attitude.

After she had gone, Rita sighed.

'Helen's awfully irritable,' she murmured. 'I don't know what's wrong with her. Sometimes she is almost rude to me. I don't think she likes the job here, and I don't think she is really suited for it. She used to be in an art school. I need someone more homely, more motherly, to look after me.'

Peter, tucking into what he thought was an excellently cooked meal, and sipping the best coffee he had tasted since his arrival in London, put his cup down and stared at his fiancée.

'Good Lord, darling! But I thought Helen ideal for you. She does everything so well. And she seems so devoted to you and the little girl.'

Rita crumbled a piece of dry toast, her long lashes veiling the sudden venom in her eyes. It maddened her to hear Peter praise Helen and confirmed her decision to get rid of her. But she gave Peter a touching sad smile.

'People aren't always what they seem to be on the surface, darling Pierrot. And you're so kind-hearted.' She lowered her voice. 'Between you and me, Helen isn't always so pleasant as she appears. When nobody else is here . . .' she broke off significantly.

There followed an uncomfortable silence. Peter ate his breakfast frowning. This piece of feminine spite was unintelligible to his honest masculine mind. He did not want to doubt

231

Rita's word, but at the same time he could not reconcile what she had said about Helen with his knowledge of the girl. He had never seen the slightest signs of ill—temper or inefficiency in Helen. She did not gush and was not demonstrative. Apart from that highly emotional side which he had glimpsed (she had once betrayed herself because of the resemblance to her dead love) he found her reticent—deeply reserved, in fact. But he admired her for that.

It seemed fairly obvious this morning that Rita did not approve of Helen. When he came to think about things, one or two remarks that his young sister had made returned to memory, and made him uneasy.

Glen loved Helen. And Glen, without expressing a definite opinion, had hinted several times lately that *Rita* was the irritable one—not Helen.

At this moment, Glen herself arrived, in her usual high spirits, breathless and apologetic because she had got up later than she intended and, unable to find a taxi at this hour, had walked round from the hotel.

'Can I cadge some breakfast?' she asked.

Rita set her teeth. This was the sort of 'merry party' that she loathed and detested. She always felt so much more able to hold Peter's attention when they were alone. But she did her best to be charming, made room for Glen, and called out quite affably to Helen:

'Another cup, ducky—it's quite a family gathering and *what* a sad occasion with Pierrot about to fly miles and miles away from us!'

Glen, perched on the arm of her brother's chair, tweaked his ear affectionately.

'It may be sad for us but I bet he'll enjoy it!'

'Oh, I shall like seeing mother and home again but I shall miss you all,' said Peter.

And the 'all' included Helen, who walked into the room with a tray and announced that she was frying another egg for Glen.

She caught that glance from Peter. Some of the bitterness and misery in her own soul rolled away. But a deep depression—a most uncomfortable feeling altogether—crept over her when she caught another look, one of unmistakable hatred, from Patty's mother. It seemed a shocking thing that such an expression should have eyes so lustrous and beautiful.

The time passed all too quickly, after the meal. Discreetly Helen and Glen retired to the little kitchen to wash up. They left the engaged couple alone. Glen chatted away blithely, with all the unconcern of seventeen. She was going to catch the eleven-thirty train down to Torquay, she told Helen. Her cousins were expecting her. But she wished, really, that she could stay here with Helen.

'Never mind. I'll be back in town the moment Pierrot gets back,' she finished.

Helen answered at random. Fond though

233

she was of Glen, she could think of nothing but those two next door—once more conscious of wild, hopeless jealousy because Rita had the right to these last moments with *him*; because it was Rita who would know the tender passion of his farewell kiss.

'What's the matter, Helen, darling,' she heard Glen's voice, 'you've gone so white?'

Blindly she thrust her hands into the bowl of soap suds and picked out some spoons and forks.

'It's nothing,' she said.

In the sitting-room, Rita clung to Peter as she had never done before—tears of genuine misery magnifying her eyes. She really was passionately in love with this charming young man who had so much to offer, and terrified of the thought of the future the ordeal of trying to escape from Nigel and keep Peter's love and faith.

'Tell your mother how much I adore you, and that I can hardly wait for you to come back, won't you?' she said, with a little sob.

Peter held her tenderly and kissed the top of the fragrant red head. He could not fail to be moved by the sight of her grief because he was going. He soothed her with caresses, and promised to return immediately after Christmas. They would be married then at once, he stated.

Yet even as he felt the passion of Rita's clinging lips and straining hands, he knew deep

234

down within him that his first wholehearted adoration for his bewitching 'glamour girl'— that blind passion which she had excited in him in Paris—had cooled down. And it worried him exceedingly. It seemed too brief a time for that *'first fine careless rapture'* to have died. Why, they were not yet married.

It had been a short tempestuous wooing. Too short and too tempestuous, perhaps. He knew that it was not humanly possible for love between a man and a woman to remain at fever heat, that it always levelled itself down to a very real if less ecstatic feeling on both sides. But not yet, surely not yet! Even while Peter held Rita and kissed her, he was filled with doubts and perplexities. But he tried to tell himself that it would be all right when he came back, and that he would find himself just as much in love with her. Besides, once they were married, there would not be all this strain—*she* would be less nervy, poor darling. After all, she had only just had a nasty operation, and she wasn't well, yet. How could he expect her to be as calm, as easy to be with, as his own little sister, for instance—or Helen.

'Tell me you still love me as much as ever,' Rita was begging him.

'Of course I do,' he said, and buried his face against the warm whiteness of her neck. But he hated himself for what he fancied to be a despicable fickleness. Every time he saw this lovely woman, she seemed more in love with him. He must be a brute to feel so differently. He was determined not to go away leaving her hurt or worried about him.

But after the last feverish kiss, the final extravagant promise—back came the feeling of unease—the relief (of which he felt ashamed) once he was no longer alone with Rita; when his young sister and Helen came back into the room to say goodbye.

Rita went into her bedroom to find hat and fur coat. She insisted on driving to see her fiancé take off.

Peter put a hand out to Helen and for an instant her cool fingers lay in his clasp. He said:

'*Au revoir*, my dear, look after yourself as well as everyone else.'

'I will, Peter,' she said.

He saw that she was very pale but that her lips smiled at him. And her eyes were soft and full of that terrible unspoken yearning which had rent his heart when she had first opened the door to him, and cried out because she thought she had seen a ghost. Impulsively his grip of her hand tightened until she winced for pain. And for the second time, he had a crazy desire to gather her up into his embrace. Then he said abruptly:

'So long—see you when I get back—' and turned and walked out of the room, followed by Glen.

All three of them left the flat together,

236

Peter, Rita and Glen.

Helen was alone—alone with her confusion of thoughts and emotions, nursing the hand which he had bruised with that last hard clasp of his fingers. Why had he looked at her like that? Why had he pressed her hand in that way? She would be mad to read more into it than there was. She felt breathless, exhausted, as though a great wave had struck her and flung her up on to a strange barren shore.

'Peter,' she said aloud, 'Peter, come back to me, to *me* and not to *her*. Oh, Peter, it's too much for me. How could I stand by and see you married to her? Peter my dear, my darling.'

The telephone rang.

It needed that sharp metallic sound to restore her composure. She picked up the instrument.

The voice that spoke to her she recognized immediately as that of Nigel Cressland. He wanted, of course, to speak to Rita.

In the curt voice which Helen reserved for Mr. Cressland, she told him that Rita was out.

'Not unusual,' came from Nigel in a sarcastic tone. 'Well, tell her that I want her to lunch with me and that I shall expect her at the 'Caprice' at one-fifteen.'

'I doubt if she can make it,' Helen volunteered, 'she may not be back from the airport.'

'What the devil is she doing there?'

'Seeing Mr. Farrington off,' said Helen.

A brief laugh from Nigel.

'Well, that doesn't break my heart. But if that's the case tell her I'll call on her later this afternoon.'

Helen put down the receiver, her face strained, her lips compressed. It was revolting, she thought—the moment Peter's back was turned, Nigel would start coming to the flat again. Rita shouldn't let him. Though, no doubt, he was forcing her hand. He had it in his power to ruin her. Let him do so, Helen thought bitterly, let them ruin each other—*but not Peter*—pray God they would not manage to ruin *him* first of all. She no longer saw even the slightest hope that he could be happy, married to Rita Wade.

Glenise came back. She had said good-bye to her brother at the Air Booking Centre.

'Peter was worried about me getting down to Devonshire, but I told him you would see me off, Helen.'

'Yes, I'll see you off,' Helen nodded.

Glen sighed.

'Poor old Pierrot! He didn't look a bit like himself. He was sort of worried and on edge. He wanted cheering up, I think, and Rita was hanging on to his arm being all gooey and pathetic.'

Helen gave a wry smile.

'But, no doubt, she was being her fascinating self.'

Glen grimaced.

'All that fascination is so laid on, it gets me down, and I don't mind telling you, Helen, darling, I'm fearfully fed up about Pierrot marrying her. I thought she was marvellous when I first saw her but now I don't, and I sometimes wonder whether Peter does, only he is so loyal, he would rather die than admit it.'

Helen's heart-beats quickened. She turned from Glen's clear gaze.

'There's nothing you can do about it,' she said in a low voice.

'Helen, I love Pierrot. He's my only brother and I think he is marvellous. I don't *want* him to marry Rita. He'll get tired of her looks and that glamour that she shovels on and off. She isn't really his type. She just *got him* in Paris. Why didn't he wait and meet you? You love him too, don't you, Helen? I asked you once before and you wouldn't answer. Now I'm asking you again. Tell me, Helen please?'

Peter's young sister was being altogether too naïve and frank for Helen who blushed burning red and exclaimed:

'Oh, Glen, be quiet, you terrible chlld!'

'No, you do love him,' persisted the young girl, 'you can tell me. I'll never tell. I'm so terribly fond of Pierrot and I'd much rather have *you* for my sister.'

Helen found it increasingly difficult to control herself. Glen was looking at her with Peter's handsome brilliant eyes. The crisp chestnut hair sprang back from her forehead the way it did from Peter's. The whole thing was too heartbreaking. And the next moment Helen had burst into tears. Glen, with her arms around her, tried to comfort her.

'Dear, darling Helen, don't cry! And don't mind me knowing about Peter—I swear I won't tell him. But I'd jolly well like to,' she added with childish fervour.

Helen blew her nose violently.

'You never, never must.'

CHAPTER SEVENTEEN

During the week that followed, Helen realized that she was working in Rita's flat 'under a cloud'; although nothing was actually said, a subtle change had taken place in Rita's attitude towards her. It ceased to be anything approaching friendly. She no longer chattered to her about her affairs. She became distant and secretive and treated Helen very much as an employee—and not a favoured one at that.

Rita avoided discussion of Peter. The one thing Helen longed to know was what sort of a trip he had had. But Rita, as though she half guessed that Helen would like that news— took a delight in withholding it.

A cable came one day while Rita was out. Helen looked at it wistfully. It was just about the time that Peter would have arrived in Nairobi. But when Rita came home, she seized it, walked away and never referred to it. Her conversations with Helen were few and far between, and mainly on the subject of Helen's work—or Patty.

Fortunately for Helen, Peter's young sister wrote to her from Devonshire. Glen had gone away that morning full of youthful affection and admiration for Helen. She promised to write and she had kept that promise. She sent a few scrappy lines out of sheer duty to the girl whom she thought would one day be her sister-in-law, but to Helen she wrote pages. She was an older edition of Patty, Helen thought, fondly, and was cheered and amused by the ardent schoolgirl epistles. From Glen she learned what had happened to Peter.

He had had a perfect flight. He found their mother well, Glen wrote. But the business was a bit trying. Undoubtedly the lawsuit would be heard before Christmas but he saw no chance of getting back to England until the end of next month. His uncle had plenty for him to do before he could return to Europe.

One line in particular, Helen fastened upon and dreamed about as she continued to lead her lonely and rather wretched existence, working in an uncongenial atmosphere.

'Peter asked me how you are and said that I was to give you his love.'

Helen could not read those words often

enough. But what he wrote to Rita, she would never know.

One morning when Rita was particularly bad-tempered and offensive, Helen took it for granted that Rita having that day received an air-mail letter from Kenya was furious because Peter had told her his return had been delayed.

And that Peter did not write as often as Rita wished was another fact apparent to Helen. Several times, Rita rushed into the flat and demanded her letters and having sorted them and found nothing from Nairobi, was in a bad mood for the rest of the day.

Helen was kept in the dark as to what was going on—she only knew that Nigel Cressland once more came regularly to the flat to see Rita. Then, one morning Rita volunteered some information.

She called for Helen, who was at that moment washing Rita's nylon stockings. It was one of those bitterly cold dark days in December, when London seemed to be shrouded in darkness even at the early hour of ten a.m. and all the lights were switched on. With a sigh, Helen wiped her hands and thought how near it was to Christmas. Only another week! Well, one thing satisfied her lonely heart. She would be going down to Bexhill to fetch darling Patty the day after tomorrow. It would be a relief and pleasure to have the child in the flat again. Patty had written an ecstatic letter this week, saying how she was longing for the 'hols' with Mummy, and *darling* Helen.

Helen walked into the sitting-room. Rita sat at her bureau, writing. She looked up as the girl entered the room, a brief indifferent glance, then down at her blotter again.

'Oh, come in and sit down,' she said. 'I want a few words with you.'

Helen remained standing.

'I'd just like to rinse your stockings first,' she said, 'you want them all ready by this evening and I'll have to get them dry.'

'Don't mind about the stockings now,' said Rita, 'what I've got to say is rather important. Perhaps it will come as a bit of a shock to you.'

Helen's heart gave a peculiar jerk.

'Is anything wrong?' she asked.

Rita avoided looking at the girl. She knew that there was nothing whatsoever to justify what she was about to do, but like all the other unkind or amoral things that she did, Rita always managed to find an excuse and exonerate herself. She said:

'You have worked very well since you came to me last September, Helen, and I have nothing whatsoever to say against you, or your kindness to Patty. But I'm afraid that circumstances have arisen which make it impossible for me to keep you on. I must ask you to leave at once. Of course, I'll give you an excellent reference.'

243

Helen stood immovable, her heart beating very fast and her face changing swiftly from white to red and red to white again. Certainly, she had not expected *this*! It was a blow that hit her so hard that she could not for a moment begin to grasp what it would mean to her. She said in a gasp:

'You want me to *leave*? But why?—'

Rita broke in, still avoiding Helen's gaze. (She could never stand up to the clear penetrating glance of those honest grey eyes.)

'I've already told you, it is through no fault of your own. You have done nothing wrong, except, perhaps, spoil Patty . . .'

Rita could not resist that gibe. She had always been jealous of her small daughter's adoration for Helen.

'But I haven't spoiled her. I've given her affection and attention but I think I have always been quite firm . . .' Helen exclaimed indignantly.

Again Rita cut in:

'That's as it may be. We are all entitled to our own opinions. But I don't think Patty will need anyone to look after her these holidays. I am taking her away.'

Helen stared. She was so thunderstruck that she could hardly concentrate. And Rita was rather enjoying the fact that she had upset Helen.

'It's something to be able to get under her skin—she is far too fond of putting over that

244

proud reserved act,' Rita thought spitefully.

She went on:

'As a matter of fact, I'm going away first thing tomorrow. That is why I asked you to wash and iron all those things for me. I'm going to start packing now, and I may say that I've let the flat.'

'Let the flat?' echoed Helen.

'Yes,' said Rita, 'also you won't need to fetch Patty from St. Cyprian's the day after tomorrow because I have arranged with Miss Ponting to send her by train and car direct to the hotel in which we shall be staying.'

'I see,' said Helen slowly.

Rita gave her a cold smile.

'I know you don't think me capable of looking after my own child. But I *am*. And I'm sure Patty will prefer country life to being here, in London. I think you have often expressed that opinion, yourself.'

Helen could not speak. But her cheeks crimsoned. Rita added:

'I am afraid I must ask you to terminate your job with me when I go, in the morning. Naturally I will pay you a month's salary in *lieu* of notice.'

That struck at Helen's pride. For a moment she felt something akin to hatred for this woman, then she tried to conquer the passionate surge of feeling. She said quickly:

'No thank you. I don't want money for work I haven't done.'

Rita gave a little tinkling laugh and twisted her fountain pen between her long pointed fingers.

'Oh, my dear, don't be silly. One can't afford to be stupidly proud in these hard times. You have got to live until you find another job.'

That struck Helen dumb again. But now her numbed brain was beginning to work, she saw the full implication of this abrupt and totally unexpected dismissal. She saw the truth in what Rita said: *she would have to live until she found another job.* And as Uncle George was dead, she had no home. She could not even go to Aunt Mary who was sharing a tiny flat with her elderly friend. Being flung out of this flat at twenty-four hours' notice presented a real problem as to where she should go. Naturally there was always plenty of domestic work available if she chose to take it. But she did not much relish cleaning and washing-up, continuing to be a servant as she had been to Rita in this flat. She had been given no scope at all for her art. All her education was wasted and Helen had been extremely well brought up at her school—she was quite wasted it this sort of menial work and she knew it and had originally taken the job only because of Patty!

Patty! Why, it would surely be a bitter disappointment for the poor little thing, not finding her, as she had longed to do, this Christmas. And even if Rita were taking her into the country, Helen could not begin to believe that Rita would devote her whole time and energy to Patty. And with that man, Nigel, around, the child's life wouldn't be worth living.

Reluctantly, but with her innate honesty, Helen burst out:

'I wish I could have stayed with Patty just over Christmas.'

Rita scribbled something on her pad.

'It would have been very nice, but I'm afraid it's out of the question,' she said with artificial brightness.

Helen bit her lip.

'May I ask where you'll be? I would like to write to Patty. I've got her little Christmas presents all ready and some decorations I bought for a tree. I know she wanted a tree.'

Rita frowned. This was the sort of thing that irritated her—that Helen should think always of the things that Patty wanted, and which she, Rita, avoided or forgot. She felt rather guilty as she remembered she hadn't bought the child a definite toy for Christmas yet. She couldn't *bear* those crushes in the big stores and toy bazaars, or the lifts, at Christmas time. She really hadn't fully recovered her strength after that beastly appendix—but she could always give Patty a pound note with which to buy something for herself, Rita reflected.

She said:

'Oh, I can take your parcels away, in my

case, and give them to Patty on Christmas Day. It was very kind of you to spend your money on her.'

Helen began to feel very unhappy—and strangely apprehensive. Was it Rita's intention to cut her off completely from the child? She stood staring at Rita, her heart thumping violently.

'You will let me come and see Patty, or have her up in town to see a pantomime one day, won't you, Rita?' she asked.

Rita rose. Walking to a small table, she took a cigarette from her nylon box and tapped one on her thumb nail. For a moment she did not answer. But she had made up her mind that there should be no further communication between this girl and her small daughter. She wanted a complete break. There were all kinds of reasons why she wished the parting tomorrow from Helen Shaw to be final.

Rita's brain, as usual, was seething with schemes—many of them wild and dangerous. But she was swimming in a positive sea of difficulties and the situation being critical, she was forced to take one or two dangerous steps and just trust that her luck would carry her safely through.

During the fortnight that Peter had been away from her, she had faced up to several disagreeable facts—first and foremost, the personal menace of Nigel Cressland.

She had seen a lot of him lately and

248

thoroughly deceived him with her charm and affability. Amongst the many lies she had told, she had assured him that she had already written to Kenya, and warned Peter that she did not mean to marry him.

She had let the flat at a handsome profit through a West End agent who was going to deal with all the business for her and would be the only person in London to know where she was going. She had instructed him that for personal reasons, her address was to be kept secret and given to nobody. No correspondence would be forwarded from this building. Peter's letters were the only ones she wanted, and of course he would know her address. She had already cabled it to him.

She had taken rooms for Patty and herself in a guest house in the remote village of West Mayling, on the Surrey—Sussex border. She had been down to see it (after reading an advertisement concerning the place which called itself the 'Old Mill'). It was an old and beautiful house situated next to a disused mill, and overlooking an attractive stream and waterfall. The village itself was tiny, too far away from any station to be spoiled, but only two miles from a nine-hole golf course. The 'Old Mill'—newly opened as a pension, catered for golfers. And the game was one of the things Rita intended to take up, to please Peter and impress Mrs. Farrington, when they arrived.

Life in a village like West Mayling would be hideously boring for her, Rita knew, but at least, she had reflected, when taking the rooms, it would please Patty. And nobody—least of all Nigel—would dream of looking for her in such a village. She could be dead to the world there. And she intended to remain dead until the day of her marriage to Peter.

Glenise was the only other person to whom she must give her address, and she had already written a careful letter to the girl, saying that she wished the address to be given to nobody who asked for it, because she, Rita, needed seclusion and a 'complete rest', for health reasons.

It was all settled and tomorrow Rita was turning her back on the London life which she adored and going into 'retreat' as she called it. She even chose to forget the unworthy motives for the said retreat and feel proud of herself for renouncing the parties and cocktails and vanities which were really the breath of existence to her.

One of her foremost worries was going to be to get Peter back quickly and nail him down to an immediate marriage. If only he would not bring that wretched mother back with him! She would be sure to hinder things. But there was no hope of Mrs Farrington not coming now. Peter had said she was arranging to fly back with him. But, at least, Rita thanked heaven, Peter had fixed the date of his return.

Money and influence had secured seats for him on a Constellation due back in England the last week in January.

Rita would have delayed her self—imposed 'exile' to West Mayling but for the fact that there was always the fear (as well as the hope) that Peter and his mother might be offered seats on an earlier plane, and surprise her—with Nigel—in London.

So she felt that it was better to get settled in her new life and make Nigel understand that this break was final and absolute long before the Farringtons arrived.

Another of Rita's immediate anxieties was Peter's attitude toward her at the moment. He wrote charming letters but they were not frequent and did not contain quite the protestations of worship for which her hungry, greedy soul craved. She had an unpleasant but definite conviction that he was no longer as madly in love with her as he used to be. Somehow, his letters were always guarded—so much too restrained to satisfy her. Rita herself sent one and sometimes two air-letters a day to Nairobi assuring Pierrot of her passionate devotion and loyalty She intended to leave no room in his mind for doubt that she considered that she belonged to him now body and soul, and that she was preparing for their marriage the moment he came back.

She had not yet told him of her intention to dismiss Helen. But she would do so tomorrow.

And because she knew that Peter liked Helen, she would be clever about it. She had already mac up her mind that she would write:

'I didn't want you to know before because you would worry, Pierrot darling, but I am very hard up, I feel what with taxation and so much of my slender means going to keep my adopted child. So I have had to let my flat and retire to a cheap little guest house in the country. And unfortunately I have had to let Helen go. I can't afford her salary. I asked her if she would accept less, but she wouldn't. Rather a blow because I thought she was fond of Patty and me and would help in a moment like this, but there you are!'

That was the letter she had already composed in her mind. It wouldn't put Helen in too good a light, and, she hoped, it would arouse Peter's chivalry and pity for herself. Being so wealthy, he would, no doubt, consider it his duty to marry her and take care of her at once.

In fact, Rita had begun to draw a beautiful picture of herself pinching and scraping in the country in order to look after Patty and she was quite enjoying the role.

Helen's voice interrupted all the thoughts that darted in and out of Rita's abnormal mind.

'You *are* going to let me see Patty, aren't you?'

Then Rita smiled at her. A cold glittering smile.

'I'm sure you will understand when I say "no"—for Patty's sake. She is rather attached to you and it might be better if you go right out of her life.'

'But I don't understand why—' began Helen hotly.

'Please,' interrupted Rita, 'don't ask me to explain. It really is my business and not yours.'

Helen went ice-cold.

'Very well.'

'I leave the flat tomorrow morning at ten o'clock. Before that I shall hand the keys over to the agent who is coming here just before ten. Don't bother to do anything more for me when you have finished the stockings. You will want time to pack for yourself, and I shall insist upon your taking a full month's money, as well as a reference from me.'

Silence. Helen felt sick and frightened. Not only was this dismissal a shock—and quite undeserved after all her patience and devotion to duty (for although she disliked Rita she had never failed to carry out her wishes) but she was deeply conscious of how hard this was going to hit Patty. Quite apart from Helen's distress that she would not be with Patty, as she had planned, the child was bound to suffer. Her mother would never understand her in a hundred years. So many things Patty said, from time to time, proved that, as well as what Helen observed for herself.

Besides—*there was Peter.*

Like a chill wind, there swept across Helen the realization that this dismissial from the houseold would cut her off completely from Peter. She would never see him again. She would never know when he cane back, or what devilish means Rita meant to employ for further deceiving and snaring him. In fact, he would go out of Helen's life just as suddenly as he had come into it, He, who was one in her mind and heart with Christopher. He, who had grown to mean so much. *Too much.*

Her heart sank to its lowest ebb. Then Rita, as though anxious to give the *coup de grâce*, said gently:

'If you're interested, you'll probably see notices in the papers when Pierrot and I are married. Now do forgive me if I run along. And if you want to go and see your aunt, you needn't bother to stay in or bother about telephone calls. I don't expect any. I have told everyone that I am going out of town. And Nigel won't ring—he is in Paris at the moment on business.'

She walked out of the room, humming a new dance-tune under her breath.

CHAPTER EIGHTEEN

About a week later, Helen sat reading a letter which had just been delivered to her in the small Earl's Court flat in which her aunt lived with old Miss Brinkley.

This was the only address which Helen could give anybody at the moment. She was homeless. After that cruelly sudden dismissal from Rita's employ, she had been forced to accept the hospitality which both the old ladies—so fond of her—had offered, despite the fact that their place was so tiny and already overcrowded.

'My niece is not going to stay alone in some cheap hotel in London,' Mrs. Shaw had declared as soon as Helen had given her the news that she was to be without a job during Christmas.

Helen gratefully accepted the offer of the sofa in the sitting-room. Indeed, just at that moment she was a blessing in disguise to the old ladies, as their faithful standby, Emily, had gone home with an attack of shingles. Isobel Brinkley's hands were so crippled with arthritis that she was unable to do any cleaning or cooking, and the domestic work was falling on the shoulders of the delicate Mrs. Shaw who, herself, was not fit for it.

So, it was after all 'an ill wind' that had

brought Helen to the little flat. She cleaned the three rooms, cooked breakfast for the old ladies and gave them their supper.

Helen loved and pitied the brave and cheerful old ladies and was glad to be of use to them. But for herself it looked like being a dreary Christmas.

It was uncomfortable in that small sitting-room, which was crammed with the belongings of both ladies (each clinging passionately to their few antiques or pieces of good china, or books and pictures that had belonged to their families for generations past).

It was like sleeping in a museum, and had the same musty smell, Helen told herself ruefully as she sat reading the letter which the porter had forwarded from Rita's flat. It was a very long letter from Peter's sister who was still in Devonshire. Glen expressed astonishment at the news which Helen had sent of her dismissal from Rita's employ. Coupled with astonishment, her indignation was expressed in the strong frank terms of youth.

'I think it's beastly of Rita to turf you out just before Christmas and I know all you had been planning for Patty. I just can't understand R., but then I never could! And I like her less now than ever for doing this to you. You were always so jolly nice to her. I feel sure Pierrot will be amazed. Even if Rita's hard up, she needn't economize on you . . . etc. etc.'

Glen's championship did much to comfort Helen. The rest of the letter, of course, interested her profoundly, as it was about Peter. Glen described his present life in Nairobi, and some of the things he had been doing, and said that he planned to get back earlier than anticipated and was definitely bringing their mother with him. The letter concluded:

'Mummy is going to meet you whether R. likes it or not. I shall make her go up to town with me to see you; because you are my friend—and Pierrot's . . .'

That line, alone—*my friend and Pierrot's*— lifted a considerable load of Helen's depression. Glen was a darling, she thought; like her brother.

She clung to this sole contact with Peter. She could not bear to feel that she might never see him again. Yet she asked herself what use it would be if she did? If he were coming back to marry Rita, Rita would not want him to meet her, Helen, and she would find no joy in watching the consequences of such a ruinous marriage.

But for the moment it was a comfort to be in touch with Glen, and Helen wrote a quick answer to the girl, giving her own personal news, explaining the present circumstances which kept her in this little flat until Emily's return (anticipated in the New Year). After which she meant, she said, to look for a job in a school. She had made up her mind to go on working with children. She would apply for a suitable post as assistant-matron—or, if she could find one, a job in a school that would recognize her art, even though she was only semi-trained.

Of Rita, she had not heard a single word since she left on that morning when Rita had shut up the flat and vanished to her secret retreat. She made it plain that she wished no further association with Helen. And as far as Rita was concerned, Helen was thankful to be away from her unhealthy atmosphere of lies, intrigues and theatrical posing. She did not care where Rita went, or what she did, but she cared about Patty. She hated being cut off from the child so suddenly; more for her sake than the affection Helen bore her. Patty did not write; or if she did, Rita did not send on the letters. It was a wretched way to walk out of the child's life, Helen thought, and it worried her incessantly. She could not beat the thought that Patty was distressed or miserable, or that she might be thinking that her Helen, whom she had loved and trusted, had just callously deserted her.

Helen could have written to Patty at St. Cyprian's. She was often tempted to. She refrained only for the child's sake. For if Helen wrote one explanation and Rita had given Patty another, it could only react unfavourably on the child's mind. She might conceivably catch her mother out in a falsehood, or it would start a mystery which would not be good for the little girl. No matter what Helen felt about Rita she would never willingly put the child against her mother.

So the curtain of silence had dropped between them.

On this grey cold morning, Glenise's cheerful letter dispelled some of the gloom in Helen's heart and soul.

Quickly Helen put Glen's letter into her bag, fetched coat and hat, and prepared to do her shopping. For the sake of her aunt and Miss Brinkley, if for nothing else, she was thankful that Rita had forced her to accept a month's salary in *lieu* of notice—the money was needed—to justify her existence here.

The flat was on the first floor of a large converted Victorian house in one of those long dreary streets leading off the Earl's Court Road. The staircase was dark and dingy. A smell of fried onions rose from the basement. As Helen opened the front door, an icy blast shivered through her. The nice white snow of two days ago had melted. The pavements were smeared with wet dirty slush, and very slippery. An east wind was tearing down the street. Helen buttoned her coat firmly around her, wished passionately that she was in Kenya with Peter whom she missed atrociously, and felt some anxiety about 'her two old dears', as she called them. Aunt Mary, in particular, was prone to bronchitis and should not be out on a day like this. But she had insisted on going out with Isobel to choose a Christmas card for an old canon and his wife, who once occupied the rectory in a village where the Shaws lived many years ago.

As Helen stood there, adjusting the collar of her coat, a taxi drove up to the door. She felt wickedly inclined to take it as far as Peter Jones; extravagant though it seemed. Then out of the taxi stepped a big smartly dressed man, and with a shock Helen recognized Nigel Cressland.

She pressed her lips rebelliously together as she saw him. She had thought he was one of the unpleasant things she had left behind her. He came up to her, raising his hat and giving that slightly ironic bow and smile which made her always want to be rude to him. He said:

'Well, well! Just the girl I have driven across London to this delectable neighbourhood to see.'

'I can't see why you should want to see me,' was Helen's curt reply.

He replaced his hat.

'Is there anywhere we can go and talk?'

'I'm afraid not. There are no convenient hotels in this "delectable neighbourhood", as

260

you call it, Mr. Cressland—at least, not near enough for me to invite you to, and in the absence of my aunt, I'm afraid I cannot ask you up to our flat.'

He looked down at her with that old hateful smile, but she could see that he was determined to make use of her, now that he was here.

'You were just about to go somewhere. May I drive you?'

'No, thank you.'

Nigel's smile turned to a frown.

'Don't be so ridiculous, my dear Helen, I'm not going to eat you.'

'That wasn't what I feared,' she said drily, 'I merely do not wish to accept any favours from you, Mr. Cressland.'

He muttered something unintelligible and then laughed.

'I can see I must shave off my moustache or change my tactics. I am losing my grip with women. I used to think they liked me.'

She flung him a contemptuous look.

'What do you want? Rita's address, I suppose.'

'Yes,' he snapped, 'but why the devil must we stand in this infernal east wind saying rude things to each other.'

Helen shrugged her shoulders.

'Very well. I am going to Peter Jones. You can drop me there if you wish.'

He opened the taxi door for her without

another word. As the taxi jolted along, he said:

'I don't want any nonsense. *Where is Rita?*'

Helen looked at him with her level grey eyes.

'You may not believe me—and I don't care whether you do or not—but I do *not* know where Rita is.'

He began to bluster, then she broke in:

'I tell you I do *not* know. I can't even buy Patty a Christmas card. Rita gave me a moment's notice and asked me not to communicate with her again.'

'Why?'

'I'll leave that for you to figure out. I know as much as you do. Or rather as little. She just said suddenly, without warning, that she was going away and leaving no address.'

Nigel sat back in the taxi, chewing savagely at his lips. He knew the truth when he heard it. He must believe what Helen said. He felt utterly frustrated.

When he had returned from Paris, where he had pulled off quite a successful little business deal, he had been in excellent spirits and had made up his mind to buy Rita a new ring which she coveted. He had been absolutely sure that he had won her back. He had taken her word that she had broken with young Farrington. It had been a complete shock to him when he called at the flat and found it tenanted by an ex-Indian Army officer and his wife. They could tell him nothing except that they had

262

rented the place through an agent for an indefinite period, and neither they nor the porter could give Nigel Rita's address. He went in a towering rage to the agents. They, of course, knew Rita's address but politely, firmly refused it. Their client, Mrs. Wade, had expressed the wish that nobody should know where she was, because she was ill and in need of a complete rest, they told him.

Of course, Nigel knew that this was not true. All his efforts to jockey the agent into giving him the address failed. He knew her bank, but they would not divulge her whereabouts. Nigel was forced to retire, temporarily beaten.

Then, at his office the next day, he found a note from Rita. In it, she said she wished to break finally with him *as well as Peter Farrington*; that she had made up her mind to remain a widow, and to devote her life to her child. She begged him not to try and find her; said that even if he did, she would not change her mind and he could spread as many stories about her as he wished—she no longer cared. She was finished with men.

If Nigel had not been so furiously angry, he would have laughed over that letter. He knew his Rita. He was convinced that she was trying on a colossal bluff. At first he had decided to put a detective on to her and trace her. Then he did nothing. He began to wonder if she was worth all the effort. She was beautiful and fascinating and as treacherous as a snake.

Twice she had let him down. She took everything and gave nothing. He began to feel that he did not much mind what she did; and convinced himself that he wouldn't mind even if she married young Farrington. He, Nigel, was well rid of her. Attractive though she was, there were limits to what a man would put up with.

Yet he could not get Rita out of his mind. That was the hell of being in love with her, he told himself bitterly; she got into a fellow's blood, like an insidious poison destroying reason and insanity. He could not forget the heady allure of her when she was soft and pliant in a man's arms; her wicked sparkling wit when she was in a good humour. The way she tossed back that flaming hair of hers; the dazzling sheen of her skin against black velvet, her clever understanding of a man's moods and requirements. And he wanted her again. He was still madly jealous of any other man whom she might admit in her life. And he wanted to get even with her for walking out on him, too.

As for all that stuff about 'devoting her life to Patty', he had never heard such tripe. Not for one moment did he believe in that. He told Helen so as the taxi drove them down the Brompton Road toward Sloane Square.

'I'd like to know where she is and what she is doing,' he muttered.

'Well, I'm afraid I cannot tell you,' said

264

Helen.

'And why did she break her engagement with her young hero from Kenya?'

Then Helen sat up and stared.

'She didn't—not that I know of—'

'But he went back to Nairobi?'

'Yes.'

'Yes,' echoed Nigel. 'I checked up on that. I called on his London branch. They said he'd gone. But I took it for granted that it was because all was over between him and Rita.'

Then Helen lapsed into a wary silence. She suspected more lies and intrigues on Rita's part. She did not want to be mixed up with it. It was all so hateful and savoured of such hideous disloyalty to poor Peter.

Nigel hurled questions at her about the engagement. At length she cut him short.

'I know nothing and can tell you nothing. Now I really must ask you to drop me and let me go on my own way,' she said.

He knew he could get nothing more out of her. He stopped the taxi in front of Peter Jones. For a fleeting instant, as he watched Helen's slim figure walk away, and looked at the beautiful ankles, the grace with which she moved, he thought, not for the first time, that the quiet little Miss Shaw had 'got something'; was really a damn pretty girl; that touch of prudery and standoffishness was quite provocative. It would be interesting to try and get through her hauteur, her reserve. Only he had other things to think about just now. *Rita* in particular.

He swore under his breath at the thought of Rita. If she had not broken with Farrington, then what *was* her game? He would dearly like to know. It would give him a malicious satisfaction to prevent that young woman doing what she wanted—when she wanted it— regardless of *his* feelings.

It was a week since he had tried in vain to bribe the porter at Rita's old flat. A whim made him turn the taxi towards Knightsbridge, and to the familiar block. Glowering, restless, he walked into the hall. The lift had just come down. The liftboy came out of it. Nigel asked for the head porter. The boy said he was out, finding a taxi for a lady upstairs.

Nigel looked at the liftboy. He was new. He had not been here in Rita's time. Nigel said:

'Listen, sonny boy, I suppose you wouldn't like to earn half a crown and tell me where Mrs. Wade has gone . . .'

The boy grinned.

'I'd like the 'arf-crown, sir, but I don't know that lady's address.'

'Never heard of her?'

'Oh yes, sir, she was the lady what lived in 52, I know because sometimes letters come for 'er and Colonel MacLeod what took over the flat gives Mr. Jackson, the 'ead porter, the letters to give to 'er agent.'

'Quite so,' said Nigel; then looking down at

a bundle of correspondence in the lad's hand, he added:

'I suppose there isn't one right now, on its way to Mrs. Wade's agent?'

The boy nodded. 'Yes, there is,' he said, with innocent candour, 'one with a foreign stamp on it.'

Nigel said:

'Let's have a look.'

The boy handed a thin envelope to him. Nigel's heart gave a sudden leap. It was an air letter from Nairobi, addressed to Rita in a man's small neat writing. No doubt it was from Peter Farrington, and had been posted before Farrington knew that Rita was quitting this flat.

Nigel looked around. The porter was not in sight. He said:

'So all Mrs. Wade's letters go to her agent?'

'Yessir.'

'Well, I am passing by the agent right now. I could drop it in for you.'

The boy looked doubtful.

He had been told, he said, to be very careful with the letters that were sent on to tenants and had orders to let nobody have them except Mr. Jackson.

Nigel whipped out a ten-shilling note.

'That's better than half a crown, isn't it?'

The boy's eyes gleamed.

'*Coo!*'

Nigel put the letter from Nairobi into his

267

pocket.

'This is just between you and me, sonny. There is no need to tell Mr. Jackson and so nobody will get into trouble.'

The boy pocketed the ten—shilling note. Nigel drove away with the letter which bore a Kenya stamp.

He did not know why he wanted the letter so much unless it was to satisfy his insatiable curiosity to find out how things were between Rita and Peter Farrington.

He had no conscience about opening the letter and reading it.

The signature was *'Pierrot'*. The letter had been posted from Nairobi. The first few paragraphs left no room for doubt that Peter was then still under the impression that he was going to marry her. So Nigel knew for certain now that Rita had lied to him about that. She had not broken their engagement. But it was a paragraph in the second half of the letter which made Nigel sit up, and which he read several times, so great was the surprise and perplexity it caused him. Most of the letter was merely the simple and rather restrained expressions of a young man in love. He said how much he missed Rita and that he was looking forward to his return. But it was an allusion to the child,

Patty, which shook Nigel to the core. Peter wrote:

'Whenever I think about your little adopted daughter it makes me realize what a wonderful and generous thing you did when you gave a home and your love to that motherless kid. I can assure you she shall never know from me that she is not your rown child, nor lack affection in my home.'

Nigel, having read that paragraph aloud in order to convince himself that it was true, that Farrington had indeed written those words, stared out of the taxi window and gave a long whistle under his breath.

Phew! There could be only one explanation. Peter Farrington had been told that Patty was Rita's adopted daughter. Adopted! Nigel was staggered. He could see in a flash why Rita had done it—because she did not want young Farrington to know how old she was. She would not admit to being the mother of a child of nearly twelve.

The little coward! Nigel's lips took an ugly twist as he folded Peter's letter and put it in his pocket. Good heavens! Even he was shocked that a mother could deny her own child, just in order to preserve the illusion of youth. Rita was worse than he had thought, yes, it was a rotten thing to have done, and what an incredible stroke of luck that he should have hit on this letter and that information.

If Rita thought she could get away with *this*

she was wrong.

Patty, an adopted child! . . . Nigel laughed harshly to himself. The last atom of soft feeling he had for Rita vanished. There remained only the desire to punish her. To turn her into a cringing slave to his own whims and desires.

Sooner or later he would find her. He might yesterday have let her go, carry on with his own life, but not now. He would make her pay for some of her lies. As for that young idiot in Kenya—if he thought that he was going to come back and marry his beautiful 'generous' Rita who had adopted a child out of charity— he, too, was heading for disaster.

There was one concrete proof to be had of Patty Wade's parentage and that lay in the records at Somerset House. For a few shillings, a copy of young Patty's birth certificate could be secured. And Nigel meant to secure one forthwith. After that—with such a weapon in his hand—he could have some fun with Rita, and he meant to have it.

CHAPTER NINETEEN

One clear cold day in mid-January, Patty Wade wearing her school coat, a green beret, woolly gloves and her gum boots, trudged over the fields that led from the 'Old Mill' in West Mayling towards Petcombe, the neighbouring village.

Patty looked pinched and miserable. She *was* miserable. And very lonely. There was nobody to play with or talk to. Mummy had promised to take her up to London for a pantomime. But she had been promising that every day since the 'hols' began, and like most of such promises given to pacify Patty at various moments when she was restless or discontented, they were seldom kept.

Patty wished passionately that she had either a companion of her own age to take on this walk, or a dog. She had to blink very hard to keep the tears from her eyes when she thought about dogs. During the first week in the 'Old Mill' (the nicest week, actually, when everything was new, Mummy was in a good mood, and the unexpected country life had been full of promise) she had found a mongrel straying in the road, cold, hungry and dejected. Her mother was out and Patty took the dog into her bedroom, made a corner for him, fed him and, within an hour, had a devoted slave. She felt very much less lonely in consequence. She called the new love 'Simon'. All her starved affections poured in a torrent over Simon. Joyously she accepted his slavish fawning, the wagging tail, the adoring golden eyes. Then Mummy came home and within half an hour Simon was a thing of the past—literally thrown out by Mummy, backed up by Mrs. Cowley who ran the guest house. Under *no* circumstances could a dog be permitted to live in the clean, newly decorated house, they said. And when Patty, in floods of tears, appealed to her mother to let her keep Simon, *somehow*, Rita had said:

'For heaven's sake don't be difficult, Patty. There's no pleasing you. You used to say you loved the country and hated the flat in town. Now you've got your way. You've plenty of things to amuse you. Why must you have a horrible—looking mongrel, full of fleas and probably sickening for distemper as well. Under no circumstances can you keep the wretched dog.'

And all Patty's bitter tears and sighs were of no avail. Simon was removed. Later it was hinted that he had been taken straight to a vet in the village, there to be what Rita called 'mercifully put to sleep'.

In Patty's opinion it was no mercy they extended to her darling, lovable, tail—wagging Simon. It was a cruel and unnecessary death. Henceforth she looked on her mother and Mrs. Cowley of the 'Old Mill' as murderers. They had *murdered Simon*. In her dramatic emotional fashion, the child built a tragedy around Simon. She wept for two days and nights, and every time Rita saw her reddened eyelids and quivering lips she reproached her; called her 'stupid, difficult and ungrateful'.

In time, Patty gave up the exaggerated mourning for her lost pet; but she did not forget Rita's complete lack of sympathy or understanding. She decided that she now hated all grown-ups. At least those who had control over her. She believed that Helen would have understood. Helen would have managed, somehow, to find Simon a home in the village where he could live and Patty could have seen him sometimes.

Unceasingly, Patty longed for Helen. Her absence had spoiled Christmas for the child. Her first question, after embracing her mother had been: 'Where's Helen? Why didn't she come to St. Cyprian's to fetch me?' And when she was told that Helen had 'left and was not coming back', it was a bitter blow to Patty. Of course, when she wept over that, she was reprimanded.

'You don't need a governess. You've got me, darling. I'm devoting myself to you, now,' Rita declared.

But Rita, as usual, misjudged the nature of a small girl. She had never 'devoted herself' to Patty in the way the child understood or wanted—as Helen had done wholeheartedly, from the start. Patty thought her mother beautiful and exciting with her lovely clothes and perfumes, and occasional bursts of generosity. But she could never be *friends* with Mummy as she was with Helen. They never giggled at the same silly things. Rita gave her money to spend, a new dress to wear on Christmas Day and took some pains to do her hair nicely and show her off to strangers. But Patty squirmed at that. She moped for Helen. And her moping infuriated Rita who, in consequence, was short-tempered and unsympathetic with the child. Her good intentions of devoting herself to Patty soon petered out. She had commenced to play golf, and had found a good-looking 'pro' at West Mayling Golf Club, to coach her. She spent all her mornings on the course, looking wonderful in her new tweeds, her red hair bound up in gay Jacqmar scarves. She felt better for the early nights, country air and wholesome food. But she was bored to death—except for the admiration and attention of the young 'pro', Dick Rowell.

Patty was soon on poor terms with her mother and no happier because she realized the fact. The cruel death of Simon was the final rift between them. She felt no further love for her mother. Only a sulky, dutiful kind of affection when it was demanded of her. She wrote passionate letters daily to Helen and was not to know that Rita burned them all. And she fretted because Helen did not answer those letters, every one of which said, *'Please, please come and see me—I'm so lonely— Mummy doesn't love me or understand me. Oh, why did you go away?'*

No answer came—and the worst thing of all that Patty had to bear was the thought that Helen had deserted her.

She did not understand. She understood so little of what was going on around her; she only knew that Mummy had changed an awful lot since Daddy died—and since Uncle Peter went away, too. Patty had liked Uncle Peter—much better than Uncle Nigel! She hoped he would come back.

This January afternoon, she felt particularly lost and wretched. She had got into a row after breakfast for saying she wanted to send Helen a telegram on the grounds that perhaps Helen was not receiving her letters but might get a wire if Patty sent one. Rita snapped:

'Oh, stop all this rubbish about Helen. She has left us and isn't coming back.'

'I want her back,' Patty said sullenly.

Rita lost her temper, slapped the child then stormed out of the room. She went up to the golf club and stayed there to lunch with Dick Rowell whose flattery and attention soothed her torn nerves. Patty, humiliated by the slapping and heartbroken, was condemned to have lunch and spend the rest of the day alone, as punishment.

The yelping of a dog distracted Patty's thoughts. She saw a golden—brown puppy scampering through a gap in the hedgerow and come bounding towards her. At once Patty's pinched little face lit up. She went down on the grass and held out her arms, whistling to the animal which leapt towards her. Patty felt a warm red tongue licking her face and a warm snuggling body against hers. The puppy reminded her so poignantly of Simon that she burst into tears.

A tall, silver—haired woman with an aristocratic face, wearing tweeds, overcoat and felt hat, and carrying a stick, now appeared through the hedge and saw the little girl in the reefer coat and beret, with the puppy in her arms. She approached her, smiling. Then, when Patty lifted a face streaming with tears, the woman exclaimed:

'Oh dear—what is it? Is anything the matter? That naughty Lindy hasn't bitten you, has she? I'm afraid she has sharp little teeth . . .'

Patty stood up, blinked back the tears, smiled and assured the lady that Lindy had not bitten her.

'Oh, no—I think she's sweet—I adore her!' she cried fervently.

The lady smiled at Patty very kindly. At once the child was comforted and began to talk to her. They introduced themselves. Lindy's mistress gave Patty her name as Lady Pilgrim and said that she lived in Petcombe and had come for a walk with her new puppy which was a thoroughbred Corgi. Lady Pilgrim had two other Corgis, Lindy's mother and father, but they were both old and fat and had stayed at home today.

In a very few minutes, the tall lady and the child were good friends, and began to walk together in the direction of West Mayling.

Patty was delighted with the company, enchanted by Lindy's yelps and gambols, and her tears dried like magic.

It was even better when Lady Pilgrim announced that she had known Mrs. Cowley of the 'Old Mill' for years and intended to stop there for a cup of tea.

'Oh, how scrumptious, then you and Lindy can have tea with me, too!' exclaimed Patty.

'Where is your mother, my dear?'

At once a shadow (which the tall lady failed to understand) fell across Patty's freckled face. She explained that Mummy was playing golf. Then when Lady Pilgrim asked if Patty had no friends, Patty broke into confidences about Helen.

Lady Pilgrim stopped, staring at the child.

'Helen! Helen *who*, did you say?'

'Miss Shaw. She was so sweet and I did love her,' said Patty with a deep sigh.

'Good gracious!' said Lady Pilgrim. 'I know Helen Shaw—very well indeed.'

Patty drew a breath of excitement.

'Oh, do you—my *Helen?* Oh, goody, *goody!*'

Then a few more questions and Monica Pilgrim was no longer in the dark. Of course, this was the child whom Helen had been looking after. Helen always wrote to Monica— at least once a month—she had told her about her job in the Wade household—and later of the strange resemblance of Mrs. Wade's fiancé to Christopher.

277

The memory of her dead son was a never—ending grief to Monica Pilgrim. Christopher had been everything to her. And she had approved so thoroughly of his choice when he became engaged to Helen Shaw. She, too, had loved Helen. But Monica Pilgrim was a woman of strong generous nature. She had been one of the first to counsel Helen not to let the bitter loss of Chris destroy her life's happiness.

'You are young. You must recover from this blow and meet and marry someone else,' she had said.

From the girl's letters, Monica Pilgrim judged that Helen was slow to forget, or replace their beloved Christopher.

What a coincidence, meeting this child! Lady Pilgrim was interested. She remembered now that Helen had hinted in her letters that she did not like her mother. Certainly from what she could glean from the little girl's chatter, Mrs. Wade seemed a selfish sort of mother; playing golf, out with young men, instead of amusing the poor child during her brief Christmas holidays.

Monica Pilgrim had received intimation from Helen during Christmas week that she had, as she drily put it, 'been sacked' by Mrs. Wade, and was now in Earl's Court, temporarily taking care of her aunt and an old lady who lived with her.

Patty began to question her new kind friend. Why had Helen left? Why had she broken her promise to spend Christmas with her and *why* didn't she write?

Lady Pilgrim gently answered each question in turn. She was positive, she said, that dear Helen had not forgotten Patty nor wilfully deserted her. It was just that Patty's mother had told her that her services were no longer required. Artlessly, the child exclaimed:

'Oh, Mummy said Helen walked out and was very mean because Mummy couldn't afford to give her more money. I knew it couldn't be true!'

Monica Pilgrim flushed. She was angry about that. She, too, knew it could not be true. It was quite out of keeping with Helen's generous character. But she said no more. She realized there was something peculiar about this whole business and that she was treading on delicate ground. She did not wish to discuss the matter with the small girl. She determined, however, to write to Helen at once and tell her what her late employer was saying about her to the child. Poor little scrap—how miserable and peaky she looked! A nice, affectionate little thing, too. It was a shame. Lady Pilgrim disliked Rita Wade before they ever met.

She was bent, however, on reassuring Patty that Helen still loved her, and when Patty asked why she supposed that Helen never answered her letters, Lady Pilgrim asked how she was addressing them.

Dolefully, the child confessed that her

279

mother would not give her the address but sent the letters on.

Monica Pilgrim pursed her lips. Then her sweet, rather lined face brightened.

'Never mind, my dear, if you've got another week in West Mayling, you'll see your precious Helen! She is coming down to stay with me at Petcombe Hall for the week-end, this very Saturday. I suppose she doesn't know where you are, but of course we're only two and a half miles from the 'Old Mill' and I'm sure she'll pop over to see her little friend. Mummy won't mind that.'

Patty was flung into a transport of happiness by this miraculous piece of news. She seized Lindy and skipped madly in circles round with the puppy who barked and wriggled and seemed to enjoy it.

Patty could hardly believe her luck. Helen— coming down here—to Petcombe—staying with this nice lady within walking distance of the Mill. Oh, what *fun!*

Just before they got back to the 'Old Mill', Monica Pilgrim could not forbear to question Patty Wade about Peter Farrington who so resembled her lost son.

All Patty could tell her was that 'Uncle Peter' was going to marry Mummy and be her new Daddy.

When they reached the house, Patty danced into her mother's bedroom and fetched a photograph of Peter which Rita now kept on her dressing—table. It was a splendid likeness, an enlarged snapshot of Peter in Nairobi, wearing an open—necked shirt, and riding breeches, standing by his horse.

'There's Uncle Peter!' said Patty.

Lady Pilgrim, who was standing in the oak—beamed, pretty visitor's lounge which was deserted at the moment, except for a maid laying tea, put on her horn-rimmed glasses and looked at the pictured face and figure. She received almost the same shock, the same poignant emotion, that had flooded Helen's soul on that night of meeting with Peter Farrington. She sat down sharply, her knees trembling. Her face had grown quite white. Her lips quivered.

'He is, indeed, like my son,' she whispered.

Then Rita Wade walked into the lounge. She looked flushed and excited and extremely lovely with a natural pink glow on her cheeks, eyes big and luminous. She carried a slip of paper in her hand. Oblivious of Monica Pilgrim's presence, she rushed up to her small daughter. She was in high spirits; quite changed from the sharp—tongued, nagging woman who had this morning condemned Patty to a lonely day.

'Patty—the most wonderful news!' she cried. 'I've just had a cable from Uncle Peter. He's leaving Nairobi today—*today*, Patty. He and Mrs. Farrington will be here in England before the week-end. We must tell Mrs.

281

Cowley and book rooms for them here at once.'

Patty suffered the kiss and embrace that followed, then in an embarrassed way, nudged her mother and indicated the woman on the sofa.

'Mummy—Mummy—this is my new friend, Lady Pilgrim, who lives in Petcombe,' she whispered.

Rita swallowed her excitement over the cable and at once turned a smiling face to the stranger. *Lady* Pilgrim—well—at least Patty had chosen sensibly for a change—and what tailoring—enviously Rita's expert eye roved over Monica Pilgrim's beautifully cut tweeds.

'How do you do. How nice of you to be kind to my little daughter,' she murmured in her sweetest way.

Gravely Monica Pilgrim looked into the dark, brilliant eyes; at the graceful figure; a shining curve of red hair escaping from the soft blue scarf swathing her head. A beauty, she thought—very much a beauty—but hard as nails. Instinctively Lady Pilgrim recoiled from all that charm. She put an arm around Patty whose gaze was fixed on her mother in an anxious uncertain way which Monica Pilgrim found pathetic.

'How do you do, Mrs. Wade,' she said.

Then Rita saw the photograph in her hand and stared. Her colour rose. Lady Pilgrim made haste to explain that she had asked Patty

282

to bring it.

'I had heard of Mr. Farrington's remarkable resemblance to my son, Christopher. Please forgive me for my curiosity.'

Rita went on staring. Then she said slowly:

'But how did you know about Peter—I don't quite understand—'

The child excitedly broke in:

'Helen used to be engaged to Lady Pilgrim's son, Christopher, Mummy. You remember—and Mummy, Helen's coming down to stay at Petcombe Hall with Lady Pilgrim this week-end. She'll be able to see me. Mummy, isn't that *wonderful?*'

CHAPTER TWENTY

Rita went positively white. For an instant she was too startled to do more than make the automatic gesture of patting the little girl on the head to quieten her, and muttering an unintelligible reply.

Lady Pilgrim saw for herself that Patty's mother was not pleased by the news that Helen Shaw was coming down here. She must dislike Helen very much. For the life of her Monica Pilgrim could not think why. She was the first to speak:

'Perhaps while Miss Shaw is with me, you would bring Patty over to tea, Mrs. Wade.'

Rita managed to find speech.

'Thank you—most kind of you. But we may not be here.'

That was a bombshell for Patty whose small excited face turned scarlet with disappointment

'Oh, but Mummy, *why?* I thought you were staying here until the end of my hols! Oh, *don't* let's go until Helen's been down. It's only a few days before the week-end!'

Rita managed to smile for Lady Pilgrim's benefit but her heart was pounding and her body trembling with anger. What a catastrophe! That *infuriating* Helen. Why on earth must she know intimately someone who lived so close to the 'Old Mill'? For a moment Rita dived wildly into a morass of thoughts and schemes, wondering if she could change her hotel, go farther from Petcombe before Helen came down. She did not want Helen to see any more of Patty. Still less did she wish her to come into contact with Pierrot again or anyone in the Farrington family. On the other hand, it would look most peculiar if she moved so suddenly. She would barely have time to make arrangements. Unless, of course, she took Patty up to London and met Pierrot up there. But then again, she was petrified of running into Nigel. That was the worst evil of all. And so far, since she had run away from him, he had not found her. Or at least, he had made no effort to do so. No, she was far safer down here in West Mayling.

Patty's childish treble pierced her frantic reflections.

'Do let us stay—*do* let me see Helen—why not—*why*? . . .'

Oh, the maddening child! Rita was in a state to swing round, scream at her and tell her to shut up. But she had to control herself in front of Lady Pilgrim. Shaking from head to foot, she murmured an excuse and bade Patty follow her to her rooms.

Lady Pilgrim sat down, one eyebrow raised. There was something very queer about that young woman. She could have sworn that a look of abject fear had dilated those big dark eyes—when Patty gave her the news about Helen. What *was* the matter? Monica was extremely curious to see Helen and question her about it. The person she was sorry for was Patty. That small freckled face looked so mortified, and she was struggling with her tears. When Rita turned away to walk across the lounge, Patty flew to her new friend's side and whispered to her urgently.

'Please, please, Lady Pilgrim, make Helen come and see me.'

'Don't worry. I'm sure she will.' The woman smiled kindly.

'But if Mummy takes me away . . .' Patty stopped and choked at the awfulness of such a thought.

Then Monica Pilgrim put an arm round the thin, quivering little figure and kissed her. She whispered:

'Don't you fret. You know where I live. You send a little note to Helen at Petcombe Hall and tell her where you get to—*if* Mummy has to move.'

Relieved and comforted, Patty darted away and joined her mother.

At Petcome that week-end, Helen learned within a very few moments of her arrival about the close proximity of her recent employer and little Patty.

As soon as the girl had taken off her things and was seated in front of the log fire with Christopher's mother, Lady Pilgrim began to relate the story of her meeting with Patty in the fields, and of the encounter with Mrs. Wade.

'I took the most violent dislike to her and I don't mind admitting it,' Lady Pilgrim said with a laugh, 'but the little girl is a darling and I don't wonder you got so attached to her, my dear.'

'Well, well!' said Helen, 'so that is where our Rita is hiding herself!'

Monica Pilgrim paused in the act of digging a needle into the tapestry on which she was working.

'So she *is* hiding from something or somebody? I was right!' she said eagerly. 'My dear, I assure you the woman looked positively frightened when Patty told her you were coming down here today.'

286

Helen nodded. She sat on a low stool before the fire, spreading her hands to the blaze. The firelight cast a glow on a face that was abnormally pale. She looked very tired. And Lady Pilgrim had already remarked how much too thin she was. But she had had a hard Christmas and New Year. First of all, the domestic work in the absence of Emily; then Aunt Mary in bed with a threatened bronchial attack; then a freeze—up of the pipes, a burst boiler, no hot water for days, everything possible to make more work and worry.

And all the time, the gnawing hunger in her heart for Peter, and disappointment over Patty's Christmas, from which she had not yet recovered.

Lady Pilgrim's news amazed and delighted her. It would really be a relief to be able to see the child and make sure that she was all right. On the other hand, she did not want to upset Patty or any other stories her mother had told her. She wanted to do what was best for the child. But it certainly was an unexpected surprise to learn that Rita had chosen West Mayling for her retreat.

Helen turned her fair graceful head and looked out of the window. It seemed so long ago, yet was such a short time since she had walked across those very fields from Petcombe to the 'Old Mill'—with Christopher.

She had not been down here for a long time because Christopher's old home used to remind her too painfully of those lost happy days. Yet now she could come here without the old pain *because he lived again in Peter*—and the voice of her heart cried for *Peter*. He, who was alive—so vividly alive—and who had brought life back to her. This afternoon it was of Peter she thought, sitting here with Christopher's mother. It gave her a queer delight to hear the older woman admit the remarkable resemblance between the two men.

'I was quite staggered when I saw the enlarged snapshot which Patty showed me. He might have been Chris's twin.'

Helen nodded, lacing her fingers together.

'Yes. An uncanny resemblance. Just one of those things! And yet when you see Peter Farrington in the flesh, you notice the little differences—for instance, the colouring—the shape of his nose—and Peter is taller.'

Lady Pilgrim sighed deeply and returned to her needlework.

'Rather too painful. I don't think I could *bear* to meet him.'

Helen bit her lip.

'You won't be likely to, Monica darling.'

'But I might, my dear, because Mr. Farrington is coming down to the 'Old Mill' this week-end unless that horrid Mrs. Wade changes her plans.'

Helen's head swung round. Her face and throat crimsoned. She stared at Lady Pilgrim.

'*Peter* coming to West Mayling? You mean he's back from Kenya?'

'Mrs. Wade had a cable the day I was there. She expects him and his mother today or tomorrow.'

Helen's heart was leaping. She turned back to the fire, but not before the older woman, who loved her and had known her for a long time, had caught that sudden vivid change in her.

'Why, Helen,' she said gently, 'have you let Mr. Farrington's likeness to our Chris affect you so much? Has he grown to *mean* something? Is that the real reason why you left Mrs. Wade?'

Helen's fair head dropped a little. For a moment she did not speak; struggling with her emotions.

At length she said:

'I admit that Peter means something to me, Monica. I never want to be anything but frank with you. You have always been so good to me ...' Involuntarily she reached out a hand. Lady Pilgrim laid aside her piece of tapestry and took the slim nervous hand between her warm fingers. Helen went on:

'But it's not because of that that I left Rita Wade. She asked me to go. But she hates me for all sorts of sinister, horrid reasons, things I know about her. Unfortunately they were told to me in confidence and so I can't repeat them. I hope you understand?'

289

'I quite understand that you would never betray a confidence, Helen,' said the older woman softly. 'Chris used to say that you were one of the few women in the world to whom one could entrust an important secret.'

Restlessly Helen drew away her fingers and laced them through her hair, face flushed, brows knit.

'Oh, I am so worried, Monica!'

'About Peter Farrington?'

'Yes.'

'I am not surprised. I quite dislike the thought of anybody resembling our darling Christopher marrying that odious creature.'

'She is very beautiful and she can be so charming . . . I can quite see how she "gets" the men. But Monica, she is wicked—unscrupulous—and Peter has another point in common with Chris. His simplicity. He really is a very simple, credulous person who would easily be caught by such fascination. One does disike the thought of him being so easily deceived.'

'Surely he can see *through* her!' said Lady Pilgrim drily.

Helen stared at the fire.

'I think he was beginning to . . . before he left England.'

Lady Pilgrim took off her horn-rimmed glasses and looked tenderly at the girl's drooping figure. Poor little Helen! She was changed . . .

290

'Helen, my dear, you will have to try and stop thinking about this young man,' Lady Pilgrim said in her quiet voice and picked up her tapestry and regarded it gravely. But she did not see the coloured wools with which she was working. Her eyesight was blurred by tears. It hurt her to know that this girl whom her son had loved should be faced with a new grief. It seemed so unfortunate.

After a moment Helen said:

'And, of course, I am worried to death about Patty.'

'And well you might be, with that apology for a mother, the poor wee thing! She made such a fuss of Lindy—she adores animals and it appears she adopted a stray mongrel which Mrs. Wade snatched away and had destroyed. It's had a bad effect on the child.'

'Typical of Rita,' said Helen darkly.

'And she misses you—talks of nothing else.'

'Poor Patty!'

'And that creature has told her a disgusting story about you leaving because you were so mean that you wouldn't accept a smaller salary.'

That brought an indignant exclamation from Helen. She rose to her feet and thrust her hands into the pockets of the cardigan she was wearing.

'How iniquitous! There was no question of salary in it. Rita gave me a moment's notice because she wanted me out of the way. And I

291

haven't communicated with Patty because I was asked not to, and, after all, Rita *is* her mother.'

'It appals me,' said Lady Pilgrim, 'that the wrong kind of women so often become mothers, and those best fitted for the role stay childless.'

Helen's thought focused upon the little girl whom she so genuinely loved.

'Monica,' she said, 'after what you have told me, I don't care whether Rita is her mother or not. Patty believed in me and my promises, and I refuse to let her think that I betrayed her out of sheer avarice. I am going to write a note to her, and perhaps you'd let Watkins run over with it when he goes down to the village in the morning.'

'Why not go over and see her yourself.'

Helen bit her lip and the colour rose to her cheeks again.

'Quite honestly, Monica, I don't want to come in contact with Rita. I wouldn't be able to keep from telling her what I think of her for putting over such an—an—*atrocious* story about me to that unfortunate child. And I—I don't particularly want to run into the Farringtons. What's the good?'

CHAPTER TWENTY-ONE

Peter Farrington and his mother did not reach London until twilight that afternoon. Mrs. Farrington had been tired by the long flight and wanted to meet her young daughter who had come up from Torquay to join them, so the family were reunited at Claridges Hotel, where they decided to stay the night.

The plane should have been in much earlier. Glenise had waited many hours at the airport. Rita had been on the telephone several times. She wanted them all to go straight down to West Mayling which was only an hour and a half's journey from Victoria. But the delay put an end to her hopes of seeing Peter that night.

She suffered one of her moments of frustration and annoyance which never improved her temper, when Peter telephoned to the 'Old Mill' and said that he would not be coming down with his family until the next morning.

'It's sickening, darling,' he said, 'but it can't be helped.'

She suggested that he should leave the two women and go down alone. That brought a very disappointing answer from Peter. He really could not leave his mother and young sister, he said. He must stay up here and bring his mother down to West Mayling tomorrow. He hoped Rita would understand.

She did not understand. She liked everybody to do what she wanted immediately and throw up all their other plans. She had no time for 'difficult old women' and she had dreaded, all the way along, that Peter's mother would be difficult and spoil things. She was furious because the dinner party she had arranged and all the hopes of seeing Peter tonight must be cancelled. However, with an effort at sweetness she assured Peter that it was 'quite all right', and that she looked forward immensely to seeing them in the morning.

'What's the earliest train you can catch?' she asked feverishly.

'Oh, my mother is an early riser so I dare say we will be down before eleven, darling. I'll look up the trains and phone you again.'

'Pierrot, it's absolutely *heaven* to have you back,' came her husky ardent voice.

Peter cleared his throat. He was not very good at expressing his intimate thoughts over a telephone. And he was uneasily aware that he could not answer Rita with a matching ardour. He struggled to make a suitable reply but was conscious that that husky voice of hers, which had once so fascinated him, scarcely moved him today. Also he felt very little thrill over this reunion which should have been so vivid and exciting after their long separation.

Her voice persisted.

'Do you love me as much as ever?'

He felt his cheeks burn. With a self-conscious laugh he answered:

'I'll tell you tomorrow.'

He hung up the receiver, moved out of the telephone kiosk and walked very slowly back to the lounge where he had left his mother and sister to order drinks. He paused a moment to light a cigarette. His hands were cold. It was perishing back here in London, he thought, and regretted the warm sunshine, and his home in Kenya. He felt depressed and unlike himself. There were so many things on his mind. And first and foremost there was *Helen.*

It had taken him that journey all the way to Nairobi and back again—during which time he had done a lot of thinking—to make him realize that it was not Rita whom he missed, but Helen.

And it was not Rita whom he wanted to see tonight. *It was Helen.*

He had been slow to make that discovery, but having discovered it, was filled with dismay. In Nairobi he had suffered more sleepless nights than he had ever known in his life. His mother had remarked that he was unlike himself. He had even lost his appetite. She had teased him, and had put it down to 'love'; to the fact that he was missing his future wife.

He had let her think it. He received all the

295

congratulations of his old friends in silence. He showed them Rita's photograph and tried to derive satisfaction from their flattering comments on her singular beauty.

But there remained in his mind and heart the inescapable realization that he no longer wanted to marry Rita, that he loved Helen Shaw.

All the time he was away, he was haunted by the thought of her—Helen, the good companion who loved the things he loved—Helen, with her sad grey eyes and courageous mouth—Helen, grieving for her dead love yet responding so sweetly to his efforts to help and restore her. Helen, working like a slave in that flat for Rita and little Patty. Always it was Helen, and the many intimate details about her, that he remembered. And when he wandered around his home, he wanted *her* there to share with him the sunshine, the flowers, the fruit, the good things that Nairobi offered. Even when he turned on his wireless and listened to a concert . . . one of the Tchaikovsky piano concertos which he and Helen had heard together in London—he was filled with nostalgia—with a peculiar, hungry need of her.

He knew definitely at last that he had missed the way—that his love for Rita Wade had been only a frightful infatuation, now fast dying—if not already dead. He loved Helen, and he believed that she loved him. She had

296

begun to love him because he resembled the man who had meant so much to her. But he knew that he could make her love him now for himself.

It was a terrible *dénouement*. He was appalled by the awfulness of it. He tried to tell himself that it was all a figment of his imagination. He reproached himself for disloyalty to Rita and did everything that he could think of to get Helen out of his mind. He had a lot of work to do in connection with his uncle's lawsuit, and he flung himself into it with an energy that worried his mother. She accused him of over—doing things.

'Your Rita won't forgive me if I take you back to her looking a wreck!' she had said on one occasion. That had drawn a faint smile from him but only made him more worried. Also he had begun to feel a hypocrite. He had always been great friends with his mother and yet now he could not confide in her. The situation was too difficult. He had pledged his word to Rita. He knew that she expected marriage the moment he got back. He decided that it would be impossible for him to sweep everything aside while he was here in Kenya, and give way easily to his persistent longing for Helen. He must go back and see Rita first. He tried to tell himself that he was a fool and a fickle one at that, just letting himself go to pieces. He had always been sorry for Helen. That was it!—connected with her in some queer intimate way because of his extraordinary likeness to that fellow she was going to marry—nothing more.

It wasn't love—it was just pity he felt for her. She was neither as beautiful nor as attractive as Rita. He was just being a b——y fool. He would forget her and carry on with his plans to marry Rita. Feverishly he wrote to her (although he could never answer her wild love letters in the same exaggerated terms). He ordered a specially lovely diamond ring for her. It was sent from Johannesburg, and set in a way which he thought would please her. And when he and his mother were offered seats for a flight returning to England at the end of the second week in January, he took them.

Long before he left Nairobi, however, fresh doubts assailed him. The slender appealing ghost of Helen haunted his working days and restless nights, and it seemed to him that she looked at him with wistful gaze and said:

'It is not pity you feel for me. It is love. And it is not Christopher whom I love, but you.'

He worked himself up into a bad mental state, and none of his old philosophies or the kind of psychology he had tried to teach Helen availed to unravel the tangle in his mind.

It was all worsened by the news that Glenise sent him of Helen's dismissal from Rita's employ.

His young sister wrote rather strongly on the subject.

'I know I oughtn't to say anything against Rita, but I do think she was jolly mean to Helen after all she had done for her and I know how Helen felt being turned out just before Christmas . . .'

Peter had been much distressed when he thought of Helen's spoiled Christmas. To him, too, it seemed an unnecessary and an unattractive action on Rita's part. Of course, once or twice in the past she had made it plain that she did not really care for Helen or fully appreciate her. And Glen's information scarcely tallied with Rita's. Rita had written a guarded note about Helen, saying she had left because she wanted more money, elsewhere, and suggesting that it had been a bit of a blow to her, Rita.

Not only was Peter worried about Helen's fate but once more dismayed by his own reaction to the thought that she would not be there when he got back. It made him realize how much he wanted to see her. Incidentally, the cold hard fact struck him that Rita was not telling the truth about the affair.

Peter knew his young sister. She was honest as daylight. Her information about Helen would be the truth. The truth which she in turn had got from Helen who was in touch with her. He believed that Rita was lying. And it was not the first time that he had found her out in a falsehood. He had long since reached the unpleasant conclusion that Rita was far from being wholly sincere or honest about things. He could never forget how secretive she had been about that child, in the first place.

Yet he knew that she loved him. He could not doubt the sincerity of her passion for him, which was overwhelming. He looked at the exquisite portrait of her constantly, seeking almost in a despairing fashion, by staring at that perfect face and form, to fan the flame of revival of his own idealistic belief and passion for her.

He took his mother to England with a heavy heart. And because he, himself, liked honesty, he decided that it was only fair to see Rita again before he did anything drastic. Then, if he really was convinced that he was doing the wrong thing in marrying her, he must have the courage to say so. That was what engagements were for—or should be for—a kind of trial—and if it didn't succeed one should have the right to back out. But it wasn't the sort of thing Peter Farrington liked doing. He could not bear to hurt anybody, especially a woman who loved and believed in him. He cherished a dismal hope that when he saw Rita again, everything would be as it used to be, and that the tormented and disquieting ghost of Helen would be banished.

All the same he felt as Glen felt—a sense of indignation on Helen's behalf at the treatment she had received from Rita, and he meant to tackle his fiancée about it.

Now that he was back, he had spoken to Rita and he knew for certain that he dreaded rather than looked forward to his meeting with her tomorrow. And he wanted to see Helen. In all London, she was the one person whom he ached to go and find.

A few words with young Glen told him her address. And Glen quickly suggested that they should look her up after 'Mummy went to bed' which Mrs. Farrington intended to do early.

Peter avoided his sister's gaze.

'Oh, I don't think so . . .' he said.

But his heart leapt in his breast at the thought of going to see Helen. Glen kept a wary eye on him. He looked tired and thin, for Peter, and not really well in spite of his tan. She was aware that he was a worried man. And she half guessed the truth. At least hoped it was the truth. She hoped that Peter would back out of this marriage with Rita Wade; she so cordially disliked her. She had told Mummy so as soon as they met and had a few moments alone. But Mrs. Farrington had said:

'Now, Glen, dear—this is Pierrot's affair and we mustn't interfere. I can't say I have ever been keen on his marrying a widow with an adopted child—nor the sort of glamour girl that Rita looks from her photos. But perhaps I am wrong, and I might like her very much.'

'I bet you won't!' said Glen bluntly.

And she had every intention of interfering. But Peter decided not to go and see Helen. So Glen, herself, went in search of her. While Peter was smoking his after—dinner cigar, talking to an associate in the lounge, Glen slipped away and took a taxi to the address in Earl's Court. She returned to Claridges half an hour later, in a high state of excitement, with the news, given her by Helen's aunt, that Helen was in Petcombe for the week-end or perhaps longer.

'I asked Mrs. Shaw where that was and what do you think she said?' Glen exclaimed to her brother breathlessly. 'She said that Petcombe is next to West Mayling. That's where *we* are going. So Helen will be only two or three miles away from us, Peter!'

Peter could not altogether conceal the fact that he was deeply interested in this news, but he waved his cigar airily at Glen and said:

'You run up and see if Mummy wants anything, and don't look at me like that, you little devil. What are you trying to do? Start something?'

'Yes!'

Glen's eyes danced at him.

'You're a little devil,' he repeated with a short laugh, but his pulses were jerking. It was good to know that Helen would be down there—both good news and bad—for it was bound to cause trouble if he went on feeling about her as he did now.

'Oh, Lord!' he thought, and groaned aloud. *'What a hellish muddle it all is and what an imbecile I was in Paris!'*

Glen came down to the lounge again to tell him that his mother wished him to go up and say good night to her.

Peter had been glad that she had consented to take this holiday with him and Glenise in England. But as he looked at her tonight, and met her grave tender gaze, his heart sank at the thought of tomorrow. Now that he was actually about to introduce her to Rita, he realized how little she was going to like his choice.

Ann Farrington reached out a hand to her son. For a moment she toyed with it, seriously regarding the long brown fingers. She loved her son very dearly. She had always felt close to him. But this engagement of his had troubled her not a little from the start. It had come between them just a bit. She was not a possessive mother. She wanted both her children to marry, and be as happy as she had been with their father. But she did so hope they would make the right choice.

Suddenly she said:

'Pierrot, tell me about Helen.'

Peter's handsome head shot up. She saw the red blood burn his cheeks, and in a flash all was made clear to her. Her heart sank . . . for him . . . So *that* was it! It was this girl, of whom she had heard such glowing accounts from

303

Glen, whom her son really loved.

'Tell me about her, darling,' she persisted gently.

Peter let go of his mother's hand, and stood up. With set lips he began to pace the bedroom. In a low voice, he said:

'You always hit on the truth with me, don't you?'

She followed the tall nervous figure with her fond gaze.

'I hope so. I love you very much.'

He swung round and faced her, brows fiercely knit.

'I could tell you a lot about Helen. She is a very unusual and very lovely person. Not so lovely physically; I mean, she hasn't Rita's incredible figure and looks, and yet she is lovely; very fair, very sweet, with the most marvellously expressive grey eyes. Sad eyes. She has had a hell of a grim time. She was going to be married and her fiancé died of infantile paralysis. He looked exactly like me, I have seen his photographs. Mums, I have made a fool of myself, and quite frankly, I don't know what to do.'

Ann Farrington drew a deep breath. Now it was all out, thank God! She leaned back on her pillows. She said:

'Stop pacing up and down like a caged tiger, Pierrot. Light your pipe and come and sit down on my bed and let's talk. No—you needn't worry about keeping me up. I can

304

sleep late tomorrow. I am not going down to West Mayling. I am going to let you go alone. I shall stay here for a few days with Glen. Then if you send for me I will come. And if you don't—I won't. But if things are wrong and there are adjustments to be made, it will be less embarrassing for you to have me out of the way.'

Peter, with a burning face, dropped on to the bed, picked up his mother's hand again and put it against his cheek. He looked frantically worried, she thought, just as he used to look when he was a small boy, facing some tremendous problem—coming to her for help.

'What a wonderful woman you are!' he said in a low voice, 'you always seem to do and say the right thing.'

She gave him the quick, sweet smile which she had bequeathed to him.

'Stop flattering your old mother and get on with telling me about Helen,' she said.

But telling his mother about Helen, although it relieved and comforted him, by no means solved the problem of having to face Rita. He loved Helen and he told his mother so but he was still engaged to Rita . . . still owed her some loyalty. Even though Mrs. Farrington agreed that the only course that he should take was a frank and open one. He must tell Rita his change of feelings and ask for his freedom.

Going down in the train alone to West

Mayling that next day—a crisp cold Sunday morning, bright with wintry sunshinehe thought of one thing his mother had said:

'Don't be quixotic and marry a woman you don't love, my dear; that would be unfair to both of you. It would never make *her* happy either—especially if you think that this girl, Helen, is really the ideal you have been looking for.'

He knew that she was right. And that Helen *was* the ideal woman whom he had been unconsciously seeking. Whereas the Rita he first met in Paris had been only an illusion—someone who did not really exist, in whose place remained a beautiful, spoiled, selfish and difficult person.

But none of these reflections made his task seem easier. To jilt a woman at the eleventh hour seemed a dastardly thing to do. Rita could not help her faults, and she still loved him, he brooded unhappily. As for Helen, she did not even know how he felt about her. And if and when she knew, she might not want anything but the desultory friendship she had given him before. She might be horrified by his change of front and despise him for walking out on Rita. Oh, it was a hell of a problem and he could not begin to share his mother's belief that everything would 'come right'. It did not seem to him this morning that anything could come right again.

It was a very dubious and unhappy Peter

who stepped out of the train at West Mayling station and saw Rita standing there on the platform, eagerly searching the passing carriages for him. Then when she saw him, she rushed towards him with a transfigured face which only added to his misery. She looked so beautiful in her short fur jacket, a jaunty feathered cap on the back of her head; and so delighted to see him, coming towards him with a fervent light of welcome in her eyes.

How the devil was he going to break with her now?

CHAPTER TWENTY-TWO

Rita was in a state of feverish excitement. She almost threw herself into Peter's arms. Then she remembered to be a woman of the world and not an hysterical schoolgirl and just gave him both hands and said in her poignant and husky voice: 'Pierrot! At last!'

Even that was too dramatic for him. He flushed uncomfortably but returned the pressure of her hands.

'Well, Rita dear—how are you?'

She put an arm through his and they walked out of the station to the old car which Rita had hired to meet him. As they got inside it and the driver put in Peter's suitcase and slammed the door, Rita sat back and examined him with her hungry gaze.

He looked more attractive and handsome to her than ever with his newly deepened tan and the rich glow of health on that fine alert face of his. But she felt her heartbeats slow down at his lack of spontaneous enthusiasm or response to her welcome. What was the matter? she asked herself fearfully. Pierrot, on the phone last night, had worried her. She had hoped that that was only the outcome of nerves and that when she saw him today he would be the same ardent lover about whom she had been so crazy that she had sacrificed truth, honour, and integrity; even her own child.

Peter, embarrassed and conscious of his changed feelings, stretched his long legs, pulled a pipe from his pocket and began to fill it, while he looked out at the country-side. They were driving away from the station and into open country. Sussex was lovely on a fresh morning like this with the sunlight sparkling on hoar-rimmed trees and bushes, and in the distance the faint outline of the downs; a belt of dark fir trees against a cloud-flecked sky.

'A real English scene,' he said, sticking the pipe into his mouth, 'and very different from the country I've just left. I'd like it, if it wasn't so cold.'

But Rita did not want him to talk about the country-side. She wanted him to take her in his arms. She wanted to be kissed and reassured that all was well between them. A horrible sinking sensation replaced her enthusiasm at meeting him, and the spurious sense of joyous youth which had accompanied it.

'How far is the "Old Mill"?' continued Peter, with that new formality which so alarmed and disappointed her.

'Only a mile or two,' she said, then added: 'Oh, Pierrot, Pierrot, my *darling . . . !*'

She thrust her hands into his, unable to control her longing, and drew closer to him.

He bit his lip, avoided looking into the melting dark eyes, and glanced uncomfortably at the driver's back.

With a gesture he indicated that they were not alone.

'I don't care,' Rita whispered recklessly, 'you must kiss me—you must . . .'

It was queer and far from agreeable, he thought, how stone cold those advances from her left him. Indeed, he was even repelled, this morning, by the beauty, the exotic perfume, all the glamour surrounding Rita. He had never felt less in love with her. Most definitely, he did not want to kiss her. At the back of his mind, he knew it was all over between them. Even the regret he had momentarily felt when he first caught sight of her had vanished; given place to the impatient wish to get the matter over quickly. *It was Helen he wanted to see.* If he felt any excitement it was because he knew that Helen was down here, staying, so Glen had told him, in a neighbouring village.

But Rita still wore the ring that he had given her and thought herself his promised wife. That thought devastated him. His natural kindness and generosity of nature, however, induced him to put an arm around her and touch her lips with his. He had meant it to be a light kiss but she clung to him fiercely, whispering again and again:

'Pierrot, oh, my darling . . . !'

He grew scarlet, then at last put her away from him, pulled out his handkerchief and wiped his lips. To cover the embarrassment of the moment, he laughed.

'Pretty startling colour, your new lipstick, isn't it?' and he looked at his stained handkerchief and laughed again.

She grew ice-cold. She felt as though a knife had been put through her heart—that sensual greedy heart which knew so little pity or kindliness towards others. And it was from that moment that retribution came upon Rita Wade, and her punishment began.

Thoroughly nervous herself now, she tried to veil her confusion by chattering feverishly during the rest of the drive. She gave him little chance to reply—telling him about West Mayling, the golf course, how she was reducing her handicap, how they must play together, and so on. But all the time she was remembering, aghast, the coldness of his kiss—the reluctance of his caresses.

He listened to her spate of words, relieved that she no longer wished to be emotional but still unhappy, contemplating the awkwardness of the approaching moment in which he must disclose his change of feelings and ask for his release.

Then he heard her say, suddenly:

'But Pierrot—good gracious!—it's only just struck me—where are your mother and Glen?'

'My mother is rather tired after the long flight. She decided to stay at the hotel for the moment, and Glen is staying with her. I hope it won't put them out too much in your guest house.'

She sat silent, clenching and unclenching her long fingers. It was not that she minded in the least that Mrs. Farrington had elected to stay in town with Glen—all the better if she could have Pierrot to herself—but it worried her—things were not going according to plan and she sensed danger in every change.

She heard Peter say:

'How's the little girl? Is she with you on her school holidays?'

'Yes.'

He longed to ask Rita to tell him, face to face, why she had dismissed Helen, but couldn't bring himself to utter that name.

Then they reached the 'Old Mill'.

For a moment, Peter was able to be quite natural in his appreciation of the beautiful old house with its roof of Horsham slab—stone,

311

yellow with lichen, its Elizabethan rosy bricks, the diamond—paned casement windows. Then the disused mill itself, the gushing waterfall, the old-fashioned garden flanked by many beautiful old trees.

'What a gem of a place!' he exclaimed.

'Oh, yes, it's sweet!' said Rita, 'not a bit like an hotel. Real country life and they've built a sun-loggia for the guests, on the other side.'

She took his arm, as though anxious to draw near to him again, and walked up the flagged path into the house. Seeing Mrs. Cowley, the manageress, in the hall, she straightway introduced Peter.

'My fiancé—oh, Mrs. Cowley, Mrs. Farrington and Miss Farrington can't get down today, but please keep the rooms,' she said.

'They won't want the rooms,' thought Peter, 'Mother and Glen will never come down here now . . .'

But he said nothing.

He had meant to tell Rita at once what lay in his mind but she made it almost impossible for him. Now Patty appeared and Rita immediately assumed a 'fond mother' attitude to impress him. She whispered gaily:

'Here comes my little adopted daughter— bless her!'

Peter, who was devoted to children, had a warm natural welcome for the small girl whose plain freckled face rather appealed to him. He liked the friendly smile with which she advanced towards him.

'Oh, hallo, Uncle Peter!'

'She'll soon have to learn to call you "Daddy" won't she, Pierrot?' put in Rita eagerly.

He felt his ears burning. This was the most damnably difficult business, he told himself. But he could not say 'No' there and then. He talked a few moments to the child. Rita said:

'Now, Patty, run away, darling. Take a little walk or something, because Mummy wants an hour to herself before lunch.'

Mrs. Cowley called from her private room:

'May I just speak to you for a moment about the reservations for your friends, Mrs. Wade.'

Rita was forced to comply with this request.

For a moment Peter stood alone with young Patty.

'Well, infant, how's school?' he asked with a smile.

Patty wrinkled her nose.

'Jolly awful.'

'Never mind. I didn't like mine either but you get used to it. And the holidays are fun down here in this lovely place, I bet!'

Patty glanced round, made sure her mother was out of earshot, then slid a confiding hand into Peter's. She whispered:

'Oh, but everything's different because Helen isn't with me any more. Oh, Uncle Peter, can't *you* ask Mummy to have Helen back?'

The man reddened.

'Well, that's rather awkward, honey—'

'She's quite near here, Uncle Peter. She's staying with Lady Pilgrim, in Petcombe—I know—Lady Pilgrim told me—but I haven't seen Helen yet, because Mummy won't let me. Oh, Uncle Peter, please, *please* . . .'

She broke off. She saw her mother rapidly returning. She dropped Peter's hand, her small face scarlet and frightened.

Peter saw the look of fear in Patty's blue eyes and was suddenly shocked by it. It was so palpable, it could not be mistaken. In Heaven's name, was she *afraid* of Rita? he wondered:

Patty escaped. Rita drew Peter into the newly-built loggia in which there were basket-chairs and tables. Through the long plate-glass windows, they could see the pretty walled-in garden sloping down towards a stream. In the middle of the lawn stood an old chipped-stone bird bath. One or two robins were shaking their wings in the water; the drops glistened like diamonds it the sun.

Peter strolled to the window and looked out upon this rustic scene, pipe between his teeth, brows knit. He had never felt more worried or miserable.

He felt Rita's hand on his shoulder.

'Pierrot—what was Patty asking you so passionately to do' I only caught the words *"Please, please"* . . .'

Then Peter put the pipe in his pocket,

314

turned and lookec straight down into that beautiful made-up face. He decided to be frank now, at all costs.

'Patty was asking me to persuade you to have Helen back,' he said quietly.

'The little *devil*,' she muttered.

'You can't be cross with her for that.'

'But I can. She has been forbidden to worry me about Helen any more, and she has no right to appeal to you.'

'It was quite natural. Any child would have done the same.'

Rita's heart beat suffocatingly fast.

'Well, I have no intention of having Helen back. So that's that. I won't do it even if *you* ask me, Pierrot.'

'I haven't asked you, Rita. It's not my business. But it seems a bit hard to have cut off the child so completely from someone she loved and trusted. I never quite understood why you got rid of Helen.'

'I didn't. She gave me notice because she wanted more money.'

Peter raised his brows.

'It's all very mystifying to me. She wrote— quite a completely different story to Glen.'

Rita caught her breath. Under the delicate rouge, her face was livid. She was trembling with nerves and anger. She would like to give Patty a sound thrashing for mentioning that wretched girl's name when her back was turned, and starting all this. Out of control for a moment, she flashed:

'You say it isn't your business, and it isn't, and after all Helen Shaw was merely an employee of mine. I don't see why it should concern you one way or the other whether she stays in my employ or not.'

'That's quite so, Rita. Let us drop the subject,' said Peter coldly.

But she was still angry and apprehensive.

'You and Glen are both mistaken in Helen's character,' she continued foolishly. 'I found out all sorts of things after you left. She wasn't nearly as angelic as she made herself out to be.'

Egged on by this, Peter said:

'Helen never tried to appear angelic, in my estimation. She was always genuine and I am sure she was devoted to you and Patty.'

'Oh, she isn't worth arguing about!' flashed Rita. 'Why, anybody would think we were quarrelling about her, and on your first day back. Good *heavens!*' She broke off and swallowed hard. Then she moved close to Peter, her lips and eyes softening.

'Pierrot, darling—darling—don't let the thought of Helen Shaw spoil our first few moments together. Oh, darling, isn't it wonderful that we are together again—that now we can go ahead and make our plans to get married and never be parted again?'

He had no answering warmth on his face. He felt that he had swung from the heat of infatuation to the coldness of complete indifference—and even dislike for Rita. Yes— he positively disliked her because of the things she had just said about Helen. Things which he knew intuitively to be lies. He said:

'Rita, I want you to sit down a moment and talk to me. No—don't try and kiss me, please. We've got to have a talk. A very serious one. But I want you, please, to be reasonable and make it easy for me. Because what I'm going to say, I shall not find too easy.'

He beckoned her to a chair. She did not take it. She felt a strange giddiness, a sickness that was of the spirit rather than of the body, as she looked at Peter's face, at the hardness and sternness of those clean-cut lips, and listened to his emotionless voice. It was as though she read therein her impending doom.

'No, no!' she said, more to herself than to him. 'No, I won't listen—'

'Come and sit down, Rita, please,' he pleaded.

But once again, Rita Wade resorted to lies—to the acting of a part—for whatever she guessed he was about to say to her—*she would not face up to it now*. She must see more of him first be given a chance to exercise her charms all over again. She could do nothing now; she could see that . . . he was in no mood for charm or physical contact. There was something deadly and purposeful in the calm way he looked at and spoke to her. She put two hands to her head.

'Pierrot—I feel ill—I didn't tell you at once—but I've been having fainting attacks—oh, Pierrot, hold on to me!'

He sprang to her side. She did, indeed, look so white in that moment that he could believe her story. She collapsed into his arms.

'Ask them—to get me—some brandy—take me—to my room. Please, Pierrot.'

And after that she shut her eyes and gave every semblance of being in a dead faint. That, of course, defeated Peter. A man could hardly break an engagement with an unconscious woman He called for Mrs. Cowley, who came running out and, in her turn, sent for a woman who worked in the guest house. Between them they carried Rita into her room.

'Poor thing!' exclaimed Mrs. Cowley. 'I'll ring up the doctor.'

But Rita, hearing that word, flickered her long lashes and whispered that she was better and did not need a doctor; all that she wanted was an hour on her bed. It was only a passing faintness, she was sure.

Before Peter left her, she gave him an agonized look, clinging convulsively to his hand.

'I'm sorry, darling—I didn't mean this to happen—don't be cross,' she whispered.

He bent over her.

'Of course I'm not cross—I'm sorry you're ill, my dear—'

'Pierrot—everything is all right, isn't it . . . ?' she panted.

That put him in a quandary again. He stammered:

'Now just lie there and be quiet. We'll talk later. I'll go for a walk until you have quite recovered.'

Because Mrs. Cowley was there, fussing around her bedroom, Rita had no alternative but to let Peter go. She felt that she had warded off something that threatened her whole life's happiness, but that it was only a temporary respite. Once she was alone, ,she pressed her handkerchief to her lips, her whole body shaken as though with fever. Her forehead was wet. She felt blind panic. She thought:

'He doesn't love me any more. He won't marry me now. That's why his mother hasn't come down. He's changed his mind. It has something to do with Helen—oh, my God! my God! I can't stand *that!'*

She turned her face to the pillow to stifle the sound of the hiccuping sobs that suddenly tore her body, choking her.

The wildest possible ideas swept through her brain. If Peter started to ask for his release, she would refuse to give it. She would threaten to kill herself. She would appeal to everything in him that was kind or generous. She would not let him escape her. *She would not.* At all costs, she would make him see that he must go through with their marriage now . . . or be her murderer.

And while these extravagant notions were chasing through Rita's mind, Peter put on his hat and coat, and walked into the garden.

He felt sick at heart. He wished he had never come down to West Mayling. It needed some courage, he thought bitterly, for a chap to deal with a person like Rita. She made things as difficult as she could. Why had he not realized her true nature right at the start; seen what a self-centred, hysterical creature she really was? Why had he ever let himself be blinded by her superficial glamour?

Mingled with his bitterness was the ever-growing knowledge of his love for Helen Shaw. The very mention of that name between Rita and himself—his resentment when Rita spoke ill of her—had proved to him yet again the change that had been wrought in him—by Helen.

He walked some way down the frost—hardened road, the cold air stinging his face, his thick hair lifting a little in the wind.

He came to a cross—roads, and suddenly noted the signpost. It said: *To Petcombe.*

He stopped dead. Suddenly he knew that he must take that road. He must see Helen. He would leave Rita to recover from her fainting fit and go back later. But he must see Helen first. *He must.*

CHAPTER TWENTY-THREE

Helen was taking Lindy for a walk that Sunday morning.

She had deliberately avoided going across the fields to West Mayling Mill, but she could not avoid walking down this road which would eventually reach the village, because any other route would lead her on to the busy main road to East Grinstead and that was a death trap for a small dog, especially at weekends.

Needless to say, Helen was thinking of Peter. She presumed that he had arrived at the 'Old Mill'. Last night she had slept fitfully, unable to banish the tantalizing memory of him. She viewed his forthcoming marriage with deepest concern, in addition to her personal longing to see him. Yet her hands were tied. She could do nothing but wish that she did not *know* that he was so close to her and—no doubt—in Rita's arms again.

After a while she slackened her pace and strolled along, her gaze fixed thoughtfully on the road. It was then she heard approaching footsteps, looked up and saw a man swinging along down the narrow little by-road. She stopped dead, every nerve in her body tingling. Her heart gave a tremendous leap. The burning colour flooded her face. She called out his name:

'*Peter!*'

He had seen her now. He hesitated for the fraction of second, then almost ran towards her; delight, surprise, relic many varying expressions darting across his face.

'Helen!' he exclaimed.

And now that he saw her again, after the long separation, he knew that his ever-increasing fondness for her amounted to soul-hunger which could be assuaged only by the actual sight of her and the sound of her voice. His ravished gaze swept from the top of that fair charming head to the small feet in their tan suede walking shoes. Then up to her face again—into eyes whicht were so brilliant with pleasure that he could not doubt what the meeting meant to *her*.

In an agony of embarrassment, just because the sight of him roused such an emotional storm in her, Helen began to stamm trite commonplace words. 'What a coincidence meeting on this road,' she said. 'How brown you look—how well—' anything to relieve the tension, although she did not know what she was saying. Here he was, standing before her again; this dear and most endearing Peter—this replica of the unforgotten Christopher who had walked this same road at her side so gaily in days gone by.

She wanted to burst into tears and throw herself into Peter's arms.

He put an end to what she was saying, to

those efforts to turn this into an ordinary encounter. She looked so adorable in her confusion, and so frankly pleased to see him, that he lost his head. And then it was all as she wanted, but had not dared hope for. She was caught close to him. He gave a muffled cry, his lips against the pale gold silk of her hair.

'Darling—Helen—Helen!'

Earth and sky seemed to melt into one and the wintry world revolved around her. This was undreamed—of ecstasy . . . the frantic passion of his arms straining her to his breast. They were alone on that small deserted road, save for the little puppy which found a gap in the hedge and scrambled through, yelping, in merry chase of a rabbit. Helen heard nothing, saw nothing, except the ardent flame in Peter Farrington's eyes just before he kissed her.

There was no more resistance left in her during that long and hungry kiss. She was utterly in love and gloriously released and happy. She could not begin to reason why this should have happened, why he should feel like this about her. She did not want to think—she had done too much thinking in the bitter loneliness of the years since Christopher's death. She wanted to *feel*—this splendid unleashed emotion, in the closeness of Peter's embrace.

It was some little time before he could bring himself to speak and risk spoiling the enchantment of this moment. Helen was no longer the cool calm aloof girl whom he had first known, she was a warm-blooded, passionate woman, her lips honey-sweet and responsive to his kisses. Her strong slim hands were locked about his neck. He could not doubt that she loved him. And what he felt for her was an emotion so far removed, so much more powerful and poignant than the brief passion Rita had awakened in him, that he was astonished. He had not thought it possible to feel as intensely as this about anyone in the world. He stood holding Helen a little away from him now, looking down to those wonderful grey eyes which had haunted him all the time he was away. They were no longer tragic, lost or lonely, as they had been on the first night that he had ever looked into them; when she had thought he was Christopher's ghost. They were as he had always wanted to see them . . . shining with happiness.

'Oh, Helen, Helen!' he said, 'I love you so much. So very much, my darling.'

That declaration, frank, simple, typical of him, was almost as intoxicating to Helen as his kisses.

'But why—why—oh, when did you first know?' she asked, stammering.

'After I left you, Helen. All the time I was in Kenya. I've tried to deceive myself into thinking otherwise, but I couldn't. I knew that I loved you. I knew that I wanted to come back to England only because you were here.'

She shook her head speechlessly. Her whole body was trembling. She was still in a state of such exaltation that she saw his lean brown face, his handsome ardent eyes, through a kind of haze. He gripped both her arms, drawing her nearer to him again.

'Helen, you love me too, don't you?'

'Yes, Peter. I ought not to, but I do.'

'And when did *you* first know?'

'Long before you left. I can't exactly tell you when. But I suppose everything has led up to it—it was inevitable.'

He nodded slowly.

'Yes, it was inevitable.'

'And yet I tried not to, because of—because of . . .' she broke off, unwilling to break the spell of the moment by mentioning that dreaded name.

But it had to be spoken. And now suddenly Peter let Helen go, groped in his pocket and pulled out a packet of cigarettes. Despite the frosty coldness of the day, little beads of perspiration were running down his cheeks. He wiped them away with a handkerchief, then gave a brief boyish laugh.

'I feel as though we have both been swept by a tornado. Let's have a cigarette and calm down, darling. We have such a lot to talk about.'

She echoed the laugh and took a cigarette from him. Then, by mutual consent, both of them smoking, they started to walk side by side down the road in the direction of Petcombe. The spell had broken—yes—Helen knew that—and some of her first tremendous happiness was fading—the very thought of Rita had spoiled everything. Although, she told herself, nothing, *nothing*, could ever take away the memory of this meeting with Peter, and the mutual spontaneity of their embrace, of their long, feverish, wonderful kisses. Nothing could alter the fact that they loved each other. Whether rightfully or wrongfully, *he* had said so. That, in itself, Helen reflected, was a miracle which even the existence of Rita could not change.

But she had come back to earth, and had to remember mundane things like Monica's dog.

'Oh, goodness, I mustn't lose Lindy,' she said, with a little laugh, and for the next few moments they were busy whistling, calling, searching for the truant Corgi. They both descended quite a long way from the pinnacle of white-hot emotion. Once having found Lindy, they walked, hands locked, slowly along the road. Helen listened while Peter told her all that was in his heart and mind.

Gradually some of her warm exaltation returned as she heard Peter candidly admit that he no longer loved Rita and that he did not intend to marry her.

'It's given me more than one headache and I feel a cur about it, but there it is, Helen darling. As my mother said, when we talked things over last night for the first time, an engagement should be a period of trial, and one doesn't always make the right and wise choice the first time. What I've felt for Rita has been an infatuation, a strong one for a time. I admit I thought her absolutely wonderful. But I made a mistake. It would be senseless to try to reason out the whys and wherefores. But I just stopped caring for her that way. And once infatuation dies, there is nothing left. I realized that when I saw her again this morning. She is beautiful, unique in her way, I suppose, but I don't love her any more, and I know now that I never did.'

Helen was silent. Her pulses were thrilling and her whole body tingled as she listened to Peter. It was such a crazy relief to know that he felt like this and that he was not going to be further deceived or victimized by Rita, that she could not find words to express it.

Peter continued:

'I don't think it was only meeting you that made me aware of my mistake, although, of course, it must have played a subconscious part. Even while I was still deluded into thinking I wanted to marry Rita, I must have known that *you* were the one I always wanted. But there are other factors. When I saw Rita in London again, she seemed different from the girl I met in Paris. I noticed alterations in her manner and habits. She produced traits of character which I did not like. To me, personally, she had always been charming, but I did not find her treatment of you at all attractive nor her outlook on a number of things. I was upset, quite frankly, by the sudden way she produced that adopted daughter. I couldn't understand why she behaved in Paris as though she had no child. And then, at times, she seemed so neurotic— so artificial—oh, I don't know, Helen, she just turned out to be a completely different being from the woman I imagined and whom I wanted for a wife.'

Helen, listening intently, nodded. She understood everything so well—she who had seen and heard, while Peter was still blind and deaf to the true Rita. At length she said:

'So you're quite sure you don't want to marry her now?'

'Quite sure,' he said, and stopped, and taking her by the hands, looked searchingly down into her eyes. 'How could I marry her, when I love you so much? It wouldn't be doing the right thing for any of us. I think my mother has convinced me of that. I came down to West Mayling today to break my engagement.'

Helen caught her breath.

'And have you broken it?'

'Not yet,' he said with a slight frown, and recounted the story of Rita's fainting fit. 'She makes it so damn difficult, but when I get back—when she is better—I shall tell her, Helen.'

Helen curled her lip. Rita's fainting fit! Another of her dramatic ruses. Typical of Rita. With something like fear in her heart, Helen said:

'Oh, Peter, she'll never let you go. She'll hang on to you if she possibly can.'

The grip of his hands tightened reassuringly.

'She can't. She may make it awkward for me, but I must be free. I *must*, feeling as I do about you.'

'I want you to be free,' she said breathlessly. 'Oh, Peter, my darling, *darling* Peter, I want you to be free from *her.* Whatever you feel about me.'

'I love you. You know that.'

She shut her eyes, clinging blindly to his hands.

'Yes.'

'Nothing can separate us now. But I shall be quite frank with Rita. Mind you,' he added, 'I wish to God I hadn't got to hurt her. She is so convinced that she still wants to marry me, and that it's all settled. It's hellish hard for a chap to have to do a thing like this. Of course, I blame myself entirely. I shouldn't have let it all go so far. Somehow, the whole thing seemed to get out of my control.'

Now Helen opened her eyes and looked up at him indignantly.

'She did not *want* you to control it. She did not want you to have breathing space. I—oh, I—' She shook her head. 'I mustn't say any more. It's between you and Rita. I have no right to interfere.'

He lifted her right hand up to his lips.

'Darling, there is no question of you interfering. We must talk things over.'

'I don't want to say too much—until you have seen her again.'

'You don't like Rita, do you?'

'No.'

'Tell me why.'

She flushed and tried to draw her fingers away from his.

'I'd rather not—'

'There is something I don't know. Something in Rita's past?'

'Don't ask me, please. I was foolish enough once to try and become Rita's friend and she confided in me. Even now I don't want to break that confidence.'

'But you do know something about her. Something you don't think I should like.'

'Please, don't question me, Peter!' Helen pleaded.

'All right, darling, it doesn't really matter. It's all ending, anyhow.'

'Thank God,' said Helen under her breath.

Peter stared perplexedly across the sunlit fields. He said

'She's a queer mixture—she seems to have such a generous side to her. Why else would she have adopted a kid like Patty?'

The old burning contempt for Patty's

mother surged through Helen. It was on the tip of her tongue to tell him the truth about that 'adoption', yet still she felt that she had no right. She said:

'Go back and see Rita. Until you have told her that you want to be free I shall not feel any peace of mind.'

'I'll go,' he said, 'but first of all I must hear you tell me again that you love me.'

'Oh, Peter, you know that I do!'

Once more she was in his arms, reaching her lips upward for his kiss. Then she hugged him close and whispered:

'Come and see me later, or telephone. I'll meet you somewhere. But go back to Rita now, please, darling.'

'I know what I'm going to do,' he said, suddenly.

'What?'

'Get that kid, Patty, over to see you somehow or other. She's breaking her heart for you.'

The tears sprang into Helen's eyes.

'Yes—do try and do that,' she said, *that*, most of all.'

Then she picked the puppy up in her arms and walked quickly away from him.

Peter watched her out of sight. Then he, too, turned and began to walk quickly back to the 'Old Mill'. He was returning to a disagreeable task. But he felt that nothing on earth could prevent him now from severing the last tie with Rita. He walked like a man on air, still thrilling from Helen's kisses. This was the love he had always wanted. This was the girl whom he could take proudly to his mother—present to her as his future wife.

But there was still Rita . . .

When he reached the 'Old Mill' he was given a message by Mrs. Cowley that Mrs. Wade was up in her room and wished him to go up and speak to her as soon as he came back.

With a sinking heart Peter walked up to Rita's bedroom. So there had to be another showdown! Helen had been right—Rita meant to hang on—

He did not know whether to be contemptuous of or sorry for her, when at length he saw her again. She was nothing like the soignée, seductive Rita who used to fire his senses. Her red hair was dishevelled, her face blotched with violent weeping. She sat up in bed, as soon as she saw him, and treated him to an hysterical outburst. He had changed, she sobbed. She had been thinking things over, and come to the conclusion that he had changed. But she would never give him up.

'You belong to me, Pierrot, and I to you,' she panted, trying to hold on to his hands. 'I've given up everything for you—all my other friends—my whole life—you *can't* walk out on me now.'

Sick at heart, he tried to calm her.

'Rita, dear—*please*—'

'You've been to see that girl—it's Helen who has put you against me!' Rita said wildly.

'Rita, please let us discuss things quietly.'

'You have seen Helen—she has put you against me!' repeated Rita.

'I have seen her but she said nothing about you—absolutely—nothing—'

'Yes, Pierrot, I know! You want to break with me because of her!'

'Rita, my dear, I've *got* to break with you. Not only because of Helen. Because of *myself.* Oh, try not to make it so hard for me, Rita.'

She fell back on the pillows, covering her eyes with her hands.

'If you leave me, now, I shall kill myself,' she said, in a voice of abject despair.

Shocked to the core, he stood up.

'Rita, you have no right to say such a terrible thing. It's iniquitous of you,' he exclaimed, and even while pity still lurked in his heart, his last shred of respect for her seemed to vanish.

'I won't go on living if you leave me for Helen,' she whispered.

'Rita, that's a form of blackmail and not worthy of you.'

'I'm not a worthy person,' she said, in a high hysterical voice. 'Just tell me, do you and Helen want my suicide on your hands?'

Alarmed and revolted, he looked down at her. He felt the sudden need for fresh air. He

333

must get out of this room which was so full of Rita's remembered perfume. He felt unable to breathe in it. He said:

'I refuse to believe what you're saying. Get up and dress and come downstairs, and talk to me like a normal reasonable human being. You *must*, Rita. If you don't, I shall go away now, however much you threaten me. I shall just walk out, go back to London, without speaking to you again.'

Those words beat through the red haze of her hysteria. She sank suddenly into the apathy of despair. Even now she tried not to admit to herself that she had lost him; after all her scheming, it was too awful to lose him . . . to let Helen Shaw win the day. She said:

'All right. I'll be quiet and come down. But please promise me you won't go.'

More gently he said:

'I promise, Rita . . .'

He went downstairs, wondering at the blind ignorance which had led him into believing that he had ever loved this woman.

Rita dressed more quickly than she had done before. Then made up her ruined face, and hurried downstairs. She was determined to make another bid for Peter. She had not lost the day yet, she told herself, feverishly.

She stopped Mrs. Cowley in the lounge.

'Where shall I find Mr. Farrington?'

Mrs. Cowley smiled.

'Ah, so glad to see you down, Mrs. Wade.

334

Are you feeling better, eh?'

'Where is Mr. Farrington?' repeated Rita sharply, ignoring the inquiry after her health.

'In the sun-loggia with your other friend.'

'*What* other friend?'

'The gentleman who has just arrived by car from London.'

Rita's dark eyes dilated.

'What gentleman? I wasn't expecting another visitor.'

'Oh, weren't you?' said Mrs. Cowley brightly, unaware of the storm that was going on in Rita Wade. 'Well, he arrived just now in a big car, and asked to see you. I told him you were indisposed but that your fiancé was here, so he joined Mr. Farrington.'

'Did he give you his name?'

'No he didn't . . .' began Mrs. Cowley.

But Rita did not wait for her to finish. Trembling as though with ague—full of fear— a fear such as she had never experienced in her life before, she walked to the sun-loggia and glanced in.

Then, when she saw the big man who wore horn-rimmed glasses standing beside Peter, she gave a little smothered moan. So it was Nigel. He had rooted out her hiding-place, at last.

And now she knew that she had lost Peter, beyond recall.

CHAPTER TWENTY-FOUR

Rita alternated between the desire to face the two men, and turn to fly to her bedroom. Never in her selfish life, so full of deceit and intrigue, had she felt more frightened. But she could not move. It was as though she were rooted to the spot. Then, suddenly, Nigel Cressland turned and saw her. Behind the horn-rims, his eyes narrowed. As he saw the somewhat astonishing sight of Rita looking ghastly and scared to death, his lips curled into an unpleasant smile. He gave a little bow.

'Ah! Enter the leading lady!' he said in a sarcastic voice and added: 'You *have* been a naughty girl, Rita, my sweet! What a drama! You have always been adept at justifying certain actions to which an ordinary person might take exception, but I don't think you can justify some of these astounding stories you have told this unfortunate young man. I'm no angel, neither am I Mr. Farrington's guardian, but I felt it my duty to come down here and throw a little enlightenment on your incredible statement about poor Patty.'

Rita's big dark eyes, dilated, full of something that approached horror, stared wildly at the man she had treated so badly— bad though he was. Then, her whole body ice-cold, her long fingers convulsively clenched, she turned her gaze to Peter. The one man for whom she had ever really cared and whom to win she had perjured herself so shamefully. He looked straight back at her. There was an expression on his frank boyish face which she was never to forget until her dying day. It was full of disgust. She opened her lips to speak and shut them again, utterly unable to get out the words. Nigel spoke once more after taking from his pocket a legal—looking sheet of paper. He tapped it with his thumbnail.

'Your child's birth certificate, my dear. I dropped in at Somerset House and got a copy of it just to show Mr. Farrington in case he might imagine that *I* was the liar. It proves so conclusively that Rita Ursula Wade, wife of Thomas Harold Wade, gave birth to a bonny little girl on the 14th day of April in the year—'

'Oh, stop!—stop it, I say!' Rita suddenly broke in hysterically.

Nigel shrugged his shoulders and returned the paper into his pocket.

'Just as you like. You know it all. But I really didn't see why a nice chap like young Farrington should marry a woman whom he thought eight or nine years younger than she is (much too young, of course, to have a child of *Patty's* age). Oh, my dear Rita, what a foolish story to put over! You disappoint me. I thought you had more brains!'

Rita gritted her teeth. If she could have murdered Nigel Cressland with a look, then

337

and there, he would have dropped dead at her feet. She felt suffocated with rage and despair. So that's what he had done—come down here and told Peter the truth about 'the adopted child'. Of course Peter now knew, as well, exactly how old she was, and how many lies she had uttered.

Peter continued to look at her with that expression of repulsion which was the worst part of the punishment which she was now forced to endure. In a trembling voice she began:

'Peter—*Pierrot*—'

He broke in:

'I don't ever want to see you or speak to you again. I shall leave this place at once.'

Nigel stood by, with that nasty little smile on his lips. He looked at Rita over the rim of his glasses. He knew her well, but he had never seen her quite so abject and it afforded him a sadistic satisfaction. She had done a good bit of lying to him in her time and, in his opinion, treated him pretty badly one way and another. He was more interested in getting his own back on her than saving young Farrington from her clutches. It amused him to watch Rita squirm.

Peter was walking away. Rita followed and caught his arm.

'Pierrot, don't go like this—please don't!' she said, in a desperate voice, 'let me speak to you alone. What has Nigel been telling you?

338

He is thoroughly bad and you can't believe a word he says. Peter . . . !'

Then be turned, his tanned face hot with shame for her.

'I don't care how bad he is. He's proved one thing to me—that you're worse than I believed it possible for any woman to be. Please don't think that I minded your pathetic effort to conceal your age—I could have forgiven that—if I loved a woman it wouldn't matter to me if she were twenty years older than myself. But what I find unpardonable was your denial of your own child just because you were afraid I might not marry you. Helen knew—of course—that's why you got rid of Helen—it's all so obvious to me now. Honestly, I never want to see you again—' His gaze flickered down to the ring on her finger. He added: 'Keep your ring. Keep anything I have given you. I couldn't care less.'

He shook off her hand without ceremony and walked out of the loggia, closing the door behind him. He himself was in a blind rage.

At first when Nigel Cressland had started to talk to Peter, unfold the fact that he was not Rita's lawyer but her former lover, he had wanted to hit the man across the face and then walk out. But when, swiftly, Nigel produced the certificate which proved that poor little Patty was not an adopted child but, in actual fact, Rita's daughter, it had directed all his anger from Nigel to the woman. He loathed her and he hated himself for having been so easily deceived. The whole thing was unsavoury, repellent to a man with his own clean record, and, particularly, his love for children. Yes, most of all he condemned Rita for her behaviour towards her child. The fact that she had done all this because she was infatuated with him left him cold. He regretted, now, not only his wasted passion for her but any pity he had ever felt . . . the pangs of conscience that had troubled him once he stopped loving her.

He packed his bag, gave the astonished Mrs. Cowley some money, told her to cancel all the rooms which had been reserved for him and his family (he had suddenly been recalled to London, he said) then ordered a car. He was going to drive to Petcombe to see Helen.

On the way there, he met the little girl, Patty, who was trudging along the road in the same direction. He felt sick with pity as he saw that lonely little figure and plain honest little face. He stared at her. Yes, he ought to have known that she was Rita's—blind fool that he had been—that red tint in her hair—the long slim legs. One day the ugly duckling might become a swan. But involuntarily he hoped to God that, even if she grew more like Rita to look at, she would never inherit her mother's nature. But it seemed to him that, fortunately, she was more like the father.

He stopped the car beside her and she ran

to it, her eyes lighting up.

'Oh, Uncle Peter, hallo!' she exclaimed breathlessly.

'Jump in, Patty,' he said brusquely. 'I'm going to see Helen and you shall come with me.'

She climbed into the car, pushing back her plaits, her small face flushed.

'Oh, Uncle *Peter*—how *super!*

As the car moved off, Peter sat back, one arm around the child, and thought of those two back in the 'Old Mill'—Rita and her ex-admirer who had betrayed her. How often had she betrayed him? Well, he no longer cared. But it did seem to him a shame that this nice kid had got to be brought up by a mothe like that. He began to wonder what he and Helen should do about it.

He and Helen. Suddenly he drew in his breath. It was as though he breathed purer, cleaner air suddenly. He was leaving the rot, the suffocating unhealthy aura surrounding Rita—he was going to Helen who stood for all that was sweet and fine in womanhood. Even to get what she wanted for herself, she had not betrayed Rita's confidences. What a girl! he thought with complete adoration.

*   *   *

In the sun-loggia of the 'Old Mill', Rita Wade had collapsed into one of the basket chairs.

She sat with her face in her hands. The agony of mind, of remorse that she was suffering in that moment was genuine enough. Once Peter had walked out of her life, she felt no more hysteria. She did not even weep. In silence she sat there, her shamed face covered and every atom of fight gone out of her. She even had not enough spirit left to abuse Nigel for the thing he had done to her.

For quite a few minutes he had been talking, standing over her, smoking, and still smiling a little as though he were enjoying himself.

It was no use her thinking up a lot of unpleasant things to say to him in due course, he warned her. She had not a leg left to stand on. She had broken all her promises to him and made a fool of him for the second time, so, if he had hit back they were quits. To which Rita made no response.

Nigel ceased to be amused. Baiting Rita when she didn't hit back, was no fun. He sat down and changed his tune. He offered her a cigarette.

'Come along—sit up and smoke. I suppose we can't get a drink in this godly dwelling that you've chosen for yourself. No licence, eh? Ugh! What a place. Not at all your mark, Rita. I reckon you had better put on a coat and I'll drive you to the 'local'. What you need is a stiff brandy.'

She did not answer, did not raise that

wonderful red head which she used to hold so arrogantly high. Nigel looked at her without pity. His sole emotion, really, was one of vague irritation that another man could reduce Rita to this state. Certainly, she must have been very much in love with young Farrington. Yet, he was surprised, knowing Rita, that she let herself go to pieces. He was also surprised at himself for not emulating Farrington's example and walking out on her. But deep down within Nigel Cressland there still lurked the old passion which he once had for this woman. When he was angry with her, he thought it dead. But it always seemed to revive again. He had been so long thwarted by her.

He knew that he had never really possessed her, body, mind and soul. That was the way he wanted her. Even now, in this hour of her humiliation, her beauty was still a flagrant temptation to him. His gaze wandered over the long, lovely lines of that languid body, hunched in the chair—the slender ankles—the dazzling whiteness of her skin. There wasn't another woman to touch her for looks and— when she was in a good mood, at her best— she was damned amusing, he thought. That fellow from Sweden wasn't the only man who admired Rita. There were others who would entertain him, Nigel, royally and do business with him, half because it suited them and half because of the immense appeal of the woman he brought along with him.

In other words, he still wanted Rita. He was not finished yet with her. *But it is going to be exquisite pleasure*, he told himself, *to be able, in future, to whistle her to heel when I choose.* She was ruined. He knew that. Financially ruined as well as deserted by the man whom she had expected to marry her. He, Nigel, was the only person in the world who could save her. Yes, his power over her now would be colossal, and he was going to get the hell of a kick out of directing her future movements.

He lit a cigarette, patted her band, and put the cigarette between her fingers, which automatically closed over it.

'Come along, my sweet. Let this soothe your jangled nerves. It's the brand you like.'

Then she raised her head. Her face was still deathly white and her eyes glittered with unshed tears. Some lipstick was smudge across her face. He added:

'Allow me—' and pulled a handkerchief from his pocket and touched the scarlet smear, 'your make—up is always so beautiful—I hate to see it spoiled.'

She shrank from his touch.

'Oh, go away, Nigel!" she said in a low voice, full of hatred.

He leaned back in his chair and chuckled.

'I don't suppose I'm too popular.'

She, too, leaned back in her chair, pushing a heavy wave of red hair back from her forehead. With a gesture of utter weariness she lifted the cigarette to her mouth. She felt broken to pieces. She would really not have cared in that moment the earth had opened and swallowed her up.

Nigel said:

'I think you had better be rational about this. You've played a very dangerous game and you've lost it. The fact that you've been a damned fool and gambled in the most outrageous fashion is neither here nor there. Of course, we know each other. Neither one of us can afford to criticize the other. Only I thought you had more brains. I'm surprised.'

Her long lashes drooped and veiled her eyes as though she were exhausted. She took a long breath of her cigarette.

'Why don't you go away?' she asked dully. 'You've done what you came down to do. Now you can get out.'

'And if I do—what becomes of you? You've gambled away everything you've had. What remains?'

'Nothing at all. Doesn't that please you? Go away,' she repeated.

Then he gave a short laugh.

'You've been a fool, Rita, but I see no reason why you should continue to be one. Your infatuation for that young man robbed you of your natural ability to get what you want in this world. You've lost him in no uncertain fashion. Cut your losses, my dear, and come down to earth.'

'What I do can't interest you, so why waste your time making poisonous remarks?' she asked.

'I'm sorry you find my remarks poisonous. I merely state facts.'

'So what?' she asked with a bitter look at him.

'Just this. I'm still your friend—yes, in spite of all you've done to me, I'm still more than a little interested in you and what you do, my dear Rita. There's always been a queer sort of—shall we call it a bond—between us. You've tried once or twice to break that bond. But you've always come back to me, and you're coming back to me now.'

At this, she sat upright and a look of real astonishment came into her eyes. A tinge of colour stole into her livid cheeks.

'You mean you still *want* me back?' she said incredulously.

He scowled and kicked his toe against the table leg with a vicious little movement. He did not altogether wish to admit that his senses were still so enchained by Rita. She filled him with contempt, and yet . . .

'Oh, go away, Nigel!' he heard her say for the third time. 'I feel ill. I'd rather be alone.'

'Oh, no, you would not,' he said smoothly, 'you hate being alone, and you know it. There is a pile of bills in your desk, waiting to be paid, and a large overdraft in your bank, and Patty's school bill for the coming term and your own clothes—the new line and all that. You're a woman of fashion and you won't want to wear short skirts when everybody else has taken to long—or vice versa!'

The sarcasm underlying this speech and her own inner conviction that this man, alone of all men, knew her as she really was, drove her to sudden fury. With clenched hands and blazing eyes, she flashed at him:

'Get out, *get out!* I hate you. You've ruined my life. I shall never forgive you as long as I live.'

He gave a laugh.

'That's better! I don't like to see you all chewed up. I prefer you with spirit and those magnificent eyes of yours are truly magnificent when you're in a temper.'

She made an attempt to speak, her throat working, then collapsed again like a deflated balloon. Her red head sank on to one arm. She began to cry.

Then Nigel knew that he was the master. He threw away his cigarette end and put an arm lightly across her shoulders.

'Come, Rita, pull yourself together. It's no use giving way. The affair with Farrington is over. You're in the devil of a mess, but I suggest you face up to it and listen to me. I still care for you in my funny way. And I have all sorts of plans for us. I think the best thing we can do is to get married at once, my dear, and try to make a success of life together. I've got the brains and you've got the beauty and that's a strong combination. I'm prepared to wipe out the past and forget it. I'll clear your debts and you can begin again as my wife, but on one condition. I will not have that kid of yours trailing around with us. I want to take you abroad on several business trips. I even have it in mind to clear out of the U.K. altogether and go with you to South America, where I have a business interest which may lead to a lot of money. You'd like the life in Rio and you would be a huge success with the locals. Now don't start a lot of mother sob-stuff about Patty because, if you were prepared to deny that she was your own daughter, you will be quite pleased to let somebody else look after her. Who should be better at it that dear Helen—oh, yes, I know you don't like her, but Patty does and you must be a nice unselfish girl and think of your poor child, for once. I don't doubt it would be a very agreeable arrangement for Helen Shaw to adopt poor little Patty, and I'm sure she will leap at it. She never did approve of you as his mother.'

Rita sat there, crying quietly—the tears of despair. She couli hardly bear to listen to that cruel, sarcastic voice. Every word, was designed to lacerate her feelings. Nigel was a past master at the art of hitting where it hurt most. And she had never disliked him more. Yet, in her despair, she was fully aware of the fact that every word he said was true. *And she could not escape from him*. She could not afford to be strong-minded and throw him out. She *was* ruined and he *was* the only friend she had left. She would be forced to allow him to drag her out of the abyss into which she had fallen. She had no choice. But the thought marriage to Nigel instead of Peter made her writhe. She tried to tell herself that she was lucky to have Nigel—that it was astounding that he should still want her. But for once her over weening vanity was not touched. She *hated* Nigel. She forgot that she had lost Peter long before Nigel appeared on the see today. She held it against him. She thought: 'If I do have marry him—knuckle under to him now, the day will come when I shall get my own back. The beast!'

'Well, my sweet.' Nigel's hated voice cut lightly across her morbid reflections. 'What do you say? How about asking the motherly and solicitous Helen to look after Patty while we toddle over to South America? I have a pal who will get us a couple of berths on a flying boat. And aren't you a shade tired of the old country and its petty restrictions? Think of the go food and unlimited drink—the night life in Rio. You'll have a damn good time. Better than you deserve, my angelic one! Rio Rita! Ha! ha! That rings a bell Most suitable!'

His sarcasm infuriated her. In helpless rage she sat listening, biting her handkerchief to shreds. A faint, very faint interest in the 'night

349

life in Rio' stirred in her sensual, pleasure—loving heart. But for the moment, Rita Wade was more sincerely in love with Peter Farrington than she had ever been before and her loss of him—the memory of that disgusted look in his eyes—agonized her. As for the idea of handing Patty over to Helen—that made her writhe. She would be handing everything to Helen—*everything*—oh, she would not give the odious girl that satisfaction. She would refuse . . .

Nigel, watching the beautiful desperate face, half guessed what was passing in that queer mind which he knew so well. He added insidiously:

'Oh, I know you don't like our Helen. But think of your "poor child". You wouldn't want to commit her to the care of strangers or leave her at school for her holidays. Even I, disliking brats as I do, take a dim view of that. No, my sweet—Helen's obviously the answer. If you want a break with me—a chance to wipe out the past—leave Patty behind with our Miss Shaw.'

Rita swallowed hard. Then she gave up struggling.

She knew that in this, at least, Nigel was right. For the first, if the last time in her life, she tried to consider her child's feelings instead of her own. She knew that Patty adored Helen, and she did not for an instant doubt that whatever happened in the future between Helen and Peter—or what Peter wanted—Helen would not refuse the care of Patty.

She said:

'Very well. I'll do as you say. Now let's go and find that pub. I need a stiff brandy—as you said.'

The man grinned. He was satisfied by his complete victory. This time he was not going to lose his Rita. He rose, and taking her hand pulled her up into his arms.

'Well—haven't I behaved damned generously to you after all you did to try and double-cross me?'

Her body stiffened in his embrace. She shut her eyes.

'Yes.'

'Don't I deserve some thanks?'

'Possibly . . .'

He chuckled. He felt the old mad passion stir in him as he held that long, languorous body—looked at the heavy eyelids, stained with blue, the sweeping lashes that glistened with recent tears—the drooping, angry red mouth. He whispered against her ear:

'Cheer up—we'll have some good times together, as we used to have. You don't belong to Farrington's righteous crowd. You belong to mine—Remember the old song?—"Don't you know, little fool, you never can win. Use your mentality. Wake up to reality . . ." And I have "got you under my skin". I always had,

Rita—always will have . . .'

He kissed her long and hard on the mouth. She suffered it. But there was no response from her. Her body was stiff and cold in his embrace. Perhaps in that moment, realizing that marriage with Nigel would mean a long brutal tyranny on his part—for he would expect slavish obedience from her now—she knew to the full what a lot she had lost. She thought of Peter's tenderness and intrinsic goodness—she thought, too, of the good man who had been her first husband, and her child whom she had betrayed, and she was horribly ashamed.

CHAPTER TWENTY-FIVE

Lady Pilgrim and Helen were in the middle of their lunch when Mrs. Bampton, the cook, announced that a car had come up the drive and that a gentleman and a little girl were stepping out of it.

Helen got up and walked to the window. When she saw Peter's tall figure and the small pathetic one of Patty holding on to his hand, she caught her breath and almost dropped her table napkin in her nervous excitement.

'Good gracious! It's Peter and little Patty Wade.'

Lady Pilgrim put down her knife and fork.

'Peter! You mean the young man who—who is so like my Chris?'

'Yes. You would rather not see him, would you?'

Lady Pilgrim also stood up. Her delicate cheeks coloured but a resolution came into her eyes.

'That's a lot of nonsense, of course. I mustn't be so silly. I expect he has come to see you, Helen. You must ask him in, anyhow.'

Within a very few moments of opening the front door, Helen knew why Peter had come. For in his impulsive rather naïve fashion, Peter broke into explanations the moment he saw the girl.

It's all over with *her!* I know every damn thing there is to know. I can't tell you now. I'll go into details later . . .' and he gave a significant glance at Patty.

Helens heart raced wildly. She felt a terrific sense of exhilaration—of liberation from all her anxieties and woes. *All over.* That meant that he had had a showdown with Rita and that somehow or other he knew the truth. He was free. He had come to her as a free man. That meant everything in the world to her.

But now she concentrated on Patty who, with a whoop of delight, flung herself into her arms.

'Helen—oh, darling, *snoochiest* Helen!' the child gasped, and smothered Helen's smiling face with kisses. At length, breathless, Helen had to disengage herself from the clinging little arms.

'Calm down, my pet. Don't go quite crazy,' she laughed.

Patty began to jabber in the most joyous fashion; one hot sticky hand still clinging to Helen's. Peter looked on, undeniably stirred by the touching sight of the small girl's pleasure. She certainly did love Helen. No wonder, Peter thought. Who would not love Helen? And his own gaze rested with unconcealed pleasure on the slim, young figure. She was looking more attractive today than he had ever seen her, wearing a pair of wine-coloured corduroy slacks which suited her slenderness, a pale yellow jumper, and soft, silky scarf. Her fair hair was loose and looked as if it had been newly washed—like pale gold silk. She had lost some of that tired look. There was a delicious freshness and innocence on her face which he found ravishing. He shuddered at the mere memory of the woman to whom he had just said good-bye. He knew that he would never stop wondering why he had been so blind.

Helen looked up at him with a nervous laugh, and apologized for her appearance.

'When I got back from my walk, I changed into slacks—I didn't expect visitors—but I don't usually wear them . . .'

'I think you look adorable,' he interrupted in a low voice.

'You must come and meet Lady Pilgrim,'

354

she said, hardly daring to meet his gaze.

'Are you in the middle of lunch?'

'It doesn't matter. I dare say we can find a scrap for you—and Patty, too. We killed a chicken yesterday.'

'Oh, poor chicken!' exclaimed Patty.

Helen laughed and ruffled her hair.

'Don't you waste your sympathy, you little imp. I bet you'll tuck into your share.'

Patty giggled. Some of the tension between Peter and Helen was relieved. Then Lady Pilgrim came into the hall. She advanced slowly toward the tall young man who was taking off his tweed overcoat. And if her heart gave an anguished lurch at the sight of him (for the amazing resemblance to her son could not fail to move her to the depths of her being) she did not show it. With admirable control she greeted Peter.

'How do you do, Mr. Farrington. Have you brought dear little Patty to lunch with us? I do hope so.'

Peter shook hands with her, immediately liking the gracious grey—haired woman who was Helen's friend and the mother of the man to whom she had been engaged.

'It's more than kind of you, Lady Pilgrim. I'm afraid it will be an imposition. I didn't realize what time it was when I came here. I—I'm afraid it all needs rather a lot of explaining.'

'Never explain anything. It saves a lot of

trouble and time,' broke in Lady Pilgrim smiling. 'Come now or our lunch will get cold. I'll tell Mrs. Bampton to lay two more places—' then she turned and put an arm around Patty and added, 'and how is my little friend?'

But she hardly heard the child's excited reply. Fascinated she continued to regard Peter Farrington as they all walked together toward the dining-room. She looked at the thick, chestnut hair, the boyish brow, the sweet-tempered mouth, the very way he carried his head. And inwardly she cried: 'Christopher—my son—my son!' And she knew why Helen had transferred her love from the dead to the living. It would have been impossible to meet Peter and not love him. The older woman most perfectly understood that. She ached with pity for Helen and all that she must have suffered.

Immediately after lunch, when they were gathered together in the drawing-room, drinking coffee, striving rather awkwardly to maintain a general, lighthearted conversation, the telephone bell rang. Lady Pilgrim went into the hall to answer it. When she came back, she looked with some excitement from Helen to Peter.

'That was Mrs. Wade from the "Old Mill",' she said.

Peter and Helen exchanged glances. The light went out of Peter's eyes.

Helen bit nervously at her lip. Patty

immediately stopped playing with Lindy, the puppy, and exclaimed:

'Oh! Is Mummy cross because I stayed for lunch?'

'No, no my dear—it's quite all right. Mummy isn't at all cross,' Lady Pilgrim quickly comforted her, 'but Patty—I want you to run along home now, at once.'

'Oh!' exclaimed the child with a long—drawn breath of disappointment, and flung Helen a beseeching glance.

'You can come back,' Lady Pilgrim added quickly, 'I'm going to send a car for you; yes, in about an hour's time, so don't worry. Just trot along over the fields, as quick as you can, because Mummy wants to see you. As a matter of fact, she has been suddenly called up to London, so you are going to come and spend a night or two here. Would you like that?'

Patty's brow cleared; she looked rapturous.

'How *super*! With you and Helen!'

'And Lindy!' added Lady Pilgrim laughing.

Quite happy again, the child put on her jacket and woolly gloves, kissed everyone in her warm, affectionate fashion, and left them.

Helen and Peter, who had been gazing at each other, some what mystified, now turned to Lady Pilgrim. She picked up her tapestry and looked at her work thoughtfully for a moment.

'Well, well,' she sat, 'events seem to be moving rapidly.'

'What has happened?' Helen and Peter chorused together.

'It's all rather perplexing. I couldn't quite gather over the phone what has occurred. Mrs. Wade seemed a trifle upset. But she asked if Mr. Farrington were here and I said yes, and that he had brought Patty, and that we had all had lunch. Then she said that she had been called up to London on urgent business and couldn't take the child and wondered if Helen would mind having her; so I said that I was sure nothing would please Helen more, and that Patty could certainly come to Petcombe Hall. Then Mrs. Wade said that she wished to say good-bye to the child so I sent her off. That's all I know, except that Mrs. Wade said she has written to Helen and was sending the letter immediately by a lad from the "Old Mill", and that it would require an urgent answer.'

Helen looked round at Peter again. He was frowning. She said:

'What does it all mean?'

'I'm not quite sure,' he said.

'Except that she is going away—' said Helen.

'Yes.'

Lady Pilgrim said:

'I'm going up to my room to rest. You two can have a little talk. If you want me for anything, Helen, just come up. I shan't be asleep. And as for you, Mr. Farrington—or may I call you Peter? You're so like my son ...'

358

He gripped her hand and held it very tightly for a moment, smiling down at her.

'Yes, Helen says I look like Christopher. I'm only too happy that you should call me "Peter", and I do hope that I shall see you again.'

Controlled though she was, Monica Pilgrim felt the tears sting her eyelids and for an instant her fingers clung to the kind, strong, young hand. How queer, she thought, the two men should look so alike. Yes, of course, there was a difference. Many differences—the mother's eye could detect them all. There could be nobody really quite like her Christopher. But she knew that having found it tolerable to meet and talk to Peter Farrington, she wanted very much to further the acquaintance. So it was with genuine warmth that she extended the hospitality of her house. With a touch of that dry humour which had helped Monica over many rough passages in her life, and endeared her to her friends, she said:

'I think you may be seeing a bit more of me than you bargain for, my dear boy. I don't know, but I wouldn't be surprised if you didn't find it agreeable to stay with us, tonight, instead of at the "Old Mill".'

Helen's pulses raced.

'Monica, you *angel!* Can he really stay?'

'If he wants to. Just see how things work out. Patty can have the twin bed in your room, Helen, can't she? Peter could go into

Christopher's room.'

Then Lady Pilgrim, very straight and tall, walked quickly out of the room.

'What a charming woman!' said Peter. 'Everything here is wonderful. How my mother would love it. It's our idea, in Kenya, of the perfect English country house and Lady Pilgrim the ideal *châtelaine*.'

'She is a wonderful person,' nodded Helen, 'and I can't tell you what an honour she has paid you in offering Chris's room. Nobody else has had it since he died.'

'Am I staying?' asked Peter doubtfully.

'Aren't you?' Helen parried with a softness in her eyes and a little tremor in her voice.

Then he came up to her and caught both her hands.

'Helen, Helen, I'm in a sort of whirl. I don't know whether I am on my head or my feet. My whole world is turning upside down!' he said in a deep husky voice.

'Don't worry, Peter darling. It's going to be all right,' she said.

'It's got to be,' he muttered, 'something good must come out of this appalling mess.'

'Come and sit down and talk to me quietly,' she said.

'Yes, there's a hell of a lot to talk about,' he said. 'But I feel frightfully churned up inside me, Helen. I can't explain but it's a sort of chaotic feeling. I just can't get over what I found out today about Rita.'

360

Helen's grave grey eyes looked at him in pity and understanding.

'It must be horrible for you.'

'It is horrible,' he said, 'I didn't think such things could happen or such women could exist. One sees it on the films—but no film-vampire can ever have been worse than Rita. And I thought I loved her. I meant to introduce her to my family this very week-end. What I have escaped appals me!'

Helen saw the sweat break out on his forehead. She did not yet know how much he had been told, but she could see that whatever it was had affected him deeply. That was natural, she thought, for a man who was as sensitive and as decent as Peter. Her own head was swimming a little, but in this hour she was full of an almost maternal solicitude for Peter—pitying profoundly his disillusionment and the sense of shame that had come with it.

'Darling Peter, don't be too upset. Sit down and talk,' she said.

For an instant he caught her in his arms and put his cheek against hers, holding her tightly, as though he feared to have her torn from him.

'Oh, Helen, Helen,' he groaned, 'I think I am upset most of all because I love *you* so much. I don't really feel I've got the right to come straight from that—that lowest of women—to *you*.'

Then she hugged him closely and of her own accord turned her lips to his mouth and gave him a long and most tender kiss.

'You mustn't think like that. I love you with all my heart and I always shall. I understand about Rita. She would have fascinated any man to begin with. You needn't feel ashamed. And don't, please, put me on a pedestal, because I'm frightfully human and I have lots of faults.'

He covered her soft hair with kisses.

'I think you're an angel.'

Then she laughed and raised a flushed face, red lips pouting.

'But I don't want to be treated like one, I'm far too much in love with you.'

'You're sweet,' he said, 'one hundred per cent sweet and lovely.'

For a moment their lips clung together; then the moment of passion, of exaltation passed. Hands locked, they walked to the big, deep chesterfield which stood at a right—angle to the fireplace in which a log fire was crackling pleasantly, sat down and began to talk about the day's events. After a while Mrs. Bampton came in with a letter.

'For Miss Shaw—a lad has just cycled over from "The Mill".' Mrs. Bampton announced. ''E's waiting an answer.'

'Ah!' said Peter under his breath.

Mrs. Bampton retired. Helen, her hands trembling slightly, opened the letter which was somewhat bulky, written in that big, scrawling writing which reminded her of the notes which

362

she used to receive from Rita from Paris; always rather blotched, and couched in flamboyant style; typical of the neurotic woman that she was. This epistle was neurotic enough, and in places the ink was blurred as though the writer had been shedding tears. It was long, disjointed, but definite. It left no room in Helen's mind as to what Rita wanted and that some of the sentiments (those expressing remorse about Patty) were genuine enough.

When she had finished reading she felt breathless. It was as though she had been actually taking part in one of the old scenes in Rita's household.

'What does she say?' Peter asked abruptly.

'Shall I read it to you?'

'No, for heaven's sake don't. I couldn't stand it. Just tell me the main points.'

Helen told him. Rita had decided to go away at once with Nigel Cressland. He was marrying her immediately, after which they were leaving for Sweden on business and then they were probably going to South America. There was every chance that Nigel would have important business there and that they might settle in Rio de Janeiro. Everything was ended between herself and Peter, of course, she said. There remained only the problem of Patty. Nigel would not tolerate the idea of the little girl travelling around with them. And it would not be good for Patty.

363

Here Rita, dropping a tear on the page, became sincere when she expressed her sorrow that she had not given Patty a better break recently. She wished to make up for this and although she loathed the idea, she said, of a long parting from her daughter, she knew that Patty would never get on with her stepfather, and that she would be much happier if she were brought up in England by someone like Helen. Patty adored Helen. Here, Helen read a paragraph aloud:

'You and I do not like each other but let us be frank and admit that that is not of great account now. It's Patty we must think of and I fully realize you are the one person in the world I can trust to do her best for Patty. So I suggest that if you will accept the responsibility of her upbringing . . . in fact become her legal guardian which I will arrange before I go . . . I will send you the necessary money for her schooling, clothes and holidays, etc. I beg you to do this. Even though you hate me, Helen, I shall never be at peace unless I can feel that Patty is with you. I can't look after her myself. I'm no good as a mother, I admit it. And I must marry Nigel. If I don't, I'm faced with ruin.'

Helen stopped reading and raised a flushed face to Peter.

'What do you think of that?'

He took the pipe from his mouth and frowningly regarded it.

'Possibly the most sensible and unselfish thing she has done in her life. I suppose she has gone over to Cressland because he offered to pay her debts. That's her funeral. As far as Patty is concerned she must know it would be hell on earth for the kid to live with them. And she also knows how much you care for poor Patty. The thing is—do you want to accept such a responsibility?'

Helen answered unhesitatingly:

'I would not have Patty go to anybody else. I understand her and she loves me. Of course, I couldn't afford to bring her up without financial help but if her mother intends to support her—'

Peter interrupted.

'Don't worry about money. I've got plenty of that and Kenya is the best possible place for a child. I only want to make sure *you* really want her. *I'd* like to have her. There's something very sweet and appealing about that funny, plain, little thing, don't you think?'

Helen sat silent, Rita's letter in her hand. Her thoughts were so deliriously happy in that moment that words failed her. Then with a gulp she said:

'What—what has it all got to do with you?'

He put his pipe down in the ashtray, took one of her hands and dropped a kiss on the

365

palm.

'Everything—if you're going to marry me, Helen. It means that we shall both be adopting young Patty.'

Still she could not answer. Her heart was hammering and in her imagination there came a vision of exquisite happiness—Peter and herself and the child—out there in the sun-light-together—always.

She thought of the final paragraph of Rita's letter which she had not read to Peter. The malicious envious touch which Rita had not been able to resist.

'You seem to have won. I don't expect Peter will go straight to you. You can never expect me to like you but I still hope you will take Patty and that you won't poison her mind against me . . . .

'A typical Rita reaction!' Helen reflected; as if she would ever poison a child's mind against her own mother!

She felt Peter's arms around her, dropped the letter and looked up at him. There was almost a humble appeal in those handsome eyes of his.

'Will you let me take care of you and Patty?' he asked, 'and take you both to Nairobi. I want you to paint again—lovely pictures for me—for our home.'

She lifted her lips to his.

366

'Oh, darling, *darling*—it sounds so heavenly!'

His ardent kiss seemed to fuse their very spirits into one flame. Then gently he released her.

'Write your answer to Rita, my darling. The boy is waiting for it.'

She sprang up, flushed and radiant.

'Yes, I will, at once.'

'And if I may, I'll accept Lady Pilgrim's very kind invitation to stay here tonight. But tomorrow I must take you up to my mother. She's waiting for this. She knew it was going to happen. She's going to love you, Helen.'

'I shall love her, too.'

'And as for young Glen, there will be no holding her in. She thinks the world of you.'

'Dear Glen. She's a poppet. We always got on well.'

'Then you'll go up with me?'

'Yes, I have to, anyhow, to see the lawyers about this guardianship of Patty.'

'Hurry up and write your letter, darling. I want you back, here, beside me in front of the fire,' he said with a long deep look at her. 'And we must put a call through to Glen and tell her to break the news to Mums.'

'I won't be long,' said Helen softly.

After she had gone, Peter stood looking down at the fire. His mind was still in a whirl. But he felt happier than he had done for many a long anxious week. He knew that in a short time he would be able to forget Rita and his brief fatal affair with her, altogether—and that life with Helen, back in his Kenya home, would be as near heaven as a man could expect on earth.

After a moment he became aware that he was looking up at a coloured photograph in a silver frame which stood on the mantelpiece. It might have been himself. But it bore the signature: *'For Mother from Chris . . .'*

A sudden sense of tranquillity and well—being stole into the heart and mind of Peter Farrington. He lifted the picture, stared at it intently, then set it back on the mantelpiece and lifted a hand in salute.

'I'll take care of Helen, old boy, I'll never let her down . . .' he said aloud.

And then half-ashamed of the deep emotion he was feeling, he moved across to the window, gazed out at the snow-whitened garden, and waited for Helen to come back.